Advance Praise for *Spanking New*

"Clifford Henderson has written a masterpiece in *Spanking New*. She explores the serious issues of our day such as heteronormativity, heterosexism, homophobia, and pro-choice in a humorous and non-threatening manner. The author's use of the unborn as the story teller generates an air of awe, wonder and hope regarding these important topics. [illegible] clever exploration of her protagonist [illegible]eelings leads [illegible] fluid. *Spanking New* should be a required reading for all gender and queer study courses.

While the author addresses serious issues, her book is fun, fun, fun! The playfulness, curiosity and fresh naivety as portrayed through the eyes of the story teller is refreshing and often humorous. It is pure genius on Henderson's part to write from this perspective. The protagonists are endearing and very human as you follow their struggles to navigate through life. The reader is able to sympathize with the antagonist's feelings as well, in this richly developed exploration of human beings' struggles to make sense of their worlds."—Anita Kelly, LGBT Coordinator, Muhlenberg College

"*Spanking New* is a book that brings the fantasy of what happened before I was born, to life. If you have ever wondered what you were, or where you came from, Clifford Henderson gives you an interesting, oft times hilarious answer…I am happy to have discovered this writer, as she is never dull, and lends much to the imagination."—*Out in Jersey*

Acclaim for *The Middle of Somewhere*

"…Henderson grabs her readers in a firm grip and never lets go. *The Middle of Somewhere* is a wonderful laugh-out-loud read filled with pathos, hope, and new beginnings…a very good read."—*Just About Write*

"Clifford Hend[illegible] [illegible]ives you the sense that h[illegible] [illegible]."—*Out In Jersey*

By the Author

The Middle of Somewhere

Spanking New

Spanking New

by

Clifford Henderson

A Division of Bold Strokes Books

2010

SPANKING NEW

ISBN 10: 1-60282-138-0
ISBN 13: 978-1-60282-138-5

This Trade Paperback Original Is Published By
Bold Strokes Books, Inc.
P.O. Box 249
Valley Falls, NY 12185

First Bold Strokes Printing: February 2010

Credits
Editors: Cindy Cresap and Stacia Seaman
Production Design: Stacia Seaman
Cover Design By Sheri (graphicartist2020@hotmail.com)

Acknowledgments

Writing a novel is like giving birth. It's a cliché, I know, but given the premise of this novel, it's one I think I'm entitled to use. *Spanking New* was a long, disobedient labor, so there are lots of people to thank.

Ellen Bass and the women in my first writing group who were there at conception. Thank you.

Duke Houston, Mary Brooks, Pipa Piñon, Mahesh Grossman, and Allegra McCarthy, who read the first version and gave feedback. Thank you.

My current writing group, who saw me through this final version: Phil Slater, the cut master; Sallie Johnson, queen of details; and Gino Danna, who asks big questions. Thank you.

Martha Corrigan for the many hats she wore. Thank you.

My editor Cindy Cresap, who helped me find the glue to hold it all together. Thank you.

Len Barot, whose business acumen has made it possible for me to make the momentous and satisfying leap to being published. Thank you.

Sheri, Stacia, Lori, Connie, Toni, and all the other insanely talented women of Bold Strokes Books who work behind the scenes to make us authors look good. Thank you.

Dixie Cox, who never stops believing in me. Thank you.

And finally, you, the reader. You make it all worth it. Thank you.

Prologue

Da-dum. Da-dum.

Crossing over: I had no idea it was going to be this hard.

Da-dum. Da-dum.

Makes these last eight and a half months of cell splitting seem like nothing more than playing with LEGOs.

Da-dum. Da-dum.

Da-dum. Da-dum.

Two hearts, Mom's and mine.

Da-dum. Da-dum.

Da-dum. Da-dum.

I'm going to miss this.

Uh-oh! Here we go! Another push!

The muscles in Mom's abdomen are squeezing me. Tighter. Tighter. She's grunting. I pull in my arms and legs, torpedo-like… Get ready, get set…

And…

And…

Nothing. Still here.

Phew.

I don't want to cross over until I figure out what I'm supposed to do once I get there. I know it's silly for me to care; I won't remember anyway. The minute I push through, the Forgetting will kick in.

But I want my life to have meaning! I want to be loved! I want to change the world!

I'll have to use these last minutes to scour the incidents that got me this far—while I can still remember them. Maybe some nugget from the past will give me the courage to sever ties with my old pal, Umbilicus.

FLOATING

CHAPTER ONE

My first thought is Why Me? Nobody asked me if I wanted to become a Floating Soul, to be yanked from my cozy blanket of absolute awareness. Maybe I didn't want to become a Me. Maybe I was happy as I was: blended into the wonderful, chaotic, alphabet soup of The Known.

The fact that I'm whining indicates there's no going back. I'm already stuck with a personality—*and* my first assignment: choosing parents. They'll provide me the body I need to negotiate my way through the Land of Forgetting. When it comes time for me to evaporate back, The Known will absorb everything I've learned and use it to evolve. This is how The Known recreates itself. It drips you out like a saturated rain cloud, then, after It's satisfied you've done everything you're going to do, It evaporates you back. Only Floating Souls have a bit more to do between dripping out and evaporating than loll around making puddles. We have destinies to fulfill.

I comb the paltry information I've been sent down with, and believe me, there's not much. Compared to the massive archives of The Known, it's like a small suitcase a frenzied mother might throw together for a departing child. But what's in it can make or break my chances at happiness. And what's left out…well, the future, for one thing. Besides that, don't even get me started.

I flip through something I can only describe as a traveler's pamphlet of current fads and social faux pas while simultaneously riffling through the personality traits I've been assigned—patience not being one of them—when I'm suddenly hijacked by The Yearn. It's programmed into us Floating Souls so we don't just waft around interminably trying to make up our minds. Once The Yearn takes control, all lofty thoughts about destiny disintegrate.

I've got to find a way to start splitting some cells!

I take a look around. Where am I?

A dimly lit alley. Must be The Known's idea of a joke. There's no one here. Just a Dumpster next to an old, ivy-covered brick building. Granted, it's a relatively affluent neighborhood, which is a relief. I've heard horror stories about Floating Souls being dripped into germ-infested, poverty-stricken hovels.

A streetlight from a nearby parking lot casts long shadows, enabling me to make out a wooden door built into the brick building. It's in need of a paint job and has a sign tacked to it that reads: CAST AND CREW ONLY BEYOND THIS POINT! Intriguing. I'm about to slip inside when I notice someone crouched in the shadow of the Dumpster. Two someones, actually. Possible parents? I zoom in for a closer inspection. Two young men smoking a mind-altering weed. So much for finding my ticket into life. I need an XX and XY to get the job done. I head on to the stage door, but something stops me. There's something alluring about one of the two men that I can't dismiss. Dad? I think tentatively.

The fellow I'm interested in has a cool goatee and a T-shirt with the words The Doors printed on the front. But it's his hands that fascinate me. They're callused, clean, and have long, tapered fingers; perfect for teaching a kid how to play ball in the backyard.

I need to be super careful about my choice in dads. A kid needs a good father figure; that's one of the things I'm sure of.

Or think I am.

This having feelings and opinions is new to me. Can I trust them?

But I'm so drawn to this guy with the caring, protective hands. I just *know* I'm supposed to be his.

Then I think about him smoking his weed in a dark alley.

Is he really Dad material?

Time for a background check. Zipping through his memory bank, I sift out these essential facts:

Name: Rick Hale
Birth order: Only child of a doting mother and stern father
Age: Twenty-one years old

Education: B.A. in music; Instrument: saxophone
Employment: Tire changer
Residence: Still lives with parents
Marital status: Single

I'm on the verge of dismissing him as a loser when I'm reminded of a warning I was issued by a returning Floating Soul who'd done her time on Earth: *Don't let assumptions and opinions pull you from your instincts.* At the time, I was sure I'd be above this simple misstep; now, I'm not so cocky. Assumptions and opinions have already begun attaching to me like barnacles—and they make things so confusing! Are my fears about alleyways, single musicians, and guys who still live at home with their parents instincts or opinions?

I zoom in on Howie, the muscular fellow Rick's hanging with, for a closer look. He's got really short hair and a ton of bottled-up rage. What is Rick doing associating with a guy like him?

Scanning Rick's memory, I find a vision of Rick and Howie jamming in a basement apartment, but Howie doesn't look scary in the memory. He looks happy-go-lucky in his worn jeans, a fringy vest with no shirt, and bare feet. He's slumped back in a beanbag chair, an electric guitar cradled in his lap, riffing off a smooth sax melody provided by my Rick. Just the kind of guy I want to be when I—

Whoa. I'm going to be a boy. How cool is that?

I'll be just like Rick when he shuts his eyes to sustain a note, or Howie when his fingers dance up and down the frets of his guitar—happy, content, grinning when we get the notes just right. Being a guy is going to be awesome!

So what's with this new muscular Howie with the short, short hair? He's completely different from the guy in the memory. His face is all hard angles, and he's constantly glancing around as if something might leap out from behind a wall.

It doesn't take long to find out. The events dominate his brain.

Two planes smashing into a gigantic tower full of people. His dad calling from one of the planes to say how much he loves his wife and two sons. Seconds later, the plane exploding. Howie following his big brother into an army to get back at the people who killed his dad, then spending grueling months training, and more grueling months in a mountainous place called Afghanistan. Now he's got orders to go to another place—Iraq—and he doesn't want to. He no longer believes the fighting has anything to do with his dad. He thinks it's being used to make some rich people richer. It's his last day of leave and he's desperate, angry.

"What time you leave tomorrow?" Rick asks, passing the rolled-up weed to Howie. As a send-off, Rick brought him to a play put on by a local women's college. A friend gave him the tickets, and Rick thought it would be fun, that maybe they'd meet some girls. But the play turned out to be about a hopeless wasteland at the end of the world, and it hit Howie a little too close to home.

"Too early," is all Howie says, though. He looks at the asphalt beneath him and sucks so hard on the weed he begins to cough. "Shit!" he says, then passes the weed back to Rick. For a split second their fingertips make contact.

This experience is so intimate. So taken for granted.

Mesmerized by the wondrous phenomenon of touch, I zoom in closer, hovering between the two men. Rick's posture stiffens.

He felt me! He felt me!

Then I realize that Rick was just reacting to an ugly scar on Howie's inner forearm. He wants to ask Howie how he got it, but doesn't.

What does he think words are for? Swishing around in his mouth like mouthwash? Words are one of the primary tools you get in the Land of Forgetting. Why isn't he using them? Howie needs to talk about the scar. How he tried to take his life, then lied to the doctor, saying it happened while training. And he needs to tell someone that if this is the way to avenge his dad, he's not man enough to do it. And he needs to say he's scared and doesn't want to go, doesn't think he should have to. If he said these things, I'll bet Rick would quit feeling so guilty, quit thinking he's betraying his friend by not joining the army too. What's more, it might give him the opening to talk about his *own* life, admit that he's having trouble finding reasons to get out of bed in the morning, admit that he feels like his life is going nowhere, that he hates his job at Jack's Tires. Howie would love it if Rick would say these things! He wouldn't feel like he was the only one who was lost and scared. But does either of them say anything? Does either of them use his words to confide in the friend who cares about him the most? Noooo. The knuckleheads just squat there using their mouths to suck on that weed.

Rick hands the smoked-down roll of weed back to Howie. "We should split."

Howie takes a final suck, then, still holding the smoke in his lungs, squeezes out, "You gotta introduce yourself to her, man."

Did he say "her?" Her who?

Rick looks around the Dumpster to the wooden door with its cast and crew sign.

Howie pinches out the roach, pockets it, and rocks onto his heels so his back is against the solid warm brick.

Who's the her? Who's the her? I want to scream.

Rick reaches down, picks up a bottle cap, and begins flipping it in the air like a coin. "Yeah right. 'Uh, Hi. I loved the performance…'"

Howie snickers.

"What?"

"You *loved* the performance?"

"Yeah…"

"What exactly about the *performance* did you love, Rick? The total depressingness of the language or the awesome lack of special effects? I mean, the fucking play was called *Endgame.* What were you thinking?"

They start laughing—hysterically. Howie bends over and hugs his arms to his chest, gasping, "I'm so glad you went out of your way to find us something uplifting to do on my last night home, man!"

"I told you," Rick sputters, "I got the tickets for free!"

I ignore their immaturity and move on to what's important. An actress? How absolutely perfect! Child of a musician father and actress mother; I'll be nursed at late-night jam sessions, go to sleep to the sound of my mother reciting lines.

I dive into Rick's memory to get a glimpse of my potential mom, but it's hard to get an accurate read. All his memory has to offer are scenes from the play where she's dressed in rags, her face covered in ashes. She's playing an androgynous character named Clov who seems to have nothing better to do than hang on a broom and listen to some girl dressed as a lame old blind guy pontificate. Bor-ring! But, as much as I can make out, she *is* pretty. Tendrils of red hair peek from beneath her filthy cap. And her voice is captivating; even with such repetitive text she reveals subtle nuances, shifts the timbre, rhythm, and pitch. She's not very tall, but I can live with that. She's an actress!

Rick pulls his car keys from his pocket. "Let's blow. This doesn't feel right."

Doesn't feel right? I think. What are you talking about? You'd be perfect together!

Rick is feeling light-headed and wishes he hadn't smoked so much weed. "You're leaving tomorrow," he says to Howie. "We should go party or play some music."

Howie positions himself between Rick and the parking lot. "No, man. You're staying."

"What?"

"You're staying."

"Why?"

Howie gives him a meaningful look, then says, "Because you *can.*"

I couldn't agree with him more. *Listen to the guy, Rick. He's right. You're craving change. Change takes risk. Meet the girl! Fall in love! Have a baby!* The desperation I feel as I screech out these unheard commands is excruciating. *You've got to be my parents! You've got to!*

CHAPTER TWO

Rick kicks at a scraggly plant growing up out of the asphalt. "You sure you don't want to go out for a beer or something? I'll buy."

Howie glares at him. "Rick…"

"Okay! I'm staying."

"For me, man. Do it for me."

Rick digs his hands into his pockets and nods.

"Promise?" Howie says.

"Promise."

"Okay, then. I'm outta here." But before leaving Howie turns and says, "And when I get back we're opening that music store."

"Music Jones," Rick says, swishing his hands out to indicate a store sign. "Quality Instruments and *Expert* Instruction."

The two slap each other's hands, then embrace, neither one wanting to let go. "I love you, man," Howie says.

"Love you too."

They pull apart. "Now go snag that actress."

Rick watches Howie leave. I watch Rick. Will he stay? Will he honor his promise to his friend? If he doesn't, what will this say about him as a man? As a dad? Surely I'm not going to take just any dad, one who would lie to a best friend, a soldier about to risk his life for his country.

Then again, I really like his hair.

I'm spared having to plumb the possibly shallow depths of my soul, for, right then, the cast and crew of St. Theresa's all-female production of *Endgame* come bursting through the stage door. They're laughing and chattering like a flock of colorful birds.

I search for the girl Rick keeps in his memory, but without the costume and ash-smudged face it's difficult. Plus, they're so full of adrenaline they won't stay still. So different from the slow moving, somber, rag-wearing women in the play.

Rick, I note, is having the same problem as me. He considers stepping around the Dumpster for a better look, but feels too introspective from the weed—way too introspective. He watches helplessly as the group ambles toward him, his mind careening with conversation starters: *Good show, ladies! Nice night. How's it going?* None of them locates his lips, getting caught in brain fuzz instead. He tries coughing and clearing his throat, shakes his head and rubs his eyes, but the dizziness won't go away.

The group of chattering women walks past without even noticing him.

Come on, Rick! You have to be my dad! Push past the fear. Remember your promise to Howie! I'm trying to figure out if it's possible to give him an astral shove, when he blurts out, "Excuse me, ladies!"

One of them turns around. Is it her, the actress?

She also has a rolled-up weed in her mouth, only it's called a cigarette and doesn't mess with her brain, and she wears thick black eyeliner. But it's not the actress. Her name is Dink Raz and she's not the mother type at all.

Still, contact has been made.

Rick focuses on Dink's thick black eyeliner, but her eyes begin multiplying, swirling around like a kaleidoscope gone haywire. He blinks. Tells himself: *breathe*. Then his knees start buckling…

This can't be happening! He's losing consciousness and dropping to the ground!

Dink shouts to her friends. They turn and come rushing back.

I spot the actress—Nina Kalina. She's beautiful. Long red hair, a random spray of freckles sprinkled across her nose and cheeks. She's got good wide hips too. Perfect for having a baby. For having me!

Mom! Mom!

She bends down by Rick's sprawled-out body, her face full of concern. She reaches out a hand. Places it on his forehead. The soft, pale skin of her fingertips ends in short clipped nails. Around her wrist, a string of shiny green beads.

Mate! Mate! Mate!

But I haven't thought out the timing. Nina won't be fertile for another twenty-two days. So even though Rick's ready to go—passed out on the cement he's still producing one thousand spermatozoa per heartbeat!—I'm going to have to wait on the laws of biology. What a bore.

Rick's eyes flutter open. He's trying to figure out what happened. Above him he sees a pool of women's faces, but the wooziness makes them look slightly deformed with giant noses and tiny foreheads. *As if they've been shot with a wide-angle lens*, he thinks. Then he spots Nina, right in the middle of the revolving pack, and remembers where he is and what happened. *How could I have let myself get so stoned?* he thinks. *Stupid, stupid, stupid!* And even though Nina appears slightly out of proportion, she's more beautiful than he remembered. Her red hair more luxuriant, her full lips more luscious, and she has on makeup that makes her eyelids sparkle.

He tries to think of something to say, something clever that will make light of this humiliating situation.

She pulls out a cell phone. "I better call Pablo and tell him we're going to be late."

Pablo? Rick and I both think, *Who the hell is Pablo?*

Chapter Three

Rick waves off the hands that reach out to him—even Nina's—grumbling, "I'm fine. I don't know what happened. It's never happened before." He tries to stand. Nina and her friends hold out their hands to steady him anyway, which I'm glad for. The last thing I need is for my future dad to crack his head open on the cement. I already want to bean him one for tipping over. What kind of impression is that to make on the girl of his dreams, my future mom? But he's beating himself up so badly he doesn't need any help from me.

Bodies can be tricky, I remind myself; sometimes they do things you don't expect.

Once standing, Rick keeps saying he's fine, even though he's majorly tripping out about fainting. He runs his fingers through his hair and laughs, trying to brush off the fact that he just keeled over. A nice touch, I think. It accentuates his pearly teeth and the way his eyes tip up at the sides when he smiles.

Now fall in love with him, Nina!

But she's pulled away from the group to call *Pablo*, leaving Rick vulnerable to a young woman I don't like at all. She's sharp-featured with a sharp voice and sharp movements to match. What's more, she looks like she has no sense of humor. In short, she's someone I would never want for a mom. Never. Her name is Missy Hooten.

"You look kind of pale," she says, sidling up to Rick and taking his arm.

"I'm fine," Rick replies, for about the zillionth time.

She grips his arm a little tighter. The other women glance at one another, amused.

What's so funny? I think. *She's taking advantage of his weakened state.*

Nina finally finishes her phone call and rejoins the group. "Pablo's saving us a table. Should we head that way?"

But Missy won't let go of Rick. "We should walk…uh…what's your name?"

"Rick."

"Rick to the parking lot. Just to make sure…"

Dink flicks her cigarette butt into the Dumpster. "Of what, Missy? That he doesn't need mouth to mouth?"

Ha ha ha, I think. *So funny I forgot to laugh.* But everyone else is laughing—except Missy, who shrieks, "In case he faints!"

It occurs to me that this Dink girl is different from the others. She isn't interested in meeting up with boys. And yet she's pretending she is. What's *that* about?

"I need to dance," Nina says, leading the pack toward the parking lot.

Rick lets Missy tote him along like a puppy on a leash. "I fainted in a confessional once," she coos into his ear. "It was horrible."

He clears his throat. "That must have been frightening."

Well, that's all Missy needs. She starts gabbing and blabbing about her "horrible ordeal," while Rick nods occasionally like he's listening. He thinks he has no choice. But he does. He could tell Missy to shove it up her you-know-what. I mean, I know he's still feeling light-headed, but surely he could muster the energy to run forward and tell Nina he loved her performance and thinks she's beautiful. Maybe even ask for a phone number, or her hand in marriage. But noooo. He just wags his head up and down, not wanting to hurt Missy's feelings.

His actions leave me feeling conflicted. Kindness and good manners are qualities I want in a dad; on the other hand, they're keeping him from making a play for Nina.

Missy, still blathering, now has him pinned against his cool car. It's royal blue and says Duster on the side. She pulls out a piece of paper inviting him to a graduation party the following Friday. "You can come if you want. The whole cast and crew will be there. I'm on the decorating committee."

I scan Rick's brain trying to figure out why he isn't kicking up his heels and saying, *Yes! Yes! Yes!* He's being given a second chance to hook up with Nina. But he doesn't see it that way. Oh no. The weed is making him paranoid and has convinced him that he's made such a bad impression there's no use trying any longer. What a wiener!

A girl with almond-shaped eyes and a plucky blue stripe in her long jet-black hair yells, "You coming, Missy? Or do you need to tend to your wounded soldier?"

When Rick hears the words "wounded soldier" he's reminded of his promise to Howie. He grabs the piece of paper and shoves it into his back pocket. "I'll be there," he says. "I will."

This must be what's called Luck! Dumb Luck, some people call it. What a strange concept this luck is. It's certainly not to be counted on… But who cares? It worked.

As the women walk off, Rick keeps his eyes trained on Nina. Even though there's no music, her arms sway back and forth above her head like she's dancing. He watches until her swaying arms blend into the darkness.

No wonder people in the Land of Forgetting cross their fingers, wish on stars, carry rabbits' feet in their pockets. Luck can make all the difference.

Chapter Four

The St. Theresa's gang is talking about Rick. They're walking down the street in a clump, talking animatedly about my man Rick. Maybe fainting wasn't as disastrous as I thought. I mean, how can you forget a guy who faints at your feet?

"I thought he was hot," one says as she makes a game of stepping over the cracks in the sidewalk.

Lottie Yang, the girl with the blue stripe in her hair, replies, "So did Missy."

Missy glares at Lottie. "The guy fainted! What was I supposed to do?"

I wish Nina were listening, but she's stopped to smell some flowers—jasmine—and just as I feared, she's thinking about Pablo. She breaks off a piece of the jasmine and tucks it behind her ear.

I dive into her memory. The man I find there has olive skin, a long black ponytail, and a strong jawline.

He's adjusting the worn lapels of her costume jacket. His hand brushes her breast as he makes his way down to her inseam. He tugs at the leg of her pants, then rocks back on his heels and places two fingers inside the waistband. A flutter races down Nina's spine and her panties moisten. Pablo gets up off his knees, lays his hands on her shoulders to turn her around, and steers her toward a full-length mirror. The two of them take her in. She glances past her reflection to his and notices his dark eyelashes. She wants him to kiss her.

Damn! This is really going to put a kink in my plans.

The St. Theresa's gang approaches a flat-roofed building with a neon Saturn on top. The words THE GALAXY blink right below. A couple is making out by some drooping foliage on the side of the building. I can't help but think how happy they're probably making some Floating Soul—some Floating Soul, that is, who had the foresight to choose parents who already knew one another.

The sound of a low thumping bass and a jangling tambourine seeps through the walls of the tacky building. "Motown Night!" Missy squeals and races toward the door.

Nina and her friends angle their way through the people smoking cigarettes on the street.

I go on ahead, determined to check out this Pablo guy, see what he has that my Rick doesn't. The place is jam-packed with young people shouting intimacies over the blaring music.

I spot him. He's sitting alone at the biggest booth in the place. I'm about to peer into his memory to see if he shares Nina's romantic feelings when she slides in next to him. The rest of the St. Theresa's gang quickly surround them, cramming into the one booth.

"Where have you been?" Pablo yells across the large kidney-shaped table to Dink Raz. His voice is smooth. Too darn smooth, if you ask me. Dink pops a peppermint in her mouth to mask her cigarette breath. I like her. Mostly because Pablo seems more interested in her than in Nina.

"A guy fainted," Dink yells back. "We had to stick around to make sure he was all right." I notice that Dink is wishing she were sitting next to Nina. Why doesn't she just move over and squeeze in between her and Pablo?

"Fainted?" Pablo asks in an obvious ploy to draw out a blow-by-blow report of Rick's moment of weakness. To spare myself this humiliation, I dive into Pablo's memory bank and land on one from just a few weeks ago.

Dink, who lives with Pablo, has just come home from a rehearsal of Endgame. *She flops on the couch. "We've pulled Lottie off costumes and put her on set. Frances turned out to be a total cornflake. But now we need someone to do costumes."*

Pablo pours her a glass of wine. "Is there any money?"

"Nope."

"Just comps?"

"Please, Pablo. I'm desperate."

Pablo swirls the wine in his glass, making him seem even more attractive.

I need a memory with Nina. I flash forward a week.

Pablo and Nina standing in a bedroom. Some guy in short shorts, Jacques, is there too. He's flipping through a magazine on Pablo's bed while Pablo watches Nina walk. "You're going to have to practice, otherwise you'll keep tripping over them." Pablo is talking about her oversized boots.

Jacques rolls onto his side and places the magazine back on the night table. He has long, golden, muscular legs. "I wore zem when I played a sailor in South Pacific. *Zey have a lift because I was too small for ze choreographer. She wanted me big."*

Pablo is focused on Nina. "Less hips when you walk. That'll make you appear more masculine."

"Speaking of masculine, did I tell you I had a date wiz Eddie?"

"I suppose you were attracted to his astonishingly high IQ?" Pablo follows this remark with a smile I don't fully understand.

"It wasn't ze size *of hiz* IQ *zat first caught my attention, I must admit."*

Pablo walks around Nina, giving her suit occasional little tugs. "Did he wear his tool belt?"

Jacques rolls onto his stomach, laughing. "Believe me, his drill was all we needed." Then he reaches over to Pablo's night table and pulls out a spent tube of something. "You're getting low," he says. "You must be getting lucky yourself."

Pablo glances up from Nina's inseam. "You're no longer welcome in my drawers, Jacques."

Jacques runs his finger around the rim of the tube. "Yes, Daddy."

I slip out of Pablo's memory.

How funny. He doesn't even like girls. Not the way Nina wants him to. Doesn't Nina know this? Doesn't she remember Jacques in the short shorts?

I scan her memory.

She's forgetting on purpose! She doesn't want it to be true, so she's simply forgetting it on purpose. That's a relief…I guess. But do I really want a mom who's prone to forgetting on purpose? Won't this make her difficult to deal with in the future? Especially when I get to my teenage years and need strong guidance. Then again, she *is* an actress and that's bound to make her a bit quirky. Having an actress for a mom is going to be so cool. I'll tell the kids at school that she didn't forget to pick me up; her *rehearsal* ran late. Yeah, her show opens this Friday. Autograph? Well sure, I can probably arrange that, for a dollar.

I return to the bar and watch smugly as Pablo pretends to listen to Nina, his attention drifting to a guy in leather pants at a nearby table.

CHAPTER FIVE

By the time I get back to Rick, he's home and sitting on the front porch step, gazing out onto the warm night, mulling over his encounter with Nina—or, more precisely, how he screwed it up. *I passed out, for Christsakes!* he thinks. *How lame!* Occasionally he allows himself a thought of Nina that isn't wrapped in self-deprecation: the sway of her body as she walked off with her friends, her resonant voice, her sumptuous red hair… The whole bohemian nature of her scene is so different from the guys at Jack's Tires and their ultra-bland girlfriends that it makes Rick feel like sprinting around the block—or howling. But he doesn't do either of these things. He just sits there, the corner of his mouth tipped up on one side. What a perfect couple they'll make. Her dramatic style coupled with his reserve and good sense is inspired. But for now it's just me and him, a couple of guys dreaming about a girl…dreaming about…

The screen door squeaks open. Rick jumps.

A slender middle-aged woman dressed in a baby blue nightgown and robe steps out. Her graying hair falls softly around her shoulders. "You're home early," she says.

"Yeah."

"Did you have a nice time?"

Gazing upon this vision of perfect grandmotherliness, I can't believe my…luck. And once again it's working in my favor. I picture myself on the couch snuggled next to this woman, a handmade afghan thrown over our knees. I'm listening to her read me a story about a troll who lives under a bridge while I munch a homemade chocolate chip cookie.

"Why are you up?" Rick asks, his voice a tad disrespectful, in my opinion.

I scan to see if he's hurt her feelings, but she's aware that her son is going through a difficult time. Ever since Howie's enlistment she's seen him struggling, as if he too wants to do something big and meaningful, but he can't figure out what. Now, after seeing Howie, the pressure has only gotten worse.

"It's such a warm night," she says, joining him on the step, "and the crickets are so loud…" She runs her fingers lightly across her upper lip, trying to think of something to say, something that will put him at ease.

Rick doesn't appreciate this. Doesn't appreciate *her*, if you ask me. Here, he can tell her anything, do anything, and all she will do is love him. She's been picking up his messes, cooking his meals, Band-Aiding his cuts for years, but instead of being beholden to her, he acts like she's some kind of intruder in his life, like she has no business sitting on her own front porch. He unlaces his shoes, takes them off along with his socks, then spreads out his toes, letting the cool air slip between them.

Someone upstairs is snoring. You can hear it from the porch.

Dorothy Hale reaches her hand out to place it on Rick's leg, but places it on the wooden porch next to his leg instead. She's searching for the right words for what she has to say. *Don't settle for less* passes through her mind. So does *Be careful in your choices.* But she says nothing, just keeps her hand next to his leg and lets her mind stray to the angling light on the severely manicured lawn.

They listen to the crickets and the snoring.

So do I. It's nice.

Then Rick stands. "I'm gonna hit the hay. 'Night, Mom," he says before slipping through the screen door into the house.

Dorothy closes her eyes and wraps one hand around her waist; the other hand, trembling, pinches the bridge of her nose.

Rick! I wanted to scream, *Come back! Gramma is about to cry!* But he's clueless, padding his way up to his bedroom, pulling his T-shirt over his head.

What's making her so sad?

The answer is buried beneath tons of useless worry. Things like: *Do I have enough butter for the casserole I promised the church? Will I have enough time to get the brakes on the car looked at before I'm due at the hairdresser's?* And *What to do about the stain on the new couch?* Underneath all this I find the cause for her tears. Rick, she fears, will be moving out soon. And then it will be just her and the snorer, Richard Douglas Hale II.

CHAPTER SIX

A week of observation later and I'm a total mess. Popping back and forth between Nina's and Rick's very different lives has made me realize what a crazy move I made when I chose parents that don't even know each other. Could I have been any less practical?

At the moment I'm watching my man Rick loll around in bed convincing himself it would be a waste of time to go to the St. Theresa's graduation party. *Nina won't be interested in a guy whose life is going nowhere*, he thinks. *So why not stay in bed all day? That will show her!* He heaves onto his side and tries to go back to sleep.

Show her? What is he talking about? He can't show her anything if he doesn't go to that ding-dang party! I'm doomed. Toast. An unmet dream drifting off on the wind…

Right in the middle of my ruminations, Richard Douglas Hale II, a.k.a. The Snorer, bursts through the bedroom door. "Rise and shine, my boy! We have work to do!" He's wearing his weekend outfit: starched khakis, black leather belt, and a bright white T-shirt stretched across his hard-earned and much-flaunted six-pack. His short silver-white hair has a razor-sharp part on the side.

After a week, I'm still trying to warm up to the idea of this guy as my grandfather. From my observations, he seems the type who will never let a kid win—not even in a friendly race to the end of the block. "Toughen up" is one of his favorite things to say. That, and "Better than a sharp stick in the eye." Rick pretty much shares my opinion of his dad and pulls the pillow over his face. "Leave me alone. I want to sleep."

"Sleep? Sleep? You think your friend Howie's sleeping in

this morning? You think he's saying, 'I think I'll sleep in instead of defending my country'? Do you?"

Rick takes the pillow from his head and opens an eye. "Leave Howie out of this."

"Well, just so you know, I dropped your name to Stan at the office. Once we're done with the reorganization, he says we'll talk."

"Sounds like I'm a shoo-in."

"You plan on wasting your life changing tires?"

Rick lets one leg drop to the floor. "I'm not going to sell insurance, Dad."

Richard Douglas Hale II places his hands low on his hips and spreads his stance, cowboy-style. "Don't suppose you noticed those rotting boards on the back porch."

Rick groans.

"Hey! No complaints, mister. You live at home, you help at home. We're burning daylight. Hop to it."

Obnoxious as Richard's tactics are, I have to give credit where it's due. He's gotten Rick out of bed. Quite an accomplishment given the circumstances.

Once dressed, downstairs, and jacked on coffee, Rick goes through the motions of ripping up old boards, measuring and cutting new ones, and nailing them down while half listening to his dad spout such bits of knowledge as: "Insurance sales are as likely to happen while you're taking a piss with a fellow as they are in the office." It's painful to watch. And I'm not the only one who thinks so.

Dorothy Hale, who's gearing up to do her weekly cleaning of her husband's home office, stands at the open window and watches too. She's worried about Rick holding in all that anger and wonders if one day he won't just explode. Exhausted from years of reining back her own anger, she lets her gaze travel across the flat oak desktop, stopping on a studio shot of her, Richard, and a pudgy three-year-old Rick standing by a tall fern. She thinks back to the day it was taken.

Before the photo shoot, she slips into the employee bathroom to check her lipstick. Over two weeks late on her period, she prays that she's pregnant. A house with just one child is too quiet, she thinks. Rick needs a brother to tussle with, or a sister to tease. "Mommy, can I have a brother?" he asks her from time to time. She doesn't know what to tell him. Her doctor says there's no medical reason they're unable to conceive again.

As she sits on the toilet, she's sure she can feel her breasts swelling. She even allows herself to believe that the next year's portrait will include a baby in her arms. Then she sees the blood on her panties. She's calm at first, going through the motions of peeing and wiping, rising from the toilet, pulling up her stockings. She runs shaky hands over her wool skirt to make sure that her slip isn't showing and walks to the sink where she reads the sign tacked there. REMEMBER TO WASH YOUR HANDS BEFORE LEAVING! *Suddenly, her throat begins to tighten; air can barely squeeze past to her lungs. She drops to her knees, her fingers tearing at her collar. Air! She needs air!*

"Everything okay, dear?" Richard asks through the door, his voice brusque, irritated. "We're all waiting out here."

"Fine," she squeezes through her tight vocal cords. "Just fine."

I watch Dorothy place the photograph back on the desk. How sad. She was begging for a Floating Soul and one never found her. She runs an absentminded hand over the back of her slender neck. *Such a perfect picture*, she thinks, *just like a Sears Catalogue family.* She picks up her bottle of Pledge and tries to get on with cleaning but, to her amazement, her finger refuses to press down on the spray button. She tries with her other hand, but it won't work the bottle either. Her hands have gone on strike! After years of toiling away, they, of their own accord, drop the dust rag to the floor, place the Pledge onto the desk, and set about finding something new to do. She reaches into Richard's top desk drawer and snatches up a pen and yellow tablet. Before she knows it, she's scrawling words at top speed. Tons and tons of words, one after the next after the next after the next all dumping out onto the page. It wasn't the den that needed cleaning out, but Dorothy herself.

She knows I'm coming. She has to. Why else would she be tidying her muddled self up? And thinking about babies?

Outside, Richard Douglas Hale II is watching his son paint a coat of primer over a new board. "Don't let it rope up like that, son. It's the mark of inexperience!"

Rick dips his paintbrush back into the primer. *Screw it!* he thinks. *I'm going to that party. It's either that or kill myself.*

Chapter Seven

Only five hours until the dance. I can't wait! Nina's friend Lottie Yang is up on the ladder holding a Styrofoam Jupiter. Missy's on the floor cutting out zodiac symbols. They're trying to make the St. Theresa's cafeteria look like it's the 1970s.

"Has anyone seen Nina?" Lottie asks.

Missy, still hoping she has a chance with Rick, sends up another stupid prayer that he'll make an appearance. "I ran into her family on the way over. They came for graduation."

"I thought she said they were coming tomorrow."

"Me too."

Lottie snickers. "I hope they can find her. Far as I know, she never made it back last night."

Oh shoot! What did I miss now? Last I saw Nina she'd just finished her theater history exam and said she was planning to sleep until the year 2020.

I zip across campus to her dorm. Her room is empty, but the stuffy common room is filled with Kalinas. All but Nina. And none of them look happy, except Hester Kalina, Nina's nine-year-old sister. She's waiting for a text message reply from her best friend. She swings her feet, causing them to bounce on the front of the couch where she sits. *Bonk! Bonk! Bonk!* Charlotte Kalina, Nina's older sister, gives Hester a look. *Grow up!* it says. Hester returns it with a sarcastic smile of her own, then takes her strawberry-flavored lip gloss from her clear plastic purse and pointedly applies it to her lips. Charlotte sighs and goes back to her needlepoint of a duck. Hester thinks it's weird that Charlotte still lives at home, but her mother has told her it has to do with Charlotte's brittle constitution.

Iris Kalina, Nina's mom, is so angry she could spit. She even shot an e-mail to Nina to remind her of their arrival, so where is she? She reaches into her purse for her Salem Lights, then remembers she's in a public building. She walks over to the window and searches for a sign of Nina. When Iris called her twenty minutes ago, she sounded as if she'd just woken up.

Harvey Kalina is drumming his fingers on his knee. His legs are so long and the couch so low, he looks like a grasshopper. "Iris, would you like a stick of Juicy Fruit?"

"No, I would not," Iris says.

Harvey twists his wedding ring round and round on his finger, and closes his eyes. The ringing in his ears is threatening to turn into a colossal headache. He hopes he hasn't picked up the flu that's going around the schools. He's seen a lot of sick kids in his doctor's office this last week.

Bonk! Bonk! Bonk! "Mom, when Nina gets here could we get something to eat? I'm starving."

Iris sighs. "We'll see, Hessy."

Bonk! Bonk! Bonk!

This is intolerable. I'm going to go find her.

After a bit of a search, I find Nina in the passenger seat of a sporty Jetta with Pablo at the wheel. His hair is rumpled, he has sleep in the corners of his eyes, and he wears pajama pants and a T-shirt. Not only did Iris's call wake him from a perfectly good sleep, but also he had to borrow the car from his apartment manager to race Nina back to the dorm. He's none too happy about any of it.

They turn into the St. Theresa's parking lot. "I'm so embarrassed about last night," Nina says checking her hair in the visor mirror. She pulls a silk necktie from her pocket.

"We were drunk."

Whoa doggies! What did I miss? I scan back in time. After Nina finished her final exam, she did not go home and go to sleep until 2020 like she said she would. Shoot!

Once back at the dorm, Nina's so wired she can't even think of sleeping. She calls Dink, but Dink's not home, Pablo is. He tells her he's on his way out to a bar called Chaps. She asks if she can join him, and he says—as a joke!—"If you dress like a man." And damned if she doesn't take him up on it, dressing in a suit, tie, red high tops and a Yankees ball cap.

The guys at Chaps—a total dive—all think she's a boy, an underage hottie who slipped past the bouncer. And does she love it. So does Pablo—at first, until she starts getting drunk. Then he begins to worry. He has to pull her away from a guy in leather who's trying to get her to join him in the men's room.

"We should go," Pablo slurs.

"Why? Are you jealous?"

"You don't know what you're getting into."

"Maybe I do," she says, but still she lets him lead her out of the bar and into a taxi.

Nina says she wants to show Dink her costume, so they head straight to Pablo and Dink's. Being a boy makes Nina feel sexy. Anything could happen tonight, *she thinks. When Dink isn't home they crank up the CD player and start dancing to a song about being too sexy for their clothes. Nina flings her arms around Pablo's neck and whispers in his ear, "Why can't all men be like you?" She follows this by kissing him right on the mouth.*

Then instead of him saying, "Nina, I'm into men," like he should *say, Pablo takes her in his arms and kisses her back. A long, slow, wet one. I watch in horror as they continue playing swirly with each other's tongues while simultaneously heading toward his bedroom. At the doorway, Pablo slides his hands from her buttock to the front of her trousers searching for her fly. But he doesn't find what he's looking for. Oh no. There's a sag where there should be a bulge. He staggers back, almost trips. "Shit!"*

Nina reaches down to help. "I'll get it."

He turns away and runs his fingers through his hair. "Whoa... this is too weird."

"What?"

"We almost..."

"So?"

"Nina, this is so not going to happen."

At first I think Nina doesn't get it, because she just smiles and begins dancing again. Then I notice that on the inside she wants to cry.

I return to the present.

Nina's still in the car with Pablo, but the car is now in the parking lot by the dorm. Nina is tying up her shirttails to make herself look a bit more feminine.

Why can't she get it through her head? Pablo's gay. Gay! Gay! Gay! Gay! He likes men! Maybe after last night she'll finally catch on. I hope so.

There was a time I never had to Hope. I *Knew*.

Hoping sucks.

❖

Nina's sister Charlotte looks up from her needlepoint and sees the Jetta pull into the parking lot. "Here she is," she sings smugly.

Iris glances at her watch, then at Harvey. Harvey's eyes are shut. "Harvey," she says sharply. "She's here."

"I heard."

Hester goes to the window. "She's with a guy!"

Charlotte rolls her eyes and says under her breath, "She would be."

Inside the car Pablo pops open the door lock. "Good luck, Neen."

Nina runs her necktie through the loops in her slacks to make it look like a sash. "Pablo, I'm so sorry—"

"Don't worry about it."

"I'm just saying."

"Forget it."

She snatches up her jacket and ball cap and takes the stairs two at a time, fighting back tears the whole way. When she enters the community room, Hester flies at her full throttle. "Nina! You look so cool!"

No one else gets up.

Nina hugs her little sister. "Hey, Hessy!" She forces a smile. "You look so grown up."

Hester holds up her new cell phone. "Look what I got!"

"Cool."

"It's 'cuz I got all As."

Nina waits for someone else to say something. They don't. "Welcome to St. T's!" she says finally.

Iris snaps open her purse and pulls out her Salem Lights and lighter. "I believe you owe us an apology."

"You were supposed to come tomorrow!"

Charlotte, clearly not going to cut Nina one bit of slack, says, "And I suppose you wouldn't have stayed at your boyfriend's house if you'd known we were going to be here?"

"At least I have a life!"

"That's enough, you two," Iris says, then gets to her feet, holding her unlit cigarette a few inches from her mouth. "Since it seems to have slipped your mind that we were coming, I suppose we will have to search out some accommodations for tonight."

Nina sighs. "We'll figure out something. But I have a party tonight."

Iris pops the cigarette in her mouth and walks to the door. "Why don't you take Charlotte? Then at least one of us will be included in your busy life."

Charlotte turns to her father. "I don't want to go to a party. I have a stomachache."

"Nonsense!" Iris says and leaves the room.

Nina flings her jacket and ball cap onto the couch. "If I have to take Charlotte to the party, I'm not going."

Harvey sighs, hoping there's a double dry martini somewhere in his immediate future.

CHAPTER EIGHT

Me and Rick are at the dance, only he wants to leave. I can see why. Missy is gripping his arm so tight she's cutting off his circulation. She spotted him the second he pushed through the cafeteria doors and has been motor-mouthing at him ever since. She's dressed in a paisley minidress and has white hoop earrings. Her eyelids are dusted baby blue, which matches the glowing zodiac signs pasted on the old plaster walls. A giant revolving mirror ball tosses coins of light onto the linoleum floor. The dining tables are all pushed to one side of the hall, making the small clusters of partyers seem miles apart. There's a slight hum in the sound system.

Rick scans the smatterings of crowd on the dance floor, then around the edges, searching for Nina. But she's not here; not yet.

I've been popping back and forth between the two of them all day, and for a while, it seemed like Nina really *wasn't* going to go to the party. Fortunately, she came to her senses. If she didn't go she'd be obliged to hang out with her whole family as well as with Charlotte. At least at the dance she can dump Charlotte.

Now if Nina would just get here.

"How about some punch?" Missy asks, guiding Rick past the floor of gyrating bodies. I want to bean her. He's already told her he's not much of a dancer. Why won't she back off?

Rick gazes at the Styrofoam solar system floating above the refreshment table and it makes him think of Howie a million miles away. *I should be with him*, he thinks. *At least then my life would mean something.*

Oh, *that's* a good idea, Rick. Patrolling a hostile area packed inside a sweltering Humvee with a bunch of foulmouthed soldiers in need of a bath, that *sure* sounds better than a college dance.

"Are you sure you're all right?" Missy asks.

"Just taking it all in," he replies and draws a ladle through the thick orange punch.

Think I'll go check back in on Nina. This is excruciating.

I find her at the motel, lying belly up on one of two double beds. Due to graduation, the Kalinas had a rough time finding a vacancy in the area. Now they're all stuffed into one small motel room. Tomorrow they'll move to the Holiday Inn where Nina has reserved them two rooms. At the moment, it's just Nina and Charlotte in the one room. The rest have gone out for dinner.

"You look *fine*, Charlotte," Nina says.

Charlotte lets her hair drop from her attempt at a bun and massages her temples. "I don't know why I feel so dizzy."

Nina picks up a laminated card full of emergency numbers by the phone. She positions it to blot Charlotte from her view. "Just because you're coming with me, don't think I'm going to hang out with you. You're on your own as soon as we get there."

"Take care of me? You think *you* have to take care of *me*?"

The key rattles in the door and the rest of the Kalinas pile into the room, all except Harvey, who's driving Nina and Charlotte to the dance. He's opted to wait in the parking lot.

"There's some leftover mu shu pork if you're hungry," Iris says.

Hester flops down on the bed next to Nina. "My fortune said 'A kiss awaits you under a night sky'! Maybe I should go with you tonight."

Nina ruffles Hester's hair. "You're too young."

Iris sits in the hotel room's only chair. "Let the girls get ready, Hessie. Daddy's waiting for them at the car." She picks up a Planned Parenthood flyer she needs to proofread.

Charlotte charges out of the room into the parking lot. "Dad, I really don't know why Mom's making me go to this stupid dance tonight! I'm not going to know anyone and I'm not feeling well. Would you check my forehead and see if I'm hot?"

Harvey wearily places his hand on her forehead. "You feel fine."

"Are you sure?"

Harvey gazes up at the neon sign that once read SADDLE UP MOTEL, but now reads SADD…P MOTEL. "Honey, you wouldn't want to stay here all night with us old folks. You should be out having fun."

Nina, who followed her sister out, tugs at her halter top so it shows a bit more cleavage. "Hmm…Fun with Charlotte…isn't that an oxymoron?"

Harvey pulls his car keys from his pocket. "Okay, you two. Let's go." He's thinking how tricky girls are. He should know—a wife and three daughters. Bet he'll be happy to have a grandson to take to a ball game…or fishing…or camping. I can see it now: me, Rick, and Harvey sitting around a campfire gutting fish and talking man stuff. I can't wait!

Speaking of Rick, I wonder if he's shaken Missy yet?

Nope. He's still by the punch bowl and she's still blabbing away.

But somebody's watching them. Dink Raz. Interesting. She's the one who noticed him fainting too; the one whose eyelinered eyes locked onto his when his world started swirling. Now here she is again. This time, though, she's hiding behind a potted ficus, using it the way a duck hunter uses a blind. She pulls out a flask of Jack Daniel's, spikes her punch, then squints her eyes to make Rick and Missy go blurry. She unsquints them, causing the couple's edges to sharpen. Squints again. Unsquints. I feel like she's important to me somehow. Maybe The Known wants me to know her. Is that possible?

I'll keep her under close surveillance.

She focuses on Rick. She's thinking, *Poor guy, he seems so… stuck.* Then, because he doesn't look like the usual jerks who hang around the St. Theresa's events, she steps around the ficus and walks over. "Aren't you the dude who passed out at our play?"

Rick is so happy to have someone besides Missy to talk to that he doesn't care that Dink brought up his fainting; he just laughs. "That would be me. It's so weird. I've never done that before." He checks out the upside-down American flag that Dink has pinned to her jean jacket and her spiky black hair and is intrigued.

Missy glares at Dink; she doesn't want to share. But Dink isn't interested in Rick the way that Missy is. She sees Rick as a buddy, not as date potential—like how Rick and Howie are with each other. Friends. For that matter, she doesn't see boys as date potential at all.

She's like Pablo, only with girls. But why would two XXs want to be together? Or two XYs? The Land of Forgetting is about reproduction and getting born.

I wonder if it's possible for a soul to get the wrong body? Like, for a boy soul to get a girl's body. That might explain why Dink doesn't want to admit to herself that she likes girls instead of boys.

Wait. The Known can't make mistakes.

Can it?

Maybe her refusal to admit she likes girls has to do with those nasty earthly assumptions and opinions I've been warned about. They could *for sure* make a girl feel like she should like boys.

Should. There's a loaded word…

But all this is pointless to even consider. Once a Floating Soul attaches to a bunch of cells, the cells and soul blend, making it impossible to tell what is soul and what are cells. The main thing is, I know *I'm* a boy.

Now, if I could just get myself born.

"Rick, this is Dink," Missy mumbles. "She directed *Endgame*."

He reaches out his hand. "Nice to meet you—officially."

Dink takes a swig of her spiked punch before reaching out her hand to meet his. She notices his calluses and wonders what he does for a living.

"I don't know much about directing," Rick says, "but it seems to me you must have done a good job, or I would have noticed."

Dink thinks this statement astute, and pairs it with the callused hand: *Blue collar but intellectual, has a good sense for theater. A nice change from the clichéd frat dudes that usually hover around St. Theresa's.* "I hate shows where all you think about is the director's concept," she says, testing him.

"It's like anything," Rick says, "the work should stand for itself."

Dink smiles. *Definitely a kindred*, she thinks.

Missy tugs at her eyebrow.

"Any word on Nina?" Dink asks her.

"Isn't Nina the actress who played the servant?" Rick asks like he doesn't already know.

Missy begins excessively blinking her heavily made-up eyes. "She may not even come tonight. Her family just sort of showed up this afternoon."

Dink flashes open her jacket. Her silver flask is tucked in like a baby. "Anyone up for a spike?"

Rick checks out her flask. "My friend had—has!—a flask just like that. He's in Iraq."

"We should drink to him, then," Dink says and pours them each a splash. She holds up her Dixie cup. "To…what's his name?"

"Howie."

"To Howie, who's risking his life so every American can drive an SUV."

"Actually, his dad was on one of the planes that blew up the Twin Towers."

Dink didn't expect this. "Oh, man…I'm sorry."

Rick shrugs.

"No," Dink says. "That was insensitive. Let me try again."

And she does, but Rick doesn't listen. *No matter what this war is about*, he thinks, *Howie's not there for oil; he's there for blood. I just hope it's not his own.* He notices that Dink and Missy are waiting to clink cups, so he lifts his to meet theirs. "To Howie," he says, then right before chugging, he spots Nina on the stairs.

They made it!

Nina looks over her shoulder to make sure her dad is gone, then turns to Charlotte. "You're on your own. Try to have a good time."

Charlotte reaches for her sleeve. "Nina!" But she isn't quick enough to stop Nina from skipping down the steps into the cafeteria. Intensely self-conscious to be standing alone, she takes in the decorations. Underneath a floating solar system she notices the punch bowl and beelines for it.

Whoa! What's going on? I feel a strange sensation—as if I'm being pulled somewhere else. Why on earth would I want to go somewhere else? Nina and Rick are in the same room. They could fall in love any minute now. I ignore the feeling and follow Nina to the dance floor. She's met by a circle of dancing friends.

Again, this pulling feeling!

I zip over to Rick. He's trying to be subtle about watching Nina, but Dink notices and feels oddly conflicted. On the one hand, Rick might be the perfect person to get Nina over her weird obsession with Pablo. On the other hand…

—Whoa! What just happened? Where am I?

Some kind of market. A small one. What the heck am I doing *here*? I glide through the aisles of canned goods and toiletries for a clue. Harvey Kalina is perusing the candy rack. He stopped off for a pack of Juicy Fruit. Okay…I'm glad to know my future grandfather likes gum. Now, I'm going back to the dance.

…

I repeat, I'm going back to the dance.

…

This is a first. I'm being kept here against my will.

I focus in on Harvey, and although he appears to be searching for gum, that's not really what he's looking for. His life seems to have slipped by him when he wasn't paying attention. He gazes at the shelf of brightly colored wrappers, wanting to postpone his return to the motel as long as possible.

A man up front is arguing with the clerk.

"How's a person supposed to know the Pepto-Bismol is in the soda aisle?"

"Well, sir, it's not just the soda aisle. If you'll notice, there's also a large array of pharmaceuticals."

"Where's the sign? Why don't you people post signs?"

What do you know? It's Richard Douglas Hale II with a monstrous heartburn he's sure is due to the grilled onions he had on his sandwich earlier in the day. But it's the distance he feels from Rick and his wife that's causing him the pain in his chest, not the grilled onions. He's upset that Dorothy didn't do her weekly shopping today. And when he told her to pick up some Pepto-Bismol, she barely even looked up from that blasted yellow pad she was writing in. *It's not just my son who's gone soft in the head*, he thinks, *my wife has too.* He yells at the pimply, big-eared clerk. "Do you want my business or don't you?"

I look down on the two men whose chromosomes are full of traits that are going to be passed on to me, and boy, am I glad Harvey chooses to avoid the ruckus in the front of the market by picking up a box of Good & Plenty for Hester. This would be a terrible first impression for him to have of Richard. And I want them to like each other. They're going to be my grandfathers.

Harvey approaches the counter only when he's certain the obnoxious customer has left. He makes an extra effort to smile and even tells the cashier his joke about the cowboy and the nun.

Once again I try returning to the dance and this time I'm able. What a relief! Still, I find myself oddly comforted by this detour. Surely it must mean my fate is lining up. Mustn't it?

As it turns out, I haven't missed much at the dance. Nina is still on the dance floor with her friends and Rick is behind the ficus with Dink, who's pouring him and Missy more Jack Daniel's. Missy is blathering about the two chaperones who she's sure are having an affair while Rick scopes out Charlotte, who's standing by the punch bowl. *Since she arrived with Nina*, he reasons, *she must have inside information.* He excuses himself from Missy's tedious monologue and pushes past the ficus.

Charlotte keeps her eyes trained on the dance floor. She's aware that a guy just stepped up to the refreshments table but thinks better of speaking to him. She doesn't want to appear forward. Her fingers tighten around her cup as she tries to look as though things are just how she wants them—standing friendless by the punch bowl—but she's acutely conscious of the length of her skirt, a good three inches longer than any one else's, and that she's about the only woman there, besides the chaperones, who isn't flaunting her naked midriff. She draws the sweet punch through her tight lips and finds it difficult to swallow.

Rick struggles with what to say to this matronly young woman. *How do you know Nina?* although direct, doesn't seem like a proper introduction. He stirs the punch with the clear plastic ladle and contemplates his first line. "Do you go here?" he finally asks.

Charlotte coughs up a little punch. "Excuse me?" She snatches up a napkin to blot her mouth.

Rick pretends not to notice the drip of punch on her chin. "Uh, I was just wondering if you go here, you know, to St. Theresa's."

"Me? Oh, no. I'm here with my sister. My family came in for her graduation."

Rick can't believe his luck. "So you're Clov's sister."

"Clov? No. You must have me mistaken. I'm Nina Kalina's sister." Charlotte pops a pretzel into her mouth, which she instantly regrets. Now she has to chew. *A case of mistaken identity*, she thinks. She runs her tongue around her mouth trying to coax the dry pretzel from her gums.

Rick, fighting the urge to stick his head in the punch bowl, forges on. "She was in a play I saw, *Endgame*."

"Oh, that's right. She mentioned something about that." Talking about Nina is not one of Charlotte's favorite topics. "Are you her boyfriend?"

"Boyfriend?"

Charlotte rubs her hands down the front of her skirt, securing it around her thighs. "Well, I guess you're off the hook, then. If you *had* been her boyfriend, I would have given you a piece of my mind. Keeping her out like that!" Charlotte goes on to give Rick a piece of her mind anyway. "My parents were so humiliated by that stunt she pulled last night, or this *morning*, I should say."

As Charlotte rambles on, my man Rick's expression freezes into one of attentiveness. Each of Charlotte's Ps becomes a mini cruise missile, each of her Ts a nuclear explosion. *I should just leave*, he thinks. While *I* think I might as well evaporate right here and now, call the whole thing quits. Charlotte is ruining everything. But before I can take action on this dire plan of mine, Dink Raz walks over to Rick and claps a hand on his shoulder. "Hey, cowboy, how are you enjoying the wonderful world of St. Theresa's?"

Dink. Again.

Charlotte's mouth comes to an abrupt halt.

Dink takes her hand from Rick's shoulder and reaches it out to Charlotte. "You must be Nina's sister. We've all heard so much about you. I'm Dink. Dink Raz. And this is Missy Hooten," she says, beckoning to a buzzed Missy. "Another friend of Nina's. And from what Nina tells me, you and she have a lot in common." I chuckle as Dink prays no one asks her *what* the two have in common. The personality of sandpaper would be all she could come up with.

Charlotte smiles a smile too big to be sincere. "Yes. I'm Charlotte, Nina's *older* sister. My family is visiting from—"

"Why don't you show Charlotte around a little?" Dink says, resting her arm on Missy's shoulders. "Introduce her to some of the gang."

Missy begins tugging at her eyebrow again. "Sure."

Dink flashes her a peace sign as if to say, *So go already*.

Missy peels herself out from under Dink's arm and addresses Charlotte in a tone just shy of rude. "Uh. Maybe you'd like to see the photography exhibit in the hall." And off they go.

"Let those two piranhas chew on each other for a while," Dink says before chugging the dregs of her punch. She smiles at Rick. "Welcome to St. T's. Land of sugar 'n spice 'n everything nice."

Rick runs his fingers through his hair. He's dying to ask Dink about Nina's boyfriend.

Dink tosses her cup. "You look like you could use some fresh air. Want to check out the patio?"

Before they push through the French doors, Lottie comes rushing up. "Dink! There you are! I've been looking for you everywhere! Something weird is happening with the light board!"

"Have you checked the dimmers?"

"What's a dimmer?"

Dink sighs and looks at Rick. "Duty calls. I'll meet you out there." Once Lottie has turned away, she whispers, "I've got an attitude adjustment rolled in my pocket. So stick around." I just pray Rick doesn't check out the dance floor. Nina's dancing with some punked-out dude in leather pants who she has no interest in, but Rick doesn't know that and it might scare him off.

The punked-out dude pulls Nina in close. "I've done a bit of acting myself," he says, his breath smelling of alcohol and cigarettes.

Nina pulls away. "I'm feeling nauseous. I think I need to go outside."

He doesn't offer to escort her to the patio, which suits her just fine. All she wanted was some fresh air and to shake him off. She begins making her way across the dance floor now crowded with dancers. I go on ahead. I can't wait to see if Rick did like Dink asked him to.

He did! He's out there waiting for her. Nina and Rick are finally going to be alone together.

Thank you, Dink! When I get born, I'll owe you one.

Chapter Nine

The sight of Nina pushing through the French doors onto the patio has me giddy beyond belief. She pauses for a moment, letting the soft summer air caress her skin. My man Rick has his back to her. He's looking out onto a small apple grove. His forearms rest on the railing. The starlight dusting his outline makes him appear mysterious to Nina and she wonders if he's someone she knows.

She saunters over, curious, but doesn't say anything. She's waiting for *him* to say something, which he doesn't. The two of them just stand there gazing out over the apple grove like a couple of mutes. Why won't she look at him? She might recognize him and then she could start up a conversation about him fainting—or maybe not that, that might embarrass him—but she could ask him about the play…or about…well, I don't know. She could say *something*.

Rick, assuming it's Dink, finally speaks. "You get it worked out?"

Nina makes a point of misunderstanding him. "I don't think life is meant to be worked out."

Rick turns, and when he sees it's Nina—and that he's standing not five feet from her—one of his elbows slips off the rail.

She laughs. "Wow. You must have been pretty lost in thought. You want to stay that way?"

He tries to regain his composure by standing up straight. "I thought you were someone else."

Nina squints her eyes and cocks her head. "Don't I know you?"

But Rick's mind is stuck on Charlotte's words about Nina's boyfriend. "I don't know," he says.

"I'm sure you look familiar."

Rick pulls a splinter from the rail and tosses it into the orchard, thinking, *Oh yeah. I'm the unconscious lump you had to step over on your closing night; a guy you'd really want to leave your boyfriend for.* He turns away from her, back to the shadowy trees. "Sometimes I don't even know if I know myself."

Rick! My life is at stake here! Is that the best you can do?

Then, to my surprise, his statement causes her to reflect on the last forty-eight hours of her life. "I know what you mean…" she whispers.

The two of them gaze out onto the orchard, afraid to look at each other, and it occurs to me that if Rick said what I'd wanted him to, "I love you, Nina. Let's get married and have a baby," she would have thought he was a kook. Rick is playing it perfectly, and he's not even trying. He's aroused her curiosity. She peeks back at him and realizes why she knows him. She fiddles with the silver bangles around her wrist. "Did you even like the play?"

He turns toward her. "I loved it. Especially you…the part you played…Clov."

Just the fact that somebody thinks she's special causes Nina's eyes to fill with tears. She clenches her jaw trying to hold them back, but an audible sniff sneaks out.

"Hey…" Rick says, softly. "What's the matter?"

She covers her face with her hands. "This is so stupid. I never cry."

Rick's arms ache to embrace her. "Maybe that's why you're doing it now."

She snort-laughs. "What? Like my tear valve got backed up?" Then she clears her throat, trying to pretend that weird noise didn't just come out of her nose. "I hate girls that cry all the time." This is followed by another surge of tears.

Rick can't figure out what he should do. He doesn't know her well enough to comfort her. Plus, he has no idea what she's crying about. He snags his pocketknife from his pocket and cuts a makeshift hanky from the bottom edge of his T-shirt. "Here."

"You ruined your shirt."

He tucks in his T-shirt, almost hiding the chunk out of the bottom. "Big deal. I've got plenty of shirts, but your tears are a rare commodity."

She smiles weakly, taking him in. Like me, she likes his hands, but she's also drawn to his sleek, muscular frame, his quiet panache. "How about all this snot?"

He smiles, making the corner of his eyes crinkle just perfectly. "I'll look the other way."

Nina blows her nose.

My first taste of family.

And speaking of family, I feel trouble brewing in an outlying post. Better go check it out.

❖

Missy and Charlotte are angling their way around the freestanding screens of the student photography exhibit in the hallway by the cafeteria. Charlotte looks about as happy as a cat on a leash. Missy is bending her ear about the illogical nature of men. "I mean, who wants a boyfriend anyway? They're too hard to figure. I don't even think *they* know what they want. Once in a while you meet a good one. But they're always taken…"

If Charlotte were listening, I'm sure she'd take pleasure in pointing out that Missy is contradicting herself. But she isn't listening. She's fuming about how she got dumped on Missy and she's certain that Nina is at the bottom of it. Missy's chatter is giving her a headache. "Missy? Where's the restroom?"

"What?"

Charlotte notes Missy's odd blink pattern, how she'll talk for minutes on end without a single blink, then punctuate a sentence or an important point with successive blinks. "The ladies' room. I need to go to the ladies' room."

"Oh, right down the hall. Do you want me to wait?"

"No, that's all right. I'm sure you want to get back to your friends."

Missy blinks a few more times, attempting to shrug off Charlotte's dismissal as nothing personal, and tugs at her eyebrow. "Oh, sure… Well, nice to meet you." She stands for a moment longer, unsure of what to do next, then strides off to the main room feeling like a random blip on an otherwise orderly radar screen.

I don't trust Charlotte. She's up to something.

Once in the ladies' room, she locks herself in a stall, kneels by the porcelain bowl, and throws up. When she lifts her head she sees a tiny penis etched crudely into the metal stall. She retches again. *That's it*, she thinks. *I'm calling Dad. He needs to pick us up early.*

She can't be serious. Nina and Rick are falling in love!

She washes up at the sink, pulls out her cell phone, and mumbles, "I'll say it's an emergency."

She doesn't know the meaning of the word. If Nina and Rick don't fall in love tonight, I'm…toast! I zip back to the deck. Nina and Rick are sitting on a rock bench obscured by ivy. They face each other with their backs pressed into the cool granite of the hundred-year-old building. Her sandaled feet almost touch his shoes. It's so tender, so shy—and I don't get to cherish it, because of stupid Charlotte.

Nina fiddles with her bracelets. "Do you go to a lot of plays?"

"Not too many. I was in one, though."

She leans forward and wraps her arms around her knees. "Really?"

"Yup. I played a tree. Third grade."

"A tree?"

"Yeah. Not just any tree. A cherry tree. *The* cherry tree. George Washington hacked me down."

"How tragic!" She laughs.

He laughs too. "Believe it or not, it was a coveted role."

Rick looks over his shoulder, worried about the boyfriend.

She gives his calf a playful kick. "Looking for someone?"

He feels blood rushing up his neck. "No. Just taking it all in. You?"

She flings her arms above her head. "I'm ready for St. T's to be history!"

"Uh, I meant waiting for someone."

She plucks an ivy leaf off the vine and twirls it. "Not consciously." She gives him a naughty look.

Kiss her! Kiss her! I want to scream.

He rubs his hand across his upper lip, then scratches the back of his neck.

I suppose I should be thankful he has so much integrity.

"So your…uh…boyfriend couldn't make it?"

Nina's ivy leaf stops twirling. "My what?"

Rick starts massaging a knuckle.

Nina looks directly at him. "Did you say my boyfriend?"

"Your sister, Charlotte, said…"

Nina crushes the leaf in her fist. "I wish she would butt out of my business! My parents have this warped idea that I can help her with her pathetic social life!" She tosses the wadded-up leaf like a piece of trash. "She told you I have a boyfriend? What else did she tell you?"

"Nothing. We talked…just barely…"

Harvey Kalina and a pale-looking Charlotte step out onto the patio. Nina spots them over Rick's shoulder. "Dad!"

Rick shoots to his feet and spins around as if he has something to feel guilty about.

Nina also stands, only defiantly. "What are you doing here? It can't be ten o'clock."

Charlotte pulls her sweater around her shoulders. "*I'm* sick. *I* need to go home."

Harvey Kalina takes in a lungful of apple-scented air. He thinks to himself that he should have known Charlotte wouldn't have told Nina he was coming.

Nina digs her hands into her hips and her heels into the stone floor. "I'm not going."

"I threw up!" Charlotte counters.

"So? You're always throwing up!"

"Dad! Did you hear what she said?"

Harvey brings his hand to his chin, clears his throat, and prepares to disappoint one of his daughters. But before he has a chance to speak, Rick steps forward. "Uh…I could give Nina a ride across campus if that would…um…help."

Until this moment, Harvey hasn't even noticed Rick. Now he makes a point to. He likes Rick, how he's not afraid of eye contact. That, and the fact that Rick is offering him a viable solution to his problem.

Nina takes Rick's hand. "Dad, this is my friend Rick."

Rick's whole arm is tingling. "It would be no problem. Really…"

But Charlotte can't keep her big mouth shut. "Tomorrow is graduation! Nina should get a good night's sleep!" Her remark hangs in the air like yesterday's balloon.

Harvey uses his dad voice: "Have her back to her dorm before midnight."

Rick squeezes Nina's hand. "Yes, sir."

"Thanks, son. Remember, no later than midnight."

Nina bites back a smile. "I'm not a pumpkin, Dad."

"Your sister's right, Nina. You should get a good night's sleep. It's a big day tomorrow." Even I know that Dr. Kalina is only saying this to pretend he has control over the situation. I watch as he and Charlotte make their way back through the patio doors, she tossing a spiteful glance over her shoulder at Nina.

Once I make it to the Land of Forgetting, I'm never going to presume to know why I'm doing what I'm doing. Look at Charlotte. Her actions tonight actually pushed Nina and Rick closer together. Without even knowing it, she helped set the stage for me. Still, I can't help thinking what a poor choice Charlotte made as a Floating Soul. If she'd just held out for a family a bit more like her, one who appreciated her sense of tradition and fairness, who was as sensitive as she is, she might be more appreciated.

❖

Dink finds Nina and Rick out on the patio.

"You ready for that joint?" she asks.

Nina looks to Rick. "You two know each other?"

"Actually, we just met," he says.

Dink throws an arm around Nina and speaks in an evil-sounding voice. "I saved him from the clutches of Missy Hooten. She wanted him bad."

Nina laughs. "Poor Missy. She's been trying to score a boyfriend all year." But secretly she's pleased that someone besides her finds Rick attractive.

"Let's smoke this joint," Dink says and pulls them back to the stone bench obscured by ivy. "We should be safe here."

The bench is too small for three to sit comfortably, so Rick offers to stand.

"No way," Nina says and plops down on Dink's lap. "You don't mind, do you, Dink?"

Dink doesn't mind at all. In fact, she likes Nina on her lap.

This worries me. Dink couldn't come between Rick and Nina,

could she? I check in with Nina and am mortified to discover that she likes the feel of her hiney against Dink's thighs. She also likes the attention she and Dink are getting from Rick. Dink lights the joint and holds it up to Nina's lips. Nina, her eyes never leaving Rick, brings her lips to Dink's fingers and takes a hit. The whole setup is definitely arousing her.

Shoot! I thought all I had to worry about with Nina was other boys. If I have to start worrying about girls now too, I'm sunk.

And I was just starting to like Dink.

Once the joint is smoked Nina wants to dance. Fortunately, Dink doesn't dance. Neither does Rick, but Nina doesn't give him a choice. She drags him out onto the dance floor and begins showing him off like a lucky penny. At least she's quit thinking about Pablo.

Later, as Nina takes Rick through the photography exhibit, she swishes instead of walks. And at the punch bowl when a bunch of Nina's friends are telling humorous stories about St. Theresa's, Nina's are sprinkled with witty expressions. Having Rick with her makes her feel beautiful. I look around for Dink and she's nowhere to be seen. Good.

At five minutes to midnight Nina and Rick are standing at the doorway to her dormitory. Nina leans against the old cherrywood door. "So, um…I graduate tomorrow."

"Yeah. I know."

"Want to come?"

Rick can't stop thinking about her lips.

"Do you?" she repeats.

"Sure. Yeah. Okay."

Nina wants him to sweep her up in his arms. "I mean, you don't really need an invitation or anything."

He scratches behind his ear. "No problem. I'll come. That would be cool."

"Okay. It's at one o'clock. At the amphitheater." She bites her lower lip, lightly.

"Sweet."

They stand, bodies sticky from dance-floor sweat, gazing into one another's eyes.

Rick's mind is on their last slow dance, how her body tucked into his like a rose in a buttonhole, how the warmth of her breath tickled behind his ear. Hers is on the little exposed patch of skin where he cut his shirt for her. She tips her head back, just slightly.

Rick! Do you think she's doing that for her health? Kiss her, for crying out loud!

He drives his hands deep into his jean pockets. "It's midnight. I should…um…probably go."

I can't believe my ears. And neither can Nina. Insecure thoughts start screaming through her head. *He's not going to kiss me? Did I misread tonight?* Then, somehow, his not kissing her makes her want him even more.

"So, you said one o'clock?" Rick asks.

"Yeah. It might start a little late, but you're going to want to get a seat."

"Okay."

"Okay."

After an excruciating moment—for all of us—she steps toward him, takes his face in her hands, and kisses him fully on the lips.

That's all my man Rick needs. He's the desert and she's the rain. He pulls her to him, his hands sliding up and down her body, drinking her up. And she loves it! She runs her fingers through his hair, up and down his back.

The kiss ends in a gasp.

"Wow," she says.

"Wow," he says.

She rises up onto her toes and brushes Rick's ear with her lips. "See you tomorrow." She turns to unlock the heavy door.

Rick's knees are threatening to collapse. "Nina…?" he says, not sure how to finish the sentence.

She looks over her shoulder right into his eyes, "Me too," she whispers and slips behind the door.

They kissed! They kissed! And they've made plans to see each other tomorrow! How good can it get?

Of course I still have to be conceived. But I've chosen well. I like these two. *Love* them! And they're going to love me. Cherish me. Understand my every eccentricity. I'll have so much love, I'll even spread some around!

CONCEPTION

CHAPTER TEN

Graduation day, I should be excited. Nina has invited Rick; Rick is planning to come. What more could I want?

A mother with a bit of foresight, that's what.

Over the last semester, Nina's rehearsals, finals, late-night tête-à-têtes, performances, parties, and committees somehow got in the way of making plans for *after* St. Theresa's. She thought things like a place to live, a job, money in the bank—in other words, a *life*—would simply fall into place by magic. Reality didn't strike until this morning over bagels and coffee with her family. Iris, starting in on her third cup of strong black coffee, announced, "Charlotte and I have fixed up the basement into a charming little room for you…" causing Nina to nearly choke on her sesame bagel with extra cream cheese.

It's not that she didn't know she'd have to move from the dorm, or that her parents were planning to take her home tomorrow, she just assumed options other than the horror of moving back with her family would present themselves. Nina, I'm learning, is a woman who *relies* on other options presenting themselves. This is what prompted her to neglect mentioning to her mother that she had no intention of moving back home. That other elusive "option" might still be out there, and she wanted to be free to grab it. Besides, if she did say she wasn't moving back home, Iris was bound to ask her silly questions like *where* she was moving to, and for this she has no answer.

Now, as Nina suits up into cap and gown with her fellow graduates, she still has no idea how she's going to get out of moving back home. She balances the mortarboard on her head. It's loose, so she has to bobby-pin it in place. She's sitting by Dink, which also has me a bit worried. Doesn't she have other friends she could dress with? The school's dance studio, which has been co-opted into a dressing room due to its close proximity to the amphitheater, is full of potential friends.

Lottie Yang hands Nina and Dink each a bottle of bubbles. "Right after you throw your cap, start blowing!"

Dink bends down to tie her duct-taped Converse high tops. "Just remember, Lottie, when you make it out there to the real world, there are no pep rallies."

Lottie draws the brows of her almond eyes together. "I can't believe you're wearing those ratty sneakers to graduation."

"Hey! These are my lucky shoes."

"Lucky shoes? That'll get you far in the real world," Lottie says and moves on to another group of graduates.

"That chick is like the Easter Bunny on speed," Dink mumbles to Nina.

"I can't move back home, Dink."

"You got a breath mint? I've got a killer case of cotton mouth."

"If I move back home, I'll shrivel up into a Charlotte."

Dink adjusts Nina's mortarboard. "That I can't imagine."

A professor walks by. "Line up! We're about to start!"

They both stand and Dink starts heading to her place in line.

Nina grabs her hand. "What am I going to do, Dink? My family thinks I'm going back with them."

"You haven't told them?"

"The right moment hasn't presented itself."

Dink likes the feel of her hand in Nina's, but tries not to let it show. She just shakes her head. "You are a real piece of work, Miss Nina Kalina." When Nina doesn't let go, she adds, "Look, why don't you crash at our place for a few nights?"

Nina releases her hand and tucks her bottle of bubbles into her cleavage. "Really?"

Dink flushes. "Just let me know, so I can warn Pablo."

"Warn him? What did he tell you?"

The band begins to play.

"We'll talk more later," Dink says and hurries off to her spot.

❖

Iris, carving a path through the crowd, leads the way up the bleachers. She's followed by Charlotte, then Harvey, then Hester. They're running late because the diner where they had lunch was crowded, on top of which they wouldn't make Iris a Caesar salad. "For Christ's sake, all they had to do was blend some anchovies into oil and vinegar!" she grumbles to Charlotte as she pushes past a bunch of people in her way.

Harvey stops to apologize to a family they've just tramped through.

Charlotte, scuttling to keep up with Iris, tries to explain that there's a little more to making Caesar salad than blending up anchovies. Iris is not the least bit interested. "What was Nina thinking?" she says searching for a place that will fit all four of them. "That we'd just drive up here this morning? The traffic would have been insane!"

Harvey points to an empty stretch of bench. "There's a spot…"

"I'll get it!" Hester says.

Iris barks, "Slow down, Hessy!"

None of this is how I imagined today would go. Everyone's so grumpy. They're not even appreciating that it didn't rain the way the forecasters predicted. Instead they're annoyed by the glaring sun and using their hands to shield their eyes. "Who would have thought they'd have it outside?" Iris asks, though it's written right there on the invitation.

Harvey gives Hester's hand a squeeze. He's feeling guilty. It's his first time to see Nina's school. He meant to visit before, but never got around to it. Now, to make up for his negligence, he's being extra observant. Focusing on strangers also helps him blot out Iris's mood. He spots Rick in the crowd. Rick is looking for a place to sit. Harvey shoots to his feet and whistles.

"Who's that, Dad?" Hester asks.

"Oh, no," Charlotte groans.

Hester turns to her sister. "What?"

"It's one of Nina's boyfriends."

Hester, biting back a smile, stands to get a better look. "She has more than one?"

Iris holds her program over her eyes and squints. "Harvey, who is this boy?"

Rick nods at Harvey and begins to walk over.

Harvey stretches out his hand. "Uh, Rick…is that right?"

"Yeah. Nice to see you again, Dr. Kalina." Rick thinks he's getting all this attention because Nina told her family that she liked him. He smiles at Charlotte.

Charlotte returns a curt smile, then buries her nose in her program.

"Join us," Harvey says. "Unless you have someone else you're meeting here." Before Rick can answer, Harvey starts introducing him around. "This is Hester, and my wife, Iris. I believe you've already met Charlotte."

Rick sits between Harvey and Hester. "Nice to meet you all."

I can't help but notice his mere presence acts like a lightning rod for this stormy family. All their words and accusations sputter out. Except for Charlotte's. She keeps hers to herself.

❖

Nina sits in her assigned chair, flicks a green bug off her blue robe, and scans the crowd. *It wouldn't be out of character,* she thinks, *for Mom not to show on account of some principle.* Then she spots her family—with Rick. She squints for a better look. *Why is he with them?*

Hester waves. The rest of the family looks up. They all smile and wave too. Including Rick. The more Nina watches, the more uncomfortable this alliance between her family and Rick makes her. She barely hears a word of the salutatorian's speech, and during Lottie's valedictorian's speech, all she can think about is the fact that Rick's folding the program. She watches him pass it to Iris, who puts it on her head. *A sunhat!*

Nina's resolve not to move back home grows stronger: *Nothing will be mine anymore*, she thinks. When her name is finally called to receive her diploma, Wanda Kasper has to elbow her in the ribs. "You're up."

Nina saunters toward the podium. Iris stands and gestures for her to smile. Harvey snaps photos. Nina reaches out to accept her diploma. Then, over the shoulder of the chancellor, she catches a glimpse of Pablo standing alone at the top of the bleachers. He wears a Panama hat and Hollywood sunglasses. *A majestic tree among shrubs*, she thinks.

She takes her diploma and returns to her seat, then spends the rest of the ceremony trying to figure out how to make things right with Pablo. After all, she needs to crash at his place.

Once she's flung her mortarboard with the rest of the graduates, Nina pulls out her bottle of bubbles, but the cap is welded on. The other girls are all having the same trouble. The audience shifts in their seats. It looks to them like a bunch of robed young women all bent over in agony.

Nina, the first to give up on her bubbles, charges off the stage, making a beeline for Pablo.

The Kalinas stand. *Where is she going? Why isn't she coming over?*

Rick stands too, wondering: *Is she blowing off her family? Or me?*

As for me, I'm not sure what to think. She does need a place to stay. But why does it have to be with Pablo and Dink? Either one of them could screw up everything.

"I adore you and you have to be my friend," she says when she reaches Pablo.

Pablo laughs, but I notice his arms are crossed in front of his heart. "I am your friend, Nina."

"Admit it, after the other night you were hoping you'd never see me again."

Pablo sighs. "True."

"You thought I was one more straight girl falling in love with you."

"Nina. We were drunk…"

"Admit it."

"Okay. I admit it. Now what?"

"Just promise me we can be friends and not be all weird with each other. And you have to do it quick because my family's waiting on me, and so is this really cute guy I kissed last night."

He uncrosses his arms. "Cute guy?"

"Promise me!"

"Okay, I promise. Now where's this cute guy?"

"Come on, I'll introduce you. But remember, he's mine." With that, she takes his hand and drags him through the crowd toward her family—and Rick.

The Kalinas, having made their way off the bleachers and onto a small grassy patch under a dogwood, watch Nina tow Pablo their way.

"Now, who could this be?" Iris asks no one in particular.

Charlotte is thrilled to be able to supply the answer. "Her *other* boyfriend, the one she spent the night with."

Rick feels as if he breakfasted on eels.

"Other boyfriend?" Iris asks, preparing herself for a tricky interaction. She's grown fond of Rick in the hour and a half they've spent together. Like Harvey, she's found that interacting with Rick has made her feel closer to Nina. She also likes the origami hat, although she takes it off now and hands it to Hester.

"Nina has two boyfriends!" Hester says excitedly.

Harvey senses that Rick is getting ready to go AWOL and places his hand on the boy's shoulder. Iris notes her husband's kindness and decides to endorse it. "Come have lunch with us, Rick. We'd like to take you out."

"I don't think that's such a good idea—"

"Nonsense!" Iris interrupts. "It will be lovely."

Harvey feels Rick's shoulder muscles tense. *He's going to bolt*, he thinks, but Nina has just stepped into hugging distance, so he releases his grip from Rick's shoulder and opens his arms to his always-complicated middle daughter. "Congratulations!" he says, all smiles.

She folds into him like a prayer, leaving everyone else to fend for themselves.

Iris reaches her hand out to Pablo. "I'm Iris. Nina's mother."

"Pablo. Nice to meet you."

"Nice to meet *you*," Iris says. "These are my daughters Charlotte and Hester. And this is Rick." She glances at Rick. "But perhaps you've met?"

"No," Rick says, the eels now performing belly flops off the edges of his stomach lining.

"Nina, we've invited Rick to lunch with us," Iris ventures.

Nina, still wrapped in her father's arms, says, "Great. Pablo should come too."

"That's okay," Pablo says. "You all should—"

"No! You have to come. It's my graduation."

Harvey, unsure of his daughter's motives, is eager to please her nonetheless. "Let us take you out."

Iris shoots Harvey a look.

Pablo shoots Nina a look.

Rick wishes he had someone to shoot a look to.

"Any recommendations?" Harvey asks.

"Pagano's is an excellent Italian restaurant on the strip," Pablo says. "If we hurry we could get a table." He suggests this place because a) he could never afford it, and b) he wants to reconnect with the restaurant owner, who he's flirted with at Chaps.

Iris asks, "Is that all right with you, Nina?"

"Sounds great. Let's go. It's an easy walk from here."

"I think I'm going to take off," Rick says.

"But we'll have so much fun," Nina says.

He lifts his chin toward Pablo as if to say, *What's with the jerk?*

She smiles flirtatiously. "Please?"

"Okay," he sighs. "But I can't stay long."

At least he's going. The way Nina's treating him, it's a wonder.

At the restaurant, Iris claps her hands together and says, "It's perfect!" causing Rick to hate Pablo even more. But the quirky family restaurant *is* perfect. It's decorated with postcards and small figurines and musical instruments covering the walls; and the scent of garlic and butter permeates the place, making them all instantly starving. In the corner, a classical guitarist hammers out passionate melodies. What's more, thanks to Pablo's warning, they've beaten the rush. A lean, dark-haired hostess guides them to their table. Pablo excuses himself and heads for the kitchen to talk to the hunky owner.

Rick pulls out a chair for Nina. "You look beautiful," he says.

Uncomfortable with her private life being on display to her family, Nina waves off the compliment. "Thanks."

Iris takes her place at the head of the table. "We seem to have lost your friend."

"He's talking to the owner," Nina says.

"How interesting," Iris says.

The truth is, nobody knows what to say. A few comments are thrown out about the décor, but besides that, the Kalinas are stumped. What is Nina up to with these two boys? Harvey glances at his wife, then folds his hands on the table as if he were a school counselor. "So, Rick, tell us a little about yourself."

Nina slumps down in her chair. *Why don't they just butt out?*

Rick, feeling about as interesting as a salt shaker, considers ways he might still be able to leave. "Well, I graduated with a degree in music."

"Music?" Iris pipes in enthusiastically. "That sounds *fas*cinating."

"My friend Howie and I are going to open a music store, but right now he's serving in Iraq."

"Music store?" Harvey says.

Nina watches her parents dodge Iraq. *That's right*, she thinks, *keep it nice and safe. We wouldn't want to risk talking politics.* She fiddles with the gold locket around her neck. Back and forth goes the locket on the chain. Back and forth. Back and forth.

Finally, Pablo returns to the table. He places his hand on the back of Iris's chair. "The owner has agreed to present the lunch family style. This is usually only done on Sundays or with advance warning, but I've persuaded him to make an exception. I hope you won't mind." Then he smiles that dazzling smile of his.

Iris is thoroughly charmed.

Rick isn't. He thinks Pablo is a big poser.

The wine helps some. Nina's iciness begins to thaw and Rick folds a flower for Nina from a napkin.

"That's so sweet," she says.

Throughout the meal, Charlotte attempts to impress everyone with her knowledge of Italian history. Even though no one really cares, they're glad she's taken over the talking. "That's really fascinating," Harvey says. "You got all that from that one novel?"

With dessert comes Iris's need to plan the future. "So, after lunch, I suppose we should come back to your room and help you pack."

Nina, caught off guard by her mother's statement, blurts out, "I'm not moving back home."

Harvey looks up from his strawberry tartlet.

Iris sets her fork down. "And what do you plan to do?"

"I'm moving in with Dink—until I get my own place, that is."

The table gets church quiet. A little piece of cannoli gets caught in the back of Pablo's throat. *Moving in with me?* he thinks. *Since when?*

Rick, whose thigh is pressed up against Nina's, bites back a smile. Good thing he doesn't know Dink lives with Pablo.

Nina looks at Pablo pleadingly as she speaks to her parents. "I mean, it won't be for long. I plan on getting my own apartment right away."

Iris places her hands palm down on the table. "With what?"

"I'm going to get a job."

Iris glances toward her husband in hopes that he'll come to the rescue, but he's intently placing his silverware into its pre-dining position, apparently trying to create the illusion that he's not there. "I see," she says, suddenly hit with the weight of two and a half decades of managing a family. "A job."

Nina nods. "And I don't need you telling me how impractical I'm being. It's my life and this is what I want to do."

Iris sighs. "Well, then...since you have it all figured out, you won't be needing *us* to hang around and get in your way. We'll leave shortly after lunch. I imagine we'll get some kind of refund on our room." She beckons the waiter to bring the bill. "If not, well, let that live in your conscience."

After that, no one has much to say and Hester is the only one who finishes her dessert.

Once out on the street, the family says their good-byes. Nina, Rick, and Pablo watch the Kalinas as they make their way down the street back to their hotel. Once they're out of earshot, Pablo confronts Nina. "Moving in with *me*?" He says this with such force that Rick almost drops Nina's box of leftovers.

"Please, Pablo, I know I should have talked to you. Dink told me I could crash at your place for a while. I'll sleep on the couch, on the floor, anywhere..."

"You know, I should probably go," Rick says, holding out Nina's box of leftovers. "Why don't you give me a call when you get your life worked out."

"But, Rick, we're finally alone!" Nina says, not taking the box.

He considers pointing out what, to him, seems obvious—they're not alone—but is afraid he'll say it in a way he'll regret, so he places the leftovers on the brick planter and says, "Whatever."

"Aren't you *glad* I'm staying in town?" she asks.

Amused, Pablo leans against a lamppost and rests the heel of one foot on the toe of the other. "It's okay, Rick, I'm not interested in your girlfriend. I'm gay."

Rick is caught completely off guard. *Pablo? Gay?* He clears his throat. Shoves his hands in his pockets. Pulls them out. Shoves them back in again. "It's cool. I'm cool with that."

Pablo shakes his head and smiles at the cement. "Riiiiight."

It's anybody's guess who will speak next.

"So, if it's a problem…" Nina finally says to Pablo.

"Dink knows about this?"

"She's the one who invited me."

"You sure?"

"Yes, I'm sure. You want to call her?"

"No need. I'll trust you. But just a few nights."

Rick reaches out his hand to shake Pablo's. "Thanks, man."

Pablo grips Rick's hand in an extra-manly way and uses an extra-manly voice. "Sure thing, *dude.* I'm glad we've got the little *lady* taken care of."

Nina punches Pablo's arm. "Don't be a jerk."

"Don't tell me what I can or can't be," he says. "You're beholden to me, remember?" Then he tells her where the spare key is hidden and that he and the restaurant guy are going for a drink. Once he's gone, Nina and Rick just stand there.

"So I guess I should go do some packing," she says.

"So Pablo's a—"

"Don't say that nasty word, or you won't get to be my friend."

"I just meant—"

"I know what you meant, and I'm saying don't be ordinary."

I knew it! There's a stigma around an XY loving another XY and an XX loving another XX. And just like I thought, it's all caught up with these silly assumptions and opinions that people in the Land of Forgetting are so attached to—Rick included.

I wonder what makes somebody gay?

But Rick doesn't seem to care, and neither does Nina.

I guess I won't either.

Rick, trying to look something besides ordinary, sticks his tongue out of the side of his mouth and crosses his eyes.

Nina laughs. "That's better."

He pulls out his car keys. "If you want some help packing, I'd be happy to oblige."

"I thought you said you had to be somewhere."

"I did. But I was lying, okay? Now, do you want some help or not? My car's parked back at the campus."

"You have a car? Oh, you *are* the man of my dreams!" she says taking his arm. "What's more, you're kind of cute when you're jealous."

"Jealous? You thought I was jealous?"

Nina laughs. "Let's just say you looked a little green."

They forget all about the leftovers on the planter.

CHAPTER ELEVEN

It's been one week since Nina started crashing at Pablo and Dink's. And she has gotten a job. Or kind of a job. It's called temp work. She doesn't like it much, but she will be able to make money. Temp work will also give her plenty of spare time, which makes me happy, because the more time she has away from work, the more chances she and Rick will have to mate—which they're just about to do for the first time.

Or at least I think they are.

It's Rick's day off and they're alone at the apartment feeding each other grocery-store sushi while snuggled on Pablo and Dink's couch, which conveniently doubles as Nina's bed. They're sucking each other's fingers, kissing between each bite, and I'm thinking: *This is good...This is good...Now rip each other's clothes off and get down to business!*

But wait. Keys are rattling in the outside lock.

Nina removes Rick's thumb from her mouth and turns around to see who it is.

Shoot! It's Dink. What's she doing home? She usually doesn't get off work until much later. She pushes through the door and drops her ten-ton backpack next to the couch, then flops down next to Rick. "I'm not interrupting anything, am I?"

"Of course not," Nina says, flashing Rick an apologetic glance. "We were just having a late lunch. Are you hungry?"

"God no," Dink says. "But I do need to get stoned." She pulls a cigar box from a shelf underneath the coffee table. "They're doing some remodeling downstairs from our offices and the electricity for the entire building shut off. There's no telling how much data we lost." She cuts up some buds. "I hadn't backed up my work for hours." She starts arranging them on a rolling paper. "Anyway, they sent us all home until it's worked out."

Rick clears his throat. "Nina tells me you write descriptions for an online mail-order sort of business."

Dink laughs. "Mostly for crap that nobody needs. Get this, today I wrote one for a battery-powered retractable back-scratcher. 'For that inconvenient itch that attacks you away from home.'" Rick and Nina smile and nod as if they're interested. It is her house, after all. Her couch, her bottle of soy sauce. Dink licks the edge of the joint to seal it. "Oh, Neen, did you pick up that package?"

Nina places her plastic sushi tray on the coffee table. "Um. I was going to, but—"

"Don't worry about it. It's just something from my mom." Dink lights the joint and takes a hit. "A box of flannel shirts perhaps? Or maybe another pair of sensible shoes. Or, I know, a pickup with a dog in back!"

Nina snickers. "Dink's mom thinks Dink's a lesbian."

"Her and Ms. Bobbi," Dink says.

"Dink's seventh-grade gym teacher," Nina says.

"Slash counselor," Dink adds.

Rick isn't sure how to respond to this. He thought Dink was a lesbian too.

It takes me a few seconds to figure out that being a lesbian is the same as being gay, but when I finally do I'm with Rick. All she thinks about is girls, especially Nina.

"Huh," he says, speaking for both of us, then takes the joint from Dink. "Ms. Bobbi and your mom are still in touch?" He takes a long hit and hands the joint to Nina.

Dink laughs. "Uh, you could say that, yes."

"They're lovers," Nina says.

Rick blows out a lungful of smoke. "Wait. Your *mom* is a lesbian?"

Nina takes a hit and says while trying to hold in the smoke, "Dink, can I tell the story?"

Dink gestures for her to go ahead.

Nina exhales the smoke and passes the joint to Dink. "When Dink was in seventh grade, the school counselor slipped her mom a pamphlet on diversity. Apparently a couple of the teachers were…worried…about her. And then her mom, always one to involve herself in her daughter's life, took it upon herself to, shall we say, educate herself about the lesbian lifestyle. A year later, she left Dink's dad for the counselor."

"No way," Rick says.

"Yes way," Dink says. "And now instead of a dad I have Ms. Bobbi, the politically correct gym teacher who believes that tofu chicken is real food and that all the problems of the world can be solved by little rainbow stickers. Do you know how hard those are to peel off?"

Rick shakes his head. "Can't say that I do." But even as he says this, he still thinks Dink is a lesbian. And so do I.

Why doesn't she 'fess up? Rick and Nina wouldn't care. They wouldn't think she's a freak. They like Pablo. Or Nina does. Rick is still kind of weirded out about Pablo, but that's because he thinks Pablo might be attracted to him. Which is plain silly. But, I'm learning, not all that uncommon with men in the Land of Forgetting. I guess they view themselves as irresistible.

Why am I thinking about this so much? It has nothing to do with me—except for the fact that it's gay people who keep foiling my intentions to get born. I'll admit I'm starting to take it a wee bit personally, imagining Dink and Pablo as the Gay Terminators, whose sole agenda is to wipe the planet free of all breeding. I mean, Dink has pretty much ruined what could have been a perfect mating situation this evening, and Pablo not only posed a real threat at the beginning of my life-seeking journey but is due home any minute, dooming the night to end the way it has for the last week: with Nina, Rick, and the two Gay Terminators doing nothing but hanging out because they're all too broke to go anywhere. Sure, Nina and Rick will head out to the apartment hall to say good-bye, and they'll kiss a lot and he'll feel her up, and they'll almost go out to his car, but then she'll say she doesn't want the first time to be in a car, and he'll understand, and then she'll say something about wishing he could spend the night but since she lives with the Gay Terminators she can't, and he'll understand that too. Erg!

At least there's still time. Nina's ovum, Miss Egg I've begun calling her, is building up estrogen the way a bride-to-be builds up her trousseau. And good old Spermy, my other half, is at work on his mode of transportation, a.k.a. his tail. But the closer we get to these two joining, the larger my list of "what-ifs" grows. What if Nina and Rick never mate? Or what if they don't mate in time? Or what if when they finally *do* they find out they don't like each other? Or they find out they like each other but they don't want a baby?

The idea that I've come this far only to evaporate back into The Known is more than I can bear. Why wasn't I more careful in my choice? Why did I have to choose two people that hardly knew each other?

❖

Two nights later.

Nina is cooking dinner for Dink, Pablo, and Rick. She says she's doing it to show her gratitude to Dink and Pablo for letting her crash at their place, but I know her *main* goal is to get Pablo and Rick to like each other. Which is going to be tricky. Whenever Rick's around Pablo he gets super quiet or overly polite, which makes Pablo feel like a "fucking alien" in his own home.

Pablo runs a spoon through a pot of nasturtiums simmering in a curry sauce. "Yuck!"

"You're going to love it. Now stop." Earlier in the day Nina found a Web site on cooking with flowers and thought it would make for a fun menu. Now she's breading daylilies.

"Maybe I should pick something up from Pagano's, just in case," Pablo says.

She looks up from a daylily. "Will you go read or something? Pack, perhaps?"

Pablo is going to see his mother tomorrow and Nina's looking forward to having a few days without him vibing her to move out.

Pablo picks up a wilted lily and wonders why he agreed to this dinner thing. *I deal with straight men every day at the flower store*, he thinks. *Straight men in love, straight men in the doghouse, straight men in last-minute rushes on Valentine's or Mother's day. Why do I have to deal with them at home too?* "Nina, maybe this isn't the best idea," he says.

No duh. As long as you're around, I can forget getting born.

Nina's about to beg him to stay when the phone rings.

He makes no effort to answer it.

She drops a floured daylily into the hot oil so he'll have to.

It rings again.

He says, "Your Prince Charming, no doubt."

"Pablo, my hands are covered. Just pick up."

He sighs dramatically, stomps into the living room, and picks up the phone. His voice is thick with martyrdom when he says, "Hello?" But his theatrics are wasted. It's Dink.

"Tell Nina I'm running late," she says.

"How late?"

"Like maybe I'll make it for dessert. The catalogue's got to be finished tomorrow and two of the gals are out sick. I'm a description-writing fool. Get this, 'Mechanical Dog—Come home to the affection without the mess!' What do you think? Would you buy it?"

"You're going to make me deal with these two lovebirds by myself?"

"I'll get there as quick as I can."

When Pablo passes on the news, Nina's beyond disappointed. She was counting on Dink to help make them like each other. "I'll save her a plate," she says, nearly burning her finger in the hot oil.

Pablo looks at the platter of greasy fried lilies and hopes for Dink's sake that she eats at the office.

The phone rings again, and Pablo assumes it's Dink. "Now what?" he says into the receiver, but when he hears it's Rick, he drops the phone onto the desk. "It's *him*."

"Well, ask him what he wants."

Pablo flops onto the couch and picks up a men's fashion magazine. "He doesn't want to talk to *me*, Nina."

Nina wipes her batter-covered hands on the dishcloth tucked into her jeans and cradles the phone between her ear and shoulder. She returns to the kitchen. "Hey, Rick. What's up?" Using tongs, she pulls a daylily from the sizzling oil and places it on a paper towel. Rick's voice sounds breathy, agitated, and she's having a hard time understanding him. "What?…I can barely hear you…" It takes a while, but Nina finally figures out what he's saying. "You're not going to make it?" She glances through the door to Pablo. He pointedly flips a page of his magazine. "Why not?" she asks, taking the receiver in her hand and pressing it to her ear. "I'm having a hard time hearing you. Is everything okay? You sound upset…Rick…Rick?"

She looks at the receiver blaring its dial tone and tries to figure out what just happened.

"Let me guess," Pablo says, tossing his magazine onto the coffee table, "he's a no-show."

"He was really freaked," she says, wandering into the living room trying to make sense of the phone call.

"Oh please, Nina. We both know what's going on here."

"You're misreading this."

Pablo reaches for his shoes. "I'm going for Pagano's takeout. Want something?"

"I'm going to try him again."

Pablo turns his loafer into a microphone and begins doing a Billie Holiday impression, singing a song about how much it costs to love a man.

But I'm with Nina. Whatever is bothering Rick, it isn't his discomfort with gays. Something is wrong.

I go looking for him and find him sitting on the floor of his bedroom, his back to his bed and his head in his hands—sobbing.

I slip into his memory.

He's on the phone with Howie's little sister Hannah. "I thought you should know…" she says, her voice barely audible.

"Who is this?"

"Howie is…he…he…"

"What?"

"It's so fucked*…"*

"Hannah?"

"I should go…"

"Hannah! Hannah!" Rick calls back and speaks to a friend of the family. The man isn't sure about the details, but a bomb penetrated Howie's Humvee and he was killed instantly. Was Rick a close friend of Howie's, the man wants to know.

Rick hangs up the phone.

Rick, still sitting on the floor next to his bed, is imagining different versions of Howie blowing up. Him dying right away. Him bleeding a lot first. Rick pulls the quilt off the bed, buries his face in it, and screams.

I'm in shock too. Howie wasn't supposed to die. He was supposed to come home and open Music Jones with Rick. I was going to call him Uncle How. "How's it going, Uncle How?" I'd say when I stopped by the store after school. And he'd slip me a five from the register and say, "Don't tell your dad." Then he'd wink. We were going to be friends.

Not knowing the future makes life so haphazard! So harsh! How do people cope?

I zip back to Nina, praying she won't give up on Rick.

"He's not picking up," she says and hangs up the phone. "This or his cell."

Pablo drops the loafer he's been singing into. "Something's burning."

"*Crap!* The lilies!" Nina runs for the kitchen and it's filled with black smoke. She wrenches the pan off the stove and drops it into the sink. Curls of black smoke billow up. She turns away and, coughing, slides down to the flour-dusted floor with her back to the cabinet.

Great. Now she's crying too.

Pablo peeks into the kitchen. "Neen?"

"Do you think this is easy for me?" she whimpers in between sobs. "Do you think watching you two play these stupid games with each other is easy?"

"Nina…"

Her face streaked with tears, she stands and begins brushing the flour from the seat of her jeans. "I'm going over to his place. Something is wrong."

"Into enemy headquarters?"

"Would you quit being such a drama queen! They're just conservative." She takes the rubber band out of her hair. "Can we borrow the apartment manager's car again?"

"Hey! How did this go from I to we?"

"We'll get a taxi! Come on."

"Why do I have to go?"

"I've never met his parents. I can't go by myself."

"This is your mess, Neen, not mine."

"Pablo, I'm totally freaking out. Look at my hand. It's shaking."

Sighing, Pablo grabs his jacket from the back of the chair. "Just remember, Neen, you owe me—big-time."

❖

By the time the taxi reaches Rick's house, Nina's beginning to wonder if foisting herself upon him and his family is such a good idea. She's seen the house once before, when Rick drove her by, but now, with the long shadows spreading across the property, the perfectly manicured hedges lining the bleached walkway, the planter boxes full of well-behaved flowers, the giant oak doorway, it scares her.

"You sure they're not the enemy?" Pablo whispers as they pass the NO SOLICITORS sign stuck in the grass and head up the walkway to the front door. They hear Rick and Richard Hale yelling inside, not the actual words, but enough to know there's a fight going on.

"I'm going home," Pablo says.

"Should I ring the bell?" Nina asks.

"They don't need us here, Neen."

"How can you say that?" She punches the bell.

The yelling stops.

Nina and Pablo listen as someone pads toward the door. It creaks open, and, wedged between the door and door frame, is Dorothy Hale dressed in elastic-waist navy blue pants and a white-collared blouse. "Can I help you?"

"We're looking for Rick."

Dorothy recognizes Nina's voice from brief phone chats they've had when Rick wasn't home. "I'm afraid this is a bad time," she says.

"It's important."

Pablo's fists, hanging at his side, are squeezed so tight his nails are making tiny crescents on his palms.

"Mom," Rick says from somewhere beyond Nina and Pablo's sightlines. "What is it?"

Dorothy holds the door open a little more so they can see inside. "You have some friends here."

Rick is standing in the living room wearing sweats, his face blotchy and red. He's about to say something when *"We are not done here, young man!"* blasts through the airways.

Rick turns toward the voice. "Yes, sir, I believe we are."

Richard Hale steps into view. He wears a tight maroon T-shirt with JUST DO IT scrawled across the front. His face is red and the veins in his neck jut out. "You walk out this door, son, and you are not welcome back here."

Dorothy gasps, "No…no…" and covers her mouth with her hands.

Rick turns toward her. "I'm sorry, Mom. I don't know what else to do."

She hugs him and doesn't want to let go, but she has to because he steps back.

"So be it," Richard Hale says and turns away.

Rick looks from his mother's tear-streaked face to his father's taut back muscles, then feels Nina's hand slide into his.

"Come on, Rick," she says, trying to keep her voice calm.

She and Pablo back out the doorway before turning and sprinting down the narrow path. Nina pulls Rick as they go. Once they're a safe distance away from the house, Nina asks breathily, "What's going on?"

For a few seconds it looks as if Rick is going to answer, but then his legs fold beneath him, causing his knees to hit the cement with a thud. He's breathing hard, which turns into sobbing.

Pablo and Nina glance at one another, then join him on the sidewalk. Nina rests her hand on his shoulder. Pablo looks back to make sure Richard Hale hasn't followed them.

"I tore up his fucking flag!" Rick chokes.

"His flag?" Nina repeats.

Head in his hands, Rick sways gently back and forth.

Nina tries again, "You tore up his flag?"

Rick covers his head as if he's trying to bury himself alive. Someone in a nearby house closes a window.

Nina strokes the back of Rick's neck. "What happened?"

"I got a call…" He starts moaning and tearing at his hair.

Pablo places a hand on Rick's other shoulder. "Calm down, bro. It'll be all right."

"No, it won't! It's fucked!"

Pablo and Nina barely hear Rick's next choked words. "Howie didn't make it…They…He's…"

"Oh my God," Nina whispers.

But how did Howie's dying turn into Rick's eviction? It doesn't make sense. Shouldn't death draw people together?

I return to Richard Hale for a clue. He's sitting in a leather wing-backed chair, the door to his den closed and locked. His mind, too, is racing. *He* thought he was honoring Howie by flying the household flag at half-mast. *The kid's a hero, for God's sake*, he thinks. *Rick should be proud.* He has no idea why Rick flew off the handle when he tried to say as much, no idea what Rick meant when he yelled, "They fucking took advantage of him! Of his pain! The fucking axis of evil doesn't exist!"

Richard looks around his office. *Look at this mess!* he thinks. *There's dust covering the dust! And my trash is overflowing! What's wrong with that woman?* He pictures Dorothy in the kitchen, her head bowed over her notebook, her fingers gripping a scribbling pen. *She always closes the goddamn thing when I get any-goddamned-where near her.* He's tried to find her notebook when she's gone, but has never been able to. *She probably buries it in the goddamned backyard!* he thinks. He pictures his son standing triumphantly, the red, white and blue scraps of the family flag at his feet. *The both of them are goddamned nutso!*

Dorothy Hale stands in the kitchen staring at a stain on a dish towel. *He's taken my son from me*, she thinks. *What else is there?* She's begun to imagine that her home has a cancerous growth—neat and orderly on the outside and slowly mutating on the inside. She wonders how much longer it has to live. She drops the stained dish towel to the floor, recalling her own mother, who upon entering the home of another woman would discreetly check the cleanliness of her dish towels and potholders. "Not much of a housekeeper," she'd conclude, or "That man did real good for himself. She's a real catch." *Dish towels and potholders*, Dorothy thinks, *the secret gauges of a woman's worth.*

She imagines the cancer cells multiplying and remembers the day Richard went so far as to make the "goddamned bed" himself, yanking the blankets up over the pillows and tucking the corners military style. *He can't hurt me anymore*, she thinks. *I'm losing substance.* She pictures the poisonous tips of his angry words slicing right though her and sticking into the dining room walls and sofa cushions, cluttering the house even further.

She goes to the baking cabinet and pulls her notebook from between two cookie sheets. She doesn't know what else to do.

Chapter Twelve

I'm back at Pablo and Dink's. Pablo is standing across from Nina and Rick, who are sitting on the couch with an afghan draped over their laps. His mind is running like a caged hamster on a wheel—with about the same results. *Where's Rick going to stay? Nina keeps reassuring him he doesn't have to go back home, and that his new life starts now, but what's her plan? That her homophobic boyfriend's going to move in too?*

Nina notices. "Is something wrong, Pablo?"

"No. Nothing." Pablo wants to at least appear sympathetic. "It's just so…awful."

"Well, you're making me nervous staring at us like that. Come sit on the couch."

Rick inches over to make some room for him.

Reluctantly, Pablo sandwiches Rick between himself and Nina. Nina reaches across Rick's lap and tosses one end of the afghan to Pablo, making the three of them look like triplets tucked into a stroller. One, two, three.

She's enjoying this too much, Pablo thinks. *It's fitting right in with her little plan to make Rick and me friends.*

Rick is oblivious. He stares at the Rousseau print on the wall: a man lying prone next to a guitar. *Sleeping Gypsy* is written beneath the image, but he thinks the gypsy looks dead, not sleeping. He hasn't thought about where he's going to spend the night; he doesn't even know it *is* night. His eyes sting, his lower lip is tender from biting down, his muscles ache. Staring at the gypsy, he takes short, shallow breaths, which turn into long, sustained gasps.

"You need to eat," Nina says and gets up from the couch. Pablo starts to get up too, but Nina says, "Stay with him. I'm going to heat up dinner."

Pablo's had lots of experience being under blankets with men, but this is different. He scrutinizes the side of Rick's head, his chestnut hair cut close around his ear, his skull tipped back onto the couch as if it's too heavy to hold up. Pablo wants an excuse to leave. "Can I get you something?" he asks.

"No. I'm okay."

Pablo notices a small mole just above Rick's ear. "I'm sorry about your friend."

Rick squeezes his eyes tight, then opens them very wide. "I—I loved him." A choke of tears rushes his throat.

Pablo fiddles with the fringe of the blanket, wishing Nina would return.

Rick stares at the ceiling.

"Nina said you guys played a lot of music together."

"He was a fucking great guitar player."

Pablo nods, the muscles in his jaw tightening. Up until now, the war in Iraq has only been something he's seen on the news, or read about, but now it's in his living room, sitting on his couch right next to him, and he doesn't like it. Not one bit. He tosses the blanket off his legs. "Maybe Nina needs some help in the kitchen."

"Please don't go," Rick says.

Pablo stays where he is, thinking Rick is going to say more, but Rick doesn't. He just gazes into Pablo's dark brown eyes without worrying if it's polite or not, or that Pablo might get the wrong idea. He doesn't care. People can die, just like that; he knows this now, and it makes him see Pablo in a new light. He thinks about all the subtle, and not so subtle, ways that Richard Hale warned him not to become a man like Pablo. Pablo's father, he realizes, probably did the same thing to him. Yet here Pablo is anyway, being who he needs to be and not giving a shit what his dad or anyone else thinks. Something in Rick's heart shifts, making a space for Pablo.

"I'm here, Rick. Don't worry," Pablo says, and eases back into the couch.

❖

Dinner is served. Pablo, Nina, and Rick sit at the oval table in the small square dining room and stare at the slimy concoction on their plates. Pablo was right, Nina should have ordered out. The meal looks disgusting. Not only was Nina much too conceptual about this menu, giving her love of unique ingredients a higher rank than flavor, but also, standing over the stove stirring was too tedious for her so she cut the cooking time down to suit her disposition. Put more simply, if the way to a man's heart is truly through his stomach, I'm in deep doo-doo.

Rick pushes the breaded and fried daylilies around on his plate and grimaces.

Pablo is not so generous. "Nina, these belonged in a vase."

"You have no sense of adventure," she quips and takes her first bite. She's also disappointed with the outcome, but doesn't say so. She reaches her toe across to touch Rick's, only his feet are tucked under his chair so her foot just hangs there.

Pablo holds a skewered lily on his fork. "This whole night has been an adventure, Nina. Must we have one on our plate as well?"

Nina ignores him and shakes a bit of salt onto her lilies.

Pablo looks over to Rick, who's chewing, chewing, chewing. "Rick, let me get you some more wine to wash it down," he says, but Rick is determined to swallow the slimy, stringy, flower encased in clumpy, greasy batter. He glances at Nina and notices a thread of lily stuck on her chin. To his horror, a snicker lurches out of his mouth and forces the bite back up his throat. Afraid he might hurt Nina's feelings, he tries to swallow again, but another snicker lurches out, this one forcing him to spit the contents of his mouth into his napkin to keep from choking. Pablo and Nina look on in amazement as Rick's snickers transform into hysterical laughter. He's like a racecar that has gone from zero to sixty in less than twenty seconds. Only he's gone from a dark, brooding melancholy to a snorting, coughing, grabbing-his-belly laugh attack.

Pablo glances at Nina. He too sees the thread of lily stuck to her chin. He bites down on his lip but can't stop himself. Within seconds, he's joined Rick, hooting and slapping his legs in fits of laughter. Nina glares at the two of them, then slices off another bite of lily. Greasy strings hang from the prongs of her fork. "It does kind of look like fried snot," she admits, holding the fork at arm's length. Pablo points to the lily on her chin. She wipes it off and bursts into laughter too.

Hyperventilating, Rick tips off his chair and falls to the floor. Pablo's eyes fill with tears. Nina wails, "What do you say we move on to the nasturtium curry?"

Pablo and Rick grab their bellies. "No! No!"

They laugh until it's painful, until their eyes gush tears, until their ribs throb. Then they laugh more, snorting out despair, worries, a future too big to comprehend. Finally, laughed empty, they sit in silence like three Zen masters around the table. Their silence is clean. Beautiful. And I think how wonderful it will be when I can join in this kind of catharsis. Astral emotion is peanuts compared to this!

The phone rings.

Pablo jumps. Rick blinks. Nina straightens up in her chair. They look at one another with a tinge of embarrassment. Nina blows her nose.

Another ring.

Pablo gets up to answer it. "Hello?"

It's Dink. She's calling to see if she should pick up anything on her way home.

"Food! Bring food. Nina's trying to poison us," he says.

Rick leans back in his chair and closes his eyes, wishing he had somewhere else to be, someplace quiet. But it's late and they left his car at his parents'. The place he used to go when he felt this way flashes through his mind: Howie's basement apartment. A momentary anger at Howie passes through him. *Why did you have to go and die?* His eyes fill with tears.

Nina gets up to massage his shoulders. He leans into her breasts. Pablo refills all of their wineglasses.

Thirty minutes later, Dink arrives with pizza, two bottles of cheap Cabernet, and a joint. Pablo and Nina are glad for the diversion. Plus, they're starving. But Rick isn't so sure. When the joint gets passed around he takes a hit anyway. He also has a slice of pizza, which he can barely taste. *I want to go home*, he thinks. *Back to my room.*

The group moves into the living room with their glasses of wine. Rick excuses himself to the bathroom. Once he's out of earshot, Dink says, "Man, that's fucked about his friend."

Pablo looks at his feet. Nina gazes into her glass of wine, adding, "And his dad is being a total asshole and kicked him out." She puts her glass on the floor. "Can he stay here for a while?"

Pablo can't believe what he's hearing. *Maybe we can find a stray dog that needs a home too*, he thinks.

"Don't panic, sweetie," Nina says. "You're going to your mother's tomorrow. We'll find him a place before you return. I promise." She adds as a precaution, "And if not, we'll be your little slaves until we do."

Pablo, too tired and fucked up to refuse, replies, "You don't have the equipment I want in a slave and your boyfriend has the wrong wiring."

Dink laughs. "It's okay by me, if you can figure out a way to share the couch."

What a turn of events! Rick is going to spend the night, with Nina, on the couch. Splitting cells, here I come! That is, if Rick isn't too sad.

Pablo lights up the roach. "No breeding on my couch."

Shoot! What did he have to say that for?

In the bathroom, Rick is looking in the mirror. He wants to see if he looks as different on the outside as he feels on the inside. Besides his bloodshot eyes, he thinks he looks pretty much the same. He splashes water on his face and returns to the dining room. "I'm beat."

Nina walks over and puts her arm around him. "We should put you to bed."

"I can't stay here," he says, glancing at Pablo and Dink.

"Of course you can," Dink says. "Pablo and I are inviting you."

Pablo nods his head. "The left half of the couch is all yours."

Rick tries to smile, but only one side of his mouth will cooperate. "Thanks, guys."

Yawning, Dink stands and stretches. "It's been a long one, comrades." She walks over to Rick and places her hand on his shoulder. "Hang in there, cowboy. And I'll see what I can do about getting Rumsfeld assassinated."

Rick hugs her. "Thanks, Dink." Then, to everyone's surprise, he walks over and hugs Pablo too. "And you, dude. I'm not sure what I'd have done tonight without you."

Pablo's eyes get big as hubcaps.

Dink picks her smokes up off the table. "*Viva la revolución*, sleep tight, and all that good shit," she says before slipping behind her bedroom door.

"I'm hitting the sack too," Pablo says. "Don't forget to brush your teeth."

The moment Pablo closes his bedroom door Rick is hit with a huge case of melancholy. He doesn't have a home anymore, and he feels awkward in this apartment, awkward with Nina. He walks over to the desk and returns a stray pencil to a jar of pencils and pens.

"You can use mine," Nina says.

"What?"

"My toothbrush."

The idea of using her toothbrush makes him feel even more like an exile. His eyes start to sting. He squeezes the bridge of his nose with his thumb and forefinger.

Nina takes his face in her hands, kisses his forehead, once, twice, then kisses each of his temples and begins a slow descent to his mouth. He lets her kiss him, his body too drained to respond, but as she continues on with her feather-light kisses his body begins to wake up, to feel an urgency so strong he can barely control it. Like a man buried alive and clawing his way to air, Rick reaches behind her head and presses her face to his. The kiss is more mouth-to-mouth resuscitation than a kiss, and this excites Nina, shifting the nature of her kisses from consoling to passionate yearning. Her fingers travel down the dampness of his T-shirt and his tight muscles beneath, then she slides her hands underneath the shirt and up his back. Rick's breathing quickens. She pulls the shirt over his head. A deep groan surges from inside him.

"Shh! Pablo or Dink might hear us," she whispers, then takes her shirt off too.

I'm thinking, *Who cares if they hear? You're about to make me! I want the whole world to know!*

Rick dives into her breasts like a kid bobbing for apples. Personally, I thought her breasts were for me, but over these past weeks I've noticed that Rick seems to think they're for him. Obviously, we're going to have to learn to share.

I watch as they make their way toward the couch, Nina walking backwards while Rick guides her; he pauses only to flick off the light. At the couch, Nina pulls him on top of her and wraps her legs around his waist. Their hearts are thudding, their breathing shallow. And then they begin to hump, which seems so pointless, especially since they both still have their pants on. But they're enjoying it, so I figure, what the hell? As long as *they* know the point of the exercise is to lose the pants.

They grope one another—pants on. Then do some more humping—pants still on.

Okay. I'm sick of the pants, already. Rick's harder than a baseball bat and Nina's vagina is so wet you'd think it was drooling.

"Shh!" Nina giggles because their moans are getting loud. "We'll wake Dink and Pablo."

Rick tries to unzip Nina's fly, but he can't get it to work, so she helps him and off go her pants. She wriggles out of her panties and lies back on the couch. Rick stands to yank down his sweatpants, while simultaneously trying to kick off his shoes. He topples over and has to right himself. Nina opens her arms to him, beckoning him to her. Suddenly he doesn't care that his sweatpants are only down as far as his knees. Neither do I. It's time for a little sperm shooting. The target is willing and ready.

Hurry up! I yell to Miss Egg. *The sperm are coming! The sperm are coming!*

She hesitates at the threshold of the fallopian tube.

Miss Egg! It's time for your trapeze act. Leap! Leap!

She doesn't budge. She's like a lazy harem girl savoring the indulgences of her lifestyle in the House of Eggs: nothing expected of her, each day melting into the next, uneventful… dreamy…

How can this be happening?

I search for Spermy among the throngs of frat boys. Where is he? Where's my other half?

I spot him in the dugout. He's sizing up his two hundred and fifty-three million competitors and gauging his chances. I try to encourage him. Let him know that Miss Egg is on her way and can't wait to meet her Prince Charming, her Knight in Shining Armor, her Barbie Dream Date, but he can't hear me over the sperm frenzy in the dugout.

Nina places Rick's hand on her inner thigh. Clumsily, he searches for the point of entry. He finds it. A low moan surges up from his belly.

I try to reassure myself: Even if Miss Egg is a little tardy, Spermy will stick around. Won't he?

Rick prepares to enter. He's got himself lined up perfectly. Then Nina grabs his wrist—hard. "Wait," she whispers.

Rick freezes, poised on top of her, one hand holding him up and the other holding his pee-pee.

"I heard something…" Nina says.

A bead of sweat drops from Rick's forehead onto her cheek.

Someone else is in the living room. Oh no! It's one of the Gay Terminators. She woke up thirsty and wants a glass of water. She has no idea what she's interrupting as she shuffles toward the kitchen.

Rick tries to position himself into a more neutral-looking pose, but accidentally kicks the coffee table and knocks an ashtray to the floor.

The Gay Terminator startles. "Shit!" She squints as if this will help her see into the dark. "Oh, it's you two. I forgot you were here. Sorry if I woke you."

Nina stifles a laugh. "You didn't."

The Gay Terminator heads to the kitchen, mumbling, "I had the weirdest dream. I was wearing this cape like I was some kind of superhero, but I couldn't figure out what my super powers were…"

Nina whispers to Rick, "We should stop."

"Stop?"

"It's not cool."

As the Gay Terminator rattles on about her dream, Rick eases off Nina. "I'm going to make a trip to the bathroom."

Nina kisses him on the nose. "Take the blanket to, uh, cover yourself."

"That's okay," he says hopping around on one foot trying to pull his sweatpants back up.

"Can you get them on over that?" she whispers.

His face grows hot. "I'll manage," he whispers back, at which point Nina pulls the blanket over herself and Rick makes for the bathroom.

This is a nightmare. He's going to shoot Spermy into the toilet. *Stop! Stop!*

The Gay Terminator stands at the sink and downs a glass of water—Gulp, gulp, gulp—then shuffles back through the living room. "'Night. 'Night."

"'Night," Nina replies. She listens for the click of the Gay Terminator's door, then focuses on the crack of light shining from beneath the bathroom door. He's thinking of me, she thinks and slides her hand between her legs and begins rubbing.

Rick is doing the same thing in the bathroom. I watch in horror as millions of sperm cascade into the toilet. I search the porcelain bowl for Spermy and have trouble spotting him in the huge school of sperm all swimming around like boys at a frat party where someone forgot to invite the girls— But wait. There he is! He's still in the dugout! He was second string!

How could I ever have doubted them? Miss Egg, Spermy, they're my champs. They've foiled the evil foe!

I remember that Pablo is leaving in the morning. And Dink has to go to work. Nina and Rick will be alone—again. I'll get another chance.Without interruptions.

Rick stumbles out of the bathroom and Nina pats the couch next to her. "Come here, you."

He slides in next to her.

"Sorry," she says.

He pulls her close. "There's nothing to be sorry about."

Time to employ Hope. I only get one window to snag life and time is running out.

Chapter Thirteen

7:45 am. Nina is startled awake by the sound of Pablo making coffee in the small galley kitchen. She considers staying put, pretending to sleep, but the smell of brewing coffee is too much. She untangles herself from Rick's floppy embrace and rolls off the couch. She has a crick in her neck.

Earlier, while she was still zonked out, I gently reminded a sleepy Miss Egg that she had an appointment with destiny. How she kept sane being cooped up with all those other eggs I can't imagine. There are close to four hundred thousand occupants in that overcrowded carton. But after bidding her girlfriends adieu—"I'll miss you! Wish me luck!"—she gracefully leapt across the moat outside Nina's ovary to the gateway of promise. Like a prom queen tingling with excitement as she descends the aisle to receive her crown, she began her float down the fallopian tube. She's spent years waiting for this moment, her aspirations focused on just one thing: to be more than just another unfertilized egg flushed down the toilet in a torrent of red.

"Are you naked under that shirt?" Pablo asks when Nina pads into the kitchen.

She rubs her eyes awake and stretches. "As a jaybird."

"Ew." He pours her a cup of coffee. "Girls."

She pinches back a grin the size of Montana. "I'm glad not everyone feels that way."

He eyes her suspiciously and shakes his head. "I don't want to know."

She massages her neck. "Can we use your bed while you're gone? It would be a little more romantic…and private…and comfortable."

"I'll need a note from your mother."

"Can we?"

"I'd rather you didn't."

"We'll wash the sheets."

Pablo doesn't respond.

He'll never know, she thinks.

They sip coffee and look through the breakfast bar at Rick lying on his back, feet protruding from underneath the blankets, snoring lightly.

"My, what big feet he has," Pablo says.

Nina punches him in the arm. "Is that all you think about?"

"Almost." He lifts his coffee mug.

Dink rushes in, buttoning a rumpled shirt. "I was supposed to be at a meeting fifteen minutes ago!"

Pablo chugs his last sip of coffee. "Maybe we can ride the bus together."

She runs her fingers through her hair. "I'll pick up a coffee on the way."

Before leaving, Pablo turns to Nina. "Don't do anything I wouldn't do."

Then I guess we can use your bed, she thinks.

Music to my ears!

8:13 a.m. Rick is still asleep on the couch. He's dreaming of dropping anchor on an island of scantily clad women, which he finds pretty entertaining…

I remind myself that he's scheduled to be at work by 10:00. It's now or never. Fortunately, Nina doesn't need coaxing. She woke up with a hankering so strong you'd think she was *trying* to create me. She walks over to the couch and kisses Rick's eyelids.

"Brrrft," he utters.

She brushes her lips lightly across his. "Wake up, sleepy boy."

The island women beckon him back into the water. The scant fabric covering their bodies, now wet with the sea, clings to their curves, hiding little.

"Wake up," Nina whispers again.

He blinks once. Twice. The island ebbs from his consciousness.

Nina pulls the blanket back and kisses his nipple.

"Uhhhnnn?" A tingle races the length of his spine. "Nina…"

She slides in next to him on the couch, traces his lips with her finger. “Hey, sleepyhead.”

He’s never seen how curly her hair is first thing in the morning. “Hey, beautiful.”

She nips his nose.

He pulls her toward him into a tongue kiss.

“That was nice,” she says.

“I’ll say,” he says.

They do another.

“You’ve had coffee,” he says.

She nods, a naughty smile on her face. “And I’ve got all this energy I just don’t know what to do with…” She reaches her hand down between his legs. “Maybe this present you have for me will help.”

He laughs and rolls her on top of him. “Is anyone else home?”

She shakes her head. “Nope. All ours.”

He does a little growl, pulls back her shirt, and dives into her breasts. And I’m thinking, *This is good…This is good…*until she says, “Oops!”

Oops? What does *that* mean? She pries herself gently from his hold and gets up from the couch. “Meet me in the bedroom.”

He makes a grab for her arm and misses. “What?”

Which is exactly what I’m thinking.

“Meet me in Pablo’s bedroom,” she says seductively.

Rick! Don’t let her out of your sight! Grab her! Grab her! But it’s too late. She’s headed for the bathroom.

Once inside, she opens a pink vanity bag and pulls out a small plastic box with a shallow rubber cup inside. Like it’s nothing, she hikes her leg up onto the side of the tub and fortresses off Miss Egg.

This makes no sense! Why is she doing this now when she didn’t do it last night? Was it the alcohol? An oversight? I watch poor little Miss Egg ready herself for a Prince Charming who will never arrive.

Nina steps into Pablo’s room. “All protected,” she says in a singsongy voice.

Rick is wrapped in a blanket and standing by the bed, his mood a bit subdued now that he remembers yesterday. “Are you sure this is okay?”

"He and Dink are both gone," she says, leading him to Pablo's bed.

Rick sits.

She kneels on the floor in front of him and slides her head under his blanket.

The irony. Spermy isn't going to wind up smashed against the despised rubber wall as I feared, but lodged behind a tooth, or spat into the sink. But Nina works her way up his abdomen one kiss at a time, then, when she reaches his mouth, he pushes back her shirt and caresses her breasts. She lets out a slight moan.

It's so tragic. Miss Egg waiting patiently, Spermy pumping himself up. They have no idea their future is doomed.

Rick rolls Nina onto her back, kissing her neck, the insides of her elbows, the palms of her hands and fingertips, little circles around her navel. Then he travels south. Nina is moaning and groaning…

8:25 a.m. Rick enters Nina, and the two begin their humping and grinding routine.

Spermy with the particularly cute corkscrew tail muscles his way through the mob of fired-up tadpoles, jockeying for position. He's not even in the first hundred million, but still the little bugger's planning to rush the gate. And…

Bang! They're off! Swells of sperm blaze down the canal at lightning speed, each one a little Ben-Hur. Then the nightmare begins. Thousands of frontrunners splat against the synthetic shell like bugs on a windshield. *Blat! Blat! Blat!* Others are extinguished by the strange poisonous goop. But something grabs my attention. A miracle! Sperm are getting though! The fortress has slipped up on the east end! What a stroke of luck! I jump back into the game like a gambler whose horse has just come up from the rear. *Go, Spermy! Go!* But where is he? Oh! Oh! My little corkscrew-tailed friend has found the breach and has made it to the other side. *Go up the fallopian, Spermy! Up the fallopian!*

To my horror, he acts disoriented, swimming this way and that, unsure of which way to go. *Focus, Spermy! Focus!* Other sperm join the fray and begin fighting each other off. It's an all-out brawl, each sperm knowing he has so little chance, each sperm fighting for life!

Some disillusioned young knights forsake their holy mission and choose to spend their one and only chance at the divine rapture of life humping any random cell they can find. But not Spermy! He's forging ahead. He's going for the gold!

A quick check-in with Miss Egg: she's fending off the onslaught of unwanted suitors. *Don't give up, Miss Egg! He's coming!* But as Spermy makes his way up the fallopian tube, a gang of belligerent sperm muscles past him. "Eat our dust!" they yell. Then another gang muscles past. "Hey, Grandma! Get out of the slow lane!" Poor Spermy is losing confidence! To my dismay, he begins flirting with a particularly tempting cell to his left.

I can't believe it! We've overcome so much, gotten so close. But Spermy's in such a funk he doesn't notice the *reason* these gangs of sperm are being so pushy. They're in striking distance of the maiden!

He's over here! I yell to Miss Egg. *Over here!* And she, bless her nucleus, allows herself to be nudged through the Fourth of July–like activities by other, more aggressive sperm, while they, unwittingly, push her right into the anemone-like cilia who gently guide her to my oblivious other half.

Miss Egg, noting that her Prince Charming is swimming in circles chasing his own tail, realizes she's going to have to take matters into her own cytoplasm. She positions herself real close and employs a tried and true tactic. "What a long, curly tail you have."

Abruptly Spermy stops the spherical dance routine. He can't believe it. The object of his desires is right there, trying to get *his* attention. And she's so compelling, so voluptuous, so, so…BIG! His tail begins to wag, propelling him through the frenzy. He searches for an entry point, but her armor-like shell is completely covered in eager sperm. He makes his way around her circumference. "What a long, curly tail I have! What a long, curly tail I have!" thrums confidence through him as he builds up speed.

He spots an opening in the crowd. *Now! Go now!* I scream and he contracts his corkscrew tail, spring-like, followed by a quick expansion, thrusting himself past the throng of sperm. *You can do it, Spermy! You can do it! You're a superstar!* But he crashes into Miss Egg's unyielding armor just like the rest of her suitors.

He panics.

I panic.

Have we come this far to be forsaken? Could it be that I was wrong? Is Spermy not the man for the job? Then he knocks politely on her outer shell. "Uh, Miss Egg? Are you in there?"

Miss Egg, not wanting to seem too easy, takes a moment for propriety's sake, then, thinking he's so cute she could eat him up, does just that, swallows him, whole— Schloop!—absorbing him right into her cytoplasm. Then she hangs out a little DO NOT DISTURB sign.

Genesis.

It's done.

My yin has found my yang. My Floating Soul has become anchored, thanks to the efforts of Miss Egg and the little fellow with the...*X chromosome*?

X? It was supposed to be a Y. *I'm supposed to be a boy!*

This doesn't make sense. How could I have not noticed?

But my cells have already begun splitting, the contract is sealed, till death do us part...and all that.

But I'm supposed to be a boy. A boy!

Rick, breathing heavily, flops onto his back. "That was amazing."

After a few seconds, Nina replies, "Amaaaaazing."

Rick asks, "What time is it?"

She checks the clock. "Eight thirty-six."

He pushes up onto an elbow and gazes at her. "Howie'd trip out to know that you and I actually...got together."

She touches his nose. "Are you?"

"What?"

"Tripping."

He draws a heart on her flat belly, then places his head where he drew it.

Does he know about me? Could he?

I check.

Nope.

Da-dum. Da-dum. Da-dum.

He's listening to her heart, which is beating so hard he can hear it in her stomach.

"It's weird," he says pondering the unsettling juxtaposition of yesterday's nightmare and today's indulgence. "But I'm happy."

He better enjoy that flat belly while he can, that's what I say.

In the meantime, what am I going to do about these XX chromosomes?

SPLITTING CELLS

Chapter Fourteen

It's been one week that I've been an Anchored Soul. I wish I could be more excited about it. I was so sure I was going to be a boy, and now that I'm not, I'm all confused. I still *feel* like a boy and consider myself a boy, but my cells are definitely going girl. As for my biological headquarters—what I've started calling this blob of multiplying cells—it's not the real me; it's just the body I've been assigned for…my…um…*mission.* I mean, there must be a reason The Known gave me a boy's soul and a girl's body. Maybe I'm supposed to be an undercover agent. All the boys will secretly know I'm one of them, but the girls will think I'm one of them. I'll be like a spy…Or maybe I'm going to be like some kind of shaman—neither girl nor boy, but mostly boy… That would be cool too. I'd be all holy.

Another thought that crossed my mind, this one a bit less welcome but gaining credibility by the second, is that The Known *didn't* give me a boy soul; I was just so jazzed to be hanging out with Rick and Howie that I made the choice myself and attributed it to The Known. Maybe we souls don't come in a sex. Maybe we're like The Known, a swirling tangle of learning and possibility—only the closer we get to the Land of Forgetting the more we get attached to its countless limitations. If that's the case, the boy/girl thing isn't quite as black and white as everyone in The Land of Forgetting seems to think…

Could this be one of the things they've forgotten?

That *I've* forgotten?

One thing's for certain. All those silly thoughts I was having about Gay Terminators are history. What a fool I was! Dink and Pablo have obviously been placed in my sphere to model the complexities of gender. And not just for me, but for Rick and Nina. They're going to need special skills to raise me; babies are highly impressionable. Parents' opinions, assumptions, and needs can either make a child's life bliss—or a living hell.

None of this changes the fact that I still wish I were a boy.

But what are the ingredients of a boy? What am I going to miss out on?

I know what they think in the Land of Forgetting: boys like to climb things, boys like adventure, boys like slugs and snails and puppy dogs' tails. But are these exclusively boy traits? And what, pray tell, are the ingredients of a…girl? Sugar? Spice? Nice? From what I've seen, there's a *whole* lot more to it than that.

Luckily, I can still travel into other people's thoughts and to other places, so I can research—even if I will forget everything once I get born. Surely there's *some* advantage to enlightenment.

Now if Nina and Rick would just figure out I'm here.

❖

Planned Parenthood. The name alone fills me with confidence. And it's so fortuitous that my own Iris should work at this place with the thoughtful moniker.

I drop into the small, overly lit waiting room with its three worn couches and racks of magazines and find it full of women.

Odd. Where are the men? Don't they need to be in on the planning too?

The next thing I notice is that not all the women look happy.

Which is also odd…

A quick scan of their thoughts provides shocking information. Some of these women don't want their babies; either they're too young, or they don't have enough money, or enough time, or the patience. For that matter, some of the Anchored Souls are having second thoughts too. The potential mom of one Anchored Soul hates the guy who forced the sperm on her—she *hates* him! Every time she thinks about the little blob of cells growing inside her all she can feel is hate. And this other Anchored Soul chose parents who came together for only that one night. They didn't even know each other's names. And they were drunk. And way young. And the potential grandmother is going to be a total nightmare. She keeps saying things to her daughter like, "Let this be a lesson to you," and "If you'd just be more like your sister..."

The Yearn sure causes us to make some stupid choices.

I notice another Anchored Soul in the corner. He's chosen a perfectly nice mother ready for a baby, but is so petrified by the sheer unpredictability of life, by the crazy gamble we each take as we try and worm our way into breathing, that he's planning to bail. Even though he totally loves his mom and dad, he's fixated on all the things that could go wrong.

Don't do it! I scream, hoping he'll tune into my thoughts and hear me, but he's so obsessed by the possibility of his umbilical cord wrapping around his neck and depriving him of oxygen that he doesn't hear me.

These sad scenarios make my gender worries seem so trivial. How could an Anchored Soul be so scared he'd choose to evaporate himself? He's so close. Or I *thought* he was close until I was hit with this whole *new* thing to worry about. What if I attached to parents who won't want me? What if they decide *not* to have me?

Yikes.

When I foisted myself into Nina's and Rick's lives, I was so desperate for life it didn't occur to me to take *their* needs into consideration.

Duh.

So I'm back to square one. Wishing. Hoping. Praying for luck.

Erg! The odds for a soul getting born are about the same as the odds for a hopeful seed blowing in the wind. Will it land on soil or cement? And if it's lucky enough to hit soil, will it rain in time? Will there be sun? Will it miss being chomped down by some hungry sparrow? Or caught in the grooves of some traveler's muddy boot?

But I *don't* want to be a burden who screws up my parents' lives, who causes them to say things like, *If only I hadn't had you*. I want to be cherished—adored! I want photo albums full of my pictures, a room full of colorful mobiles. We need to be a team. We *all* need to want me. So if Nina and Rick decide to want me, I'll go for it. But if they don't, I'm outta here. I'll evaporate myself just like that—Poof!—right back into the coziness of The Known.

Could be worse.

I could get born only to be left in a Dumpster.

I decide not to stick around and visit with Iris. I need to find Nina and Rick. Now!

I locate Nina right where she was when I last saw her: lying on the couch in the living room with a cool washrag on her head, her feet propped on Rick's lap, thinking she has a stomach flu.

Not exactly the secure loving embrace I was hoping for.

At least she and Rick have started looking for a place of their own. I wish I could say it's because they're completely in love and ready to have a baby, but that wouldn't be accurate. Pablo, back from his mom's, is making it pretty clear that he wants them to move out. Rick's grieving makes him difficult to be around—unless you're Nina, who likes processing, which she and Rick have been doing *a lot*. They snuggle on the couch having whispered conversations about loss and life. She encourages him to cry, something he's not that comfortable with, and he keeps hoping all this "feeling" will lead to more sex.

At the moment, Pablo is in the kitchen making a racket as he cooks himself dinner. He's had a bad day at the flower store where he works. It's the Fourth of July, and besides never wanting to see another red, white, or blue carnation as long as he lives, he's sick of people. Especially Rick and Nina.

Rick whispers to Nina, "When did Dink say she'd get back?" They're waiting for Dink to get back with some pot, which Nina thinks will calm her stomach.

"Soon, I hope."

Rick looks over his shoulder to the kitchen. He hates feeling beholden to Pablo. "We've got to get our own place."

"Everything's fine," Nina says. "Pablo's just had a bad day." She unfolds a small sheet of paper she pulled off a bulletin board at the Laundromat. It's decorated with hand-drawn flowers around the edges. SUNNY, PARTIALLY FURNISHED, ONE BEDROOM APARTMENT. MUST LIKE DOGS. "When did that lady say she'd call back?" she asks.

A cabinet door slams in the kitchen.

"Shortly," he says.

Nina crosses her fingers.

Rick massages her socked foot. "You doing okay?"

"Not too bad—today. At least I was able to get a little food down around lunch."

Being mistaken for a stomach flu isn't doing my self-esteem a world of good, but I'm trying to approach it with a sense of humor.

Rick's phone rings. "Hello?" Then he mouths to Nina, "It's her," and sits up straight and changes his voice to sound more professional. Nina removes her feet from his lap and also sits up straight. She wants this place to work. So do I, but for different reasons. She wants a real bed and a good night's sleep, sure that a home is all she needs to help her kick this flu. As for me, I want her and Rick to get in the mood to make a family. It doesn't have to be a big family, just the two of them and a jaw-droppingly adorable baby.

Nina takes a bottle of lavender-scented lotion off the coffee table, pumps a bead onto her hand, and massages it in as she listens to Rick make arrangements to see the apartment—*tonight!* She silently claps her newly moistened hands.

Rick hangs up the phone. "She sounded really nice. And old."

Dink pushes through the front door and holds up a baggie. "Wait until you get a whiff of these primo buds. If this doesn't help your stomach I don't know what will."

Nina turns around so she can see Dink. "You're the best."

Dink sits on the floor next to the coffee table. She's unsure about the affectionate look that Nina is giving her. "Hey, no problem," she says fumbling to fill the pipe. "You're my best friend."

"We just got a call about an apartment," Nina says in a singsongy voice. "We're gonna look at it tonight."

"I wanna go," Dink says handing the pipe to Nina. "Who knows? If Pablo's mood doesn't lighten up, I might decide to move in with you two." Everybody laughs except Pablo, who's just come into the living room with his bowl of chili. He grabs a magazine and flops onto the floor to eat.

"Excuse me. Some of us had to *work* today."

"All the more reason for you to come with us," Dink says. "We can go out after they get the apartment and celebrate our independence."

Pablo smiles for the first time since he got home.

Dink lights the pipe for Nina. "Here, sweetie."

Nina takes the pipe from Dink, intentionally grazing her hand.

Dink blushes.

"Wouldn't it be fun if we could all move in together?" Nina says before sucking on the pipe.

Pablo drops his spoon and it clanks when it hits the edge of the bowl. "I think it might get a *bit* complicated," he says pointedly to his roomie.

"What's that supposed to mean?" Dink shoots back.

He chuckles and shakes his head. "If you don't know, you're even more of a lost cause than I thought."

❖

The landlady meets them on the street, and just like Rick thought, she's old. But not old old; she's feisty old and her name is Viola Waltz and she has on the craziest clothes! She's wearing an old-fashioned ruffled blouse covered in primrose buds, accompanied by a seventies-style floor-length skirt with giant sunflowers spiking up from the hemline. But her sneakers take the cake. They're covered in hand-painted daisies. She's a walking flower garden. And right next to her is a porky dachshund named Franklin who's sporting a little checkered bowtie.

Running her bony, wrinkled fingers over the peeling plaster-molded wainscoting, Viola Waltz ushers the four of them into the foyer. "This old building holds some stories!" she says. "Sometimes, if you really listen, you can hear the laughter of those who came before. Women in fine furs, men in tuxedos coming back from a night out!" She pauses then, as if they're all supposed to listen for this. Franklin dutifully sits and cocks an ear, his tail thudding against the floor.

Viola is a kook!

Satisfied they've paid proper homage to those who came before, she says, "Onward!" and begins marching toward a narrow stairwell. They all follow. "It's on the third floor," she says, "right next to mine. People are often surprised I don't live on the first floor. They worry I'll have a heart attack walking up all these stairs. But it's these stairs, I tell you, that keep me young. Besides, I like being close to the sky. Figure it'll give me a head start on reaching heaven." She stops on the stair to slap her knee and laugh at her joke.

Pablo, Dink, Nina, and Rick exchange amused glances. What have they gotten themselves into?

By the third floor, Franklin is panting feverishly. Dink whispers to Pablo, "That hot dog is the one who's going to have a heart attack."

We make our way down a dimly lit hallway. "Honestly, Mr. Cromley was supposed to replace these lightbulbs months ago. We need more wattage!" Viola shoves the key in the lock, gives it a wiggle and a turn, then, kicks the door smartly.

It doesn't open.

"The fellow who used to live here slammed this door one too many times, I'm afraid," she says, then kicks it again, more vigorously this time. "I'm glad he's moved on. He wasn't very nice. Was he, Franklin?" One more kick and it opens. "Keeping up with this place is a lot, but she's a good old building. It would break my heart to sell her."

Nina takes hold of Rick's hand. She feels shaky from the day's nausea, but excited as well. "Shall we?"

Franklin yips at Nina's ankle.

Everyone jumps but Viola, who says, "He's an excellent judge of character. I should have listened to him about the last fellow."

Nina smiles politely, unsure of Viola's meaning. Does Franklin like her or not? She starts through the door, but Franklin cuts her off, trotting into the apartment first, his toenails clicking on the hardwood floor. Once inside, he turns to look back, his tail wagging like a cranked-up metronome.

Viola chuckles. "Don't rush us, Franklin."

Franklin spins around once and sits down, his tail slapping the floor repeatedly.

"Well, that does it," Viola says. "The apartment's yours if you want it. I've never seen Franklin so sure of tenants in my life."

The first thing that Nina sees when she heads into the apartment is a bay window with a window seat. The first thing Rick sees is a bad patch job in the wall. Nina checks out the avocado-colored couch. Rick notes the chipped crown molding and need of paint.

"All this furniture comes with it?" Nina asks.

"If you want. I can have the stuff put…"

"We want it," Nina says.

"We do?" Rick says under his breath.

"I'll have to get Mr. Cromley to come in and straighten it up. He's in a bit of a crisis. Seems his granddaughter has not been well for some time now. But he promised me as soon as he gets things sorted out, he'll fix those shutters and replace the linoleum on the kitchen floor."

This gives Rick an idea. "I'm pretty handy with stuff like that."

Viola claps her hands. "Really? You're just what I was praying for! I'd certainly adjust the rent. And there are other things in the building that need attention as well…I could keep you busy."

Rick decides it wouldn't be a bad place to live after all. If he plays his cards right, he could work off the rent.

He and Viola start talking terms while Nina walks over to the tiny kitchen. Pablo and Dink follow. "What a cute window," Nina says, unruffled by the fact that it looks out onto a dingy stairwell. "I could sew little curtains."

Dink raises an eyebrow. "Little curtains?"

Nina grunts as she tries to force the window open. "What's that supposed to mean?"

"Here," Dink says, stepping over. "Let me help you, Little Miss Homemaker."

"Don't be condescending."

Dink forces the window open. "Then quit with the little curtains routine."

"I'm just talking window coverings…maybe with a ruffled valance…"

Dink's eyes flick toward Pablo, but Pablo's inspecting the broom closet and doesn't notice. She makes a mental note to talk to him later. *Something weird is going on with Nina.*

Nina wanders over to the bedroom. "Oh, you guys have to see this! It's adorable! It even has a sweet built-in dresser."

Rick walks up behind her and slips his arms around her tummy. Together they take in the queen bed and unmatched nightstands. "I could do this," he says.

"The repairs?" Nina asks.

"All of it," he says nuzzling her hair. "The apartment, us…"

And so it's decided. For a reduced rent they're going to move in to 448 Delight Street, Apartment #3C, directly down the hall from the kooky Viola Waltz and her weird dog, Franklin.

I'm trying not to get too attached. I mean, I'm not a done deal yet, not until they for sure want me.

But it is a cool place—even if I wouldn't get my own room.

❖

Three days later is moving day. After work, Rick stops by his family's house to get the rest of his stuff, especially his iPod speakers, his vintage Led Zeppelin poster collection, and the rest of his clothes. It's his dad's club night, so he's not worried about running into him.

Wringing her hands, Dorothy follows him around as he gathers up his stuff. "It's going to be just the two of you?" she asks.

"Yup," he says.

"Just you and this girl."

"Her name is Nina."

"It seems awfully quick."

Rick looks up from his dresser drawer. "Mom, I know what I'm doing."

"Are you in love with her?"

"What kind of question is that?"

"An important one, if you're moving in together."

Having filled one grocery bag of clothes, Rick begins on another. "Sure. I love her. She's amazing…An actress."

Rick, your enthusiasm is killing me. And it's not doing much to build Dorothy's confidence either.

She sits on his bed. "I worry that this is all about losing Howie. You haven't been yourself since…"

Rick flings an armful of jeans to the floor. "Mom!"

"I'm sorry, but it's what I think. You've suffered a terrible blow."

Rick sits next to her. "I can't live here anymore, not with *him*."

"But to move in with this girl."

"I told you, her name is Nina."

"Nina, then. Do her parents know?"

"Yeah, she told them. And they're being a lot mellower about it than you."

Rick is stretching the truth a bit. Iris and Harvey told Nina that moving in with Rick was "rash" and they "wish she'd reconsider," "move in with some girlfriends or find a place of her own." The main thing is they don't want her moving back home. When Nina didn't return with them after graduation, Iris was quick to convert the basement into the home office she's always wanted, and now she can't imagine living without it.

Rick writes his new address on a slip of paper. "It's a really great place. The landlord is this cool old lady." He doesn't tell her that Viola is batty and acts like her dog understands English. "She's really sweet," he says and kisses Dorothy on the cheek. "Like you."

Which makes Dorothy feel a little better.

Once the car is loaded, Dorothy slips Rick a hundred dollar bill. "For…whatever. Just keep in touch."

"Thanks, Mom," he says and hugs her. Then he gets into his car.

She puts her hand on the car door keeping him from shutting it. "And sometime, if you get a chance, you might stop in on Mrs. Hartman. There's so much red tape involved in this military funeral, not the least of which is they can't locate Howie's older brother. The whole thing is a real mess. Anyway, I'm sure she'd love to see you."

"Will do," Rick says.

"And one more thing…"

"Mom! Quit! I'll be fine!"

She leans in and kisses him one more time. "Don't forget to call."

From there, Rick picks up Nina, Pablo, and Dink. They're going to celebrate at the new place. They stop to pick up pizza and beer on the way. Nina's craving anchovies.

Rick carries Nina over the threshold. Pablo and Dink stand on either side of the door applauding. Nina's embarrassed to admit that the smell of anchovies is now making her sick. When they sit down to eat, she subtly tries to pick them off her piece, but everyone notices.

"You okay, hon?" Rick asks.

She smiles weakly. "I've felt better."

Dink gives Pablo a look like the one she gave him a few days ago when Nina was talking about sewing curtains. He shrugs and takes another huge bite of pizza. Dink makes a mental note that she really must talk to him later and holds up her beer. "To your new home!"

Nina and Rick hold theirs up. "To our new home!"

"To having my old home back!" Pablo says.

Laughing, they all clink beers.

❖

Dink and Pablo are walking down the maple-lined street. They've just said good-bye to Rick and Nina.

"What do you say we go find a martini?" she says.

"I don't know…"

"We need to talk."

"About what?"

"You should be sitting down for this."

Pablo stops in his tracks. "God. Sounds ominous."

"It could be," she says.

I knew it! Dink is on to me.

❖

The Galaxy is fairly dead. The neon Miller sign with an undulating waterfall casts an unhealthy hue upon the patrons at the bar. Pablo and Dink grab martinis and tote them to a back booth. Dink takes a swig then leans across the table toward Pablo. "It's about Nina."

Pablo takes a sip, swirls it around his mouth, and swallows. "Why am I not surprised?"

He's about to ask if it has anything to do with Dink's obvious infatuation with her when Dink says, "Haven't you noticed anything?"

"She moved out. I noticed that."

"The nausea that comes and goes? Her cravings?" She leans in. "Her desire to sew curtains?"

Pablo coughs in the middle of a swallow. "Oh shit!"

"I'll say." Dink searches her pockets for some ChapStick.

He blots martini from his shirt. "You think Rick knows?"

"No way. He's too freaked about his friend dying." She locates her ChapStick and uncaps it.

"Nina?"

"Oblivious." She rubs ChapStick on her lips. "Someone needs to tell her."

They look at each other for a moment. "Forget it!" Pablo blurts. "It's completely out of my precinct."

"Hey, the only reason I know about any of this is my sister just hatched a baby."

"Then you should tell her. You're the expert."

"Pablo, I'm completely devoid of maternal instincts. I have no idea how to do all that coo-cooey stuff. In fact, it makes me damned nervous."

"Why do we have to tell her at all? I mean, sooner or later, won't she figure it out?"

"We've got to get her to take care of herself," Dink says, counting out her cash for another drink.

They sit in silence for a few minutes and watch the small crowd huddling around the pool table. A lively game is under way and people are hooting it up.

When it quiets down Pablo says, "I wonder if she'll want to keep it?"

It? Did he just call me It?

❖

Back at the apartment, Nina and Rick are making up their bed. Nina's dorm sheets aren't quite the right size, but they make do. Rick wraps his arms around her. "Welcome home."

She lets her head rest on his chest. "Not much help from me."

"Now that we have our own place, you'll have a chance to kick this flu."

She holds him a little tighter. "I love you."

He kisses her hair, scoops her up, and lays her gently on their new bed. "Me too."

I wish one of them would say: Wouldn't having a baby make everything perfect? I don't suppose it's all that likely, though. But a little flu can wish.

❖

Back at the bar, Pablo and Dink are getting drunk. They ro-sham-bo to see who's going to tell Nina. Then do two out of three. Then three out of five. Finally they decide to bear the responsibility together. What's more, they've come up with a plan: Tell Rick. Let him tell Nina.

Chapter Fifteen

All this puking sure makes a rotten impression. By noon the following day I'm so discouraged by this new phase of Nina's and my relationship that I zip over to Jack's Tires to hang with Rick. What a difference! He actually seems happy. He's popping tires on and off like bottle caps. He's *excited* about his new home. And about Nina.

At quitting time he sheds his greasy coveralls and punches out his time card, humming the whole time. He wants to pick up his sax tonight. Nina's been asking to hear him play, but he hasn't been able to since Howie's death. Maybe tonight he can.

In the parking lot, he's just opened his car door when he hears someone yell his name. It's Dink. She and Pablo are sprinting off a bus. He watches them run toward him, Pablo holding a huge bouquet of star lilies. "Hey, you guys! What's up?" he asks, searching their faces for a clue.

Pablo waits for Dink to say something. Dink waits for Pablo to say something.

"Is something wrong? Is Nina okay?"

Dink kicks Pablo's shoe. "Well, go ahead."

Pablo clears his throat and is clearly avoiding making eye contact.

Rick's eyes flick back and forth between his two new friends. "What? Tell me." His mind is starting to make things up: Nina hit by a car, Nina at the bottom of the stairs, Nina shivering in a hospital bed, Nina…

"*We* think—" Dink begins.

"What?" Rick snaps. "You think what?"

"That Nina's pregnant," Pablo finishes.

Rick's world jerks into slow motion, like in a soundless dream where you're trying to run but your legs won't move. The traffic light changes. Silent cars begin moving. A group of school kids cross the street silently laughing.

"Pregnant?" he finally utters. Just saying the word makes his neck flush.

He can see Dink mouth the word "pregnant," and he watches her as she glances at Pablo.

Rick wags his head back and forth, trying to make the world return to normal. "Pregnant," he hears himself say. "Wow. Does Nina know?"

Dink says something, but the only reason he knows this is because he can see her lips moving. Another group of soundless school children gathers by the light. Rick begins to run his fingers through his hair, but winds up yanking it between his fists. "Yeah…I, uh…" He releases his fists and slides his hands down to the nape of his neck where he locks them, then looks straight up. The world clicks back. The power lines against the blue sky begin buzzing, the pigeons making their low warbling sounds.

Dink nods toward the star lilies. Pablo thrusts them forward. "I thought these might help."

"Good idea." Rick takes the lilies. "Wow…Maybe that's why she's been so—"

"Uh-huh," Dink interrupts. "Just like my sister. You know…the anchovies…"

"The curtains…" Pablo offers.

"It's just…We've been so careful." He takes in a huge swallow of air and blows it out through rubbery lips. "Well, I guess I should go talk to her."

"Could you give us a ride home?" Pablo asks.

"Yeah, sure."

When Rick drops them off, Dink makes him promise to call once he's told Nina. "We'll wait to hear from you."

"All right. And thanks, guys." He chooses a back route home. His palms sweat against the steering wheel; his mind races. *Is she really pregnant? Maybe they're wrong.* Someone blows a horn at him for not noticing the green light. He presses down on the accelerator. *But what if they're not*... A car whizzes past him. By the time he gets to the apartment, we're both nervous wrecks.

Nina, however, is chipper. "I'm finally over this flu," she says when she hears him enter the kitchen. She's standing on a chair applying floral shelf paper into the cabinet shelves. "Viola gave me this. She had it left over. I never thought I'd see the day I'd be doing shelf paper, but it's transforming these shelves. Check it out."

Rick is struck simultaneously by two conflicting possibilities. One: it seems very unlike Nina to be putting shelf paper down in their cabinets; maybe she *is* pregnant. Two: she says she's healthy again; maybe she *isn't*. And, although her pattern of feeling better and then worse has been asserting itself for weeks, he finds it so much more convenient to believe that she isn't pregnant. *She doesn't look pregnant*, he thinks. And to my bewilderment, he decides to ignore the shelf paper altogether. Handing her the flowers, he wipes me completely from his mind. "For the most beautiful woman in the world," he says.

She steps off the chair, and kisses him. "They're gorgeous! You know, I'm feeling so good that tomorrow I'm going to look for a real job. I've circled some in the paper. And I talked to my dad on the phone today. I told him the reason I haven't found a real job yet is that I've been sick and he said he'd put some money in my account. Oh, and Lottie stopped by to see our place. It's been such a great day."

Rick's heart swells. "Cool."

They go on with the rest of their night as if it's like any other. It's not until they're heading for bed, after a dinner of leftover Chinese and pizza, that Rick remembers he's supposed to call Pablo and Dink. He waits until Nina is in the bathroom and dials. Pablo answers.

"Hello?"

"It's Rick," he whispers.

"How did it go?"

"She's better."

"What?"

"It *was* a flu and she's better. She's going to look for a job tomorrow."

"Rick—"

"You should see her. She shelf-papered the cabinets."

"Shelf-papered the cabinets? Rick—"

Rick can hear Dink in the background asking, "What? What?"

Rick closes out the conversation. "Look, I've got to go. We'll talk tomorrow."

I zip over in time to see Pablo saying "Shit!" to the dial tone.

Dink reaches for her Marlboros. "What happened?"

"He didn't tell her."

"What?"

"He's decided it was just a stomach flu."

"Rickie!" she groans. "Don't be such an ignoramus." She taps out a smoke and lights it.

"And get this, she's shelf-papering cabinets."

Dink takes a drag off her Marlboro and drops her head into her hands. "Rickie, Rickie, Rickie..."

Pablo goes to warm up an old pot of coffee. "I say we give it a day."

❖

The next morning, Nina beelines to the bathroom.

Rick, waking from a fitful sleep, rolls onto his back and listens to her puke. "Honey?"

"I can't believe it!" she whines between retches. "It must be the adhesive from the shelf paper."

His stomach begins its own anxiety-provoked assault. "Um... sweetheart?" He slides out of bed and heads to the dining room.

She shuffles from the bathroom and climbs back into the empty bed, rests her hands on her belly, and closes her eyes. A strand of sweat-soaked hair is stuck to her face. "Where are you?"

He returns to the room with the vase of lilies, puts it on the dresser, and breaks one newly opened star lily off the stem. He sits on the edge of the bed and peels the hair from her forehead and tucks a strand behind her ear. "I, um, love you, you know that."

She speaks with her eyes closed. "I love you too."

He pulls the sheet up to cover her exposed shoulder and then rests his hand on her chest. "There's something we need to think about..."

"Not now, Rick. I feel like doo-doo."

"I know you do. But I...well, I was talking to Pablo and Dink... and...I mean, have you thought about...that you might be pregnant?"

He feels her stop breathing. He stops too. And there they stay, the two of them—one lying flat out like a corpse, the other sitting with a lily in his hand—depriving themselves of oxygen for a whole forty-two seconds. It's excruciating. I mean, it's like he just told her the end of the world was near. Which in my case, I guess, could be true.

Please want me. Please, please, please.

Nina finally inhales. "Pregnant..." slips out on the exhale.

Rick follows suit on the air thing, but his brings with it an onslaught of things he might say, but doesn't: *I thought you were using a diaphragm. Don't panic, we don't know for sure yet. You don't want to keep it, do you? Do you?*

"You talked to Dink?" Nina says.

"And Pablo. They gave me the heads up."

She pushes herself up to sitting. "I need to be alone."

"But—"

"I want some space." She hugs her knees to her chest and drops her head.

Rick's unsure if she really wants him to leave or she's just saying that. He places the lily on the foot of the bed. "You want me to go?"

Nina doesn't even look up. *I've been so careful*, she thinks. *How could my body betray me like this?*

"Honey?" Rick asks.

Nina thinks about what Iris would want her to do. Iris, she's sure, would tell her it isn't the right time. Iris would say she still has her whole life in front of her. Iris would say she should have a plan.

I wish she'd quit thinking about Iris and think about how much fun we could have. Cuddling, doing *goo-goo ga-gas* together, practicing saying words, playing open-your-mouth-here-comes-the airplane are just a few of the things that come to mind.

Rick is still standing by the bed. "Okay then," he says, gathering up his work clothes from the chair and heading to the bathroom. He cuts himself shaving and can barely calm his hands to button his shirt. He makes a pot of coffee and brings a cup in to Nina. "You sure you don't want me here?"

She wraps her fingers around the warm cup of coffee. "This is *my* body, Rick. I need to make this decision myself."

Part of him wants to yell, It might be *your* body, but it's *my* future we're talking about!

Your future, I think. Give me a break!

Rick hovers by the door, hoping she'll change her mind about wanting him to leave.

She doesn't.

I resign myself to a day spent popping back and forth between them as they try to figure out what to do about me.

❖

Throughout the day Rick seems to try on new possible futures with each tire he changes. He and Nina with a baby. He and Nina without a baby. He and *no* Nina. He and Nina getting married… He worries about the financial situation. Does he make enough money to support Nina and a baby? And how much does it take exactly? He'll have to leave Jack's, but he's been ready to do that anyway.

On his break he tries calling Nina, but she doesn't pick up.

He goes back to tires and thinking about me. Having a baby could be the impetus to open the music store he and Howie talked about, only now he'd call it Howie's Notes, instead of Music Jones. Or maybe he should become a firefighter. He's always thought about that. He also thinks about what it's going to mean to be a father. He pictures himself holding me to his chest and bouncing me up and down. He pictures helping me with homework.

At lunch, he tries calling Nina again, but she still doesn't pick up.

One thing he's sure of: if they do decide to have me, and if I'm a boy, he wants to name me Howie.

Back at 448 Delight Street, Nina hides out in bed, getting up only when she has to, i.e., to puke. Having children is something she's always planned on; she just never thought it would be now. Does she love Rick enough? Will she be able to continue acting? She imagines herself at rehearsal with me, the perfect baby, sleeping contentedly in the front row. *It wouldn't change my life that much*, she thinks. Then she thinks about a woman and a baby she sat next to on a plane once. The baby cried the whole four hours. By the time the flight was over, Nina wanted to strangle both mother and child.

She decides to cook something healthy.

At five thirty, Rick is climbing the stairs to the apartment. He's come to the decision that he could handle a baby *if* Nina wants me.

Nina is in the kitchen standing over a pot of vegetable stew. She, to my total despair, is leaning in favor of *not* having me, but it's not me she's unsure of, it's Rick. Could he get his shit together? She hears the door click open and Rick toss his keys on the bookshelf.

"Nina?"

She fishes out the bay leaf and drops it into the trash. "In here."

He comes up behind her and kisses her neck. "Something smells great."

"I thought I should make us something healthy."

Rick wonders if there's a hidden message in her words. "You're not feeling queasy?"

"I'm okay."

"I tried to call."

"I know." Nina takes his hands, gazes into his eyes. "I did a pregnancy test…"

"And?"

"It's for real."

"But…"

She wrinkles her nose. "Can we not talk about this until after we eat?"

Rick's sick of waiting, but says, "Sure. I'll go shower." He walks past the table and notices that the lily he left on the bottom of the bed is now in a bud vase on the table between two candles. He wonders at its meaning. Once showered, he returns to the table. His bowl is already filled. He sits.

She sits.

He waits for her to pick up her spoon.

She does.

So he does as well, spooning up a bite of overcooked zucchini that he can barely taste. "This is delicious."

Nina smiles. "Thanks. I considered throwing in the lilies…"

They both laugh in a fake-sounding way.

Unable to stand their namby-pamby conversation one second longer, I plunge into Nina's thoughts.

She's watching Rick butter a second piece of bread and asking herself: *Is he up to the task?* She loves his hands. Even though he works with tires, he keeps his fingernails clean. She tries to imagine those fingers changing diapers, wiping spit-up from his shoulder. *Is he man enough?* He mops his bowl with a hunk of dark bread, folds his napkin, taking the cotton square and creasing it in half once, twice, then one more time smoothing it out and placing it next to his bowl. She reminds herself how briefly they've known one another. *I must be crazy to even be considering having a baby with him*, she thinks.

Rick, at a loss for what to do next, looks up. "Are you okay?" Nina nods. He notices she's barely touched her stew. "Shall I clear your plate? I mean, are you done? Or…" She nods again. "How about some nice calming tea, then?"

"That would be wonderful."

They both stand. He goes into the kitchen, she into the living room.

❖

Ten minutes later, he places the tray with teapot, mugs, and honey on the coffee table. "It needs to steep," he says, lowering himself onto the couch facing her. She turns toward him, and all I can think is they're like two side-by-side pages in a closed book.

The tea continues to steep.

After what seems like forever, she pours. "Honey?" she asks.

"Yes?"

"I mean do you want any."

"Oh. Yes…please."

She stirs a dollop into his mug and hands it to him, then does the same with hers. She brings the mug to her heart. He holds his on his knee.

She sips her tea.

He sips his.

She picks a stray tea leaf from her tongue.

He doesn't.

"I'm not opposed to abortion," she says at last, her tone as mundane sounding as if she's talking about paper or plastic.

He puts his mug on the table, misjudging the distance just a hair. A splash of tea burns his knuckle. "Is that what you want?" he asks sucking the burn.

"I didn't say that. It just seems the most logical. I mean, we haven't known each other very long."

Come on, Nina! Think about the way he folded that napkin.

"I guess," he says.

She picks a piece of lint off the couch and rolls it between her fingers. "Do *you* want the baby?"

Rick lets out a huge lungful of air. "It could be okay."

Rick, you're killing me here. You feel more alive, more vital, than you've felt in months. Why won't you admit it? Just cut the crap and tell Nina that the idea of having me is giving meaning to your life.

She picks up a purple throw pillow from the floor and hugs it. "I know it's totally impractical, but for some reason I keep thinking I'm supposed to have this baby."

Whoa. *That* was unexpected. Even Nina had no idea she was going to say it. I tell myself I should be happy—She wants me!—but I can't let go of her impulsiveness. Couldn't she just as easily decide that she *doesn't* want me, say, tomorrow?

Rick takes one of her socked feet in his hand and begins massaging. "Really? You think you might want the baby?" He waits for an answer, but Nina's closed her eyes. She's letting herself "feel the moment" like she does in her acting. Outside, someone walks by whistling. "We should probably get you to a doctor to make sure," he adds.

"I know I'm pregnant," she says. "I can feel it."

He takes the pillow from her and reaches over to place a hand on her belly. He's trying to comprehend the idea of me. "I think we could do a good job."

She holds his hand to her belly. "Me too," she whispers.

They sit this way for a few seconds, him with his hand on her belly, her with her hand on his. Then Rick slides off the couch onto one knee. "You're going to have to marry me."

Nina whacks his arm. "Now you're freaking me out."

"Why? If we're going to have a baby we should be married."

"It's too crazy," she says. "I haven't even been to the doctor."

"You said you knew."

"I do, but…"

"Then marry me."

"What if it turns out I'm wrong?"

Having no answer for this, Rick shrugs.

Nina slides down next to him on the floor and takes his face into her hands. "Let's just take one thing at a time, okay?"

He nods, but in his mind a baby and marriage have to go together—and marriage should come first.

"So are we really going to have a baby?" she asks.

"You tell me."

She searches his eyes. "*I* want to."

"So do I, so let's get married."

She stretches her legs out on the floor and looks at her toes. "I *so* can't make this decision right now."

He rolls off his knee and faces forward, his back to the couch. "Then don't."

"Are you sulking?"

"I just think…" He turns and kisses her on the lips, and I think they're going to talk some more about me, but they don't. Instead they do a bunch more kissing—and I mean a *bunch*. And they're doing a lot of rubbing too, and the usual humping and rolling around. Before long their clothes are strewn all over the place and Rick is shooting his sperm in her again. Ho hum. At least it's doesn't take too long. Or that's what I think, until Rick starts in with a bunch *more* kissing although this time it's between Nina's legs. It's like he's trying to prove something to her, or to himself, I'm not quite sure. And don't really care. She moans and bucks up and down, then does this giant shiver and pushes him off. He tries to kiss her some more, but she won't let him. Resigned, he rolls onto his back, winded, smiling, leaving Nina sprawled on the floor, her head propped against the couch and breathing hard.

"Wow. Who knew a goatee could do that?" she laughs.

Rick arranges his lanky body so he can lay his head on her belly. "Not just any goatee," he says, staring up at the ceiling.

She laughs, running her fingers through his hair. "I came three times."

"Show-off," he says reaching a foot over to the coffee table and picking up a felt-tip pen with his toes.

"The boy has prehensile toes too," she says.

He transfers the pen to his hand and traces a ring around her finger. "Now what do you say, Miss Nina Kalina?"

She looks at the thin black line circling her fourth finger. "You sure you can put up with me?"

"Positive."

She kisses him on the palm of his hand, then gives the tip of his finger a little nip. "Well then, I guess the answer's yes."

Rick grins, flips over, and presses his lips to her belly and whispers his first words to me. "Welcome to us," he says. After that, he and Nina fold into one another like an origami sculpture with me right in the middle.

It's times like these I wish I didn't have to forget.

Chapter Sixteen

Just as I feared, early next morning Nina is lying wide-awake in bed next to a sleeping Rick, thinking: *What am I doing? Marrying Rick...having a baby... This is crazy.*

She gets up and pukes.

"You okay, honey?" Rick croaks from the bedroom.

Nina rests her forearms on the rim of the toilet. "No, I am *not* okay. I'm puking."

Rick sighs and rolls out of bed, wondering how long the puking part will last. He squats next to Nina and puts his hand on the small of her back.

Nina lifts her throbbing head. "*What* are you doing here?"

"What does it look like I'm doing?" he says yawning. "I'm sitting next to a toilet with you while you puke."

"But it's gross."

He pulls the sweaty hair away from her face. "So? You're having our baby. The least I can do is join in the gross part of it."

The idea that Rick is so committed to me causes Nina to panic even more; she feels cornered. "I'm going back to bed," she says.

❖

An hour later, Rick is sitting at the table with a cup of coffee and yesterday's classifieds. Nina shuffles in wearing her robe, and stretches. "Morning."

He looks up from the paper. "Feeling any better?"

"Much. Sorry about earlier."

He pulls her over and nuzzles his head against her belly.

She stiffens. "I was thinking we should invite Dink and Pablo over for Sunday brunch. It's still early. I bet they haven't eaten."

He looks at her quizzically. *Why does she always want those two around?* "You up to it?"

"Yeah. I feel pretty good. And I want to tell them the news."

So she says, but I think she should 'fess up to Rick that she's having second thoughts. I don't want her to wind up regretting me.

"Whatever you say," Rick says and starts rooting through the cabinets for what they could serve. Not only is he a little put out that she doesn't want to make the morning a special one, he also doesn't trust her cooking.

She makes the call. "They're on their way," she says.

"What do you say to pancakes?" he says.

Half an hour later the doorbell rings and Nina, who's been reading on the couch, gets up to answer it.

"I should still be sleeping," Dink says, shuffling in. Her hair looks even more unkempt than usual, almost flat on one side, and her black T-shirt is rumpled.

"Dink, it's twelve thirty," Nina says.

Pablo, as usual, is pressed and alert in linen pants and a raw silk shirt, which he wears open at the collar. His silky black ponytail is pulled neatly back and he has a thin gold bracelet around his slender wrist. "Morning, Neen."

"Coffee's in here!" Rick yells.

They head for the kitchen where Rick is flipping pancakes. "Cream and sugar's on the counter."

"Why dilute it?" Dink says, filling a chipped mug. "At this hour I should just inject it."

Pablo pours a cup for himself. "Such the drama queen."

"*You're* the queen, sweetie. I'm just the drama."

Pablo picks up the classifieds. "Either of you know someone looking for a room? I'm praying the one in my apartment is about to be vacated."

Dink laughs. "Oh, it's *your* apartment now? When did that happen?"

Rick flips the last of the pancakes onto a plate. He's delighted they've turned out so well. "Everyone hungry?"

"We'll tell you the news after we eat," Nina says, pinching a wilted lily off a stalk in the wine bottle vase. "Sparkling cider, anyone?"

Why is she putting on this show? Who is she trying to convince?

The four of them sit and begin helping themselves to pancakes and fresh cantaloupe.

"So, you're not too sick to eat," Dink ventures.

"Nope." Nina shoves a huge bite into her mouth and smiles.

Rick chuckles. He doesn't realize this is all an act to try to convince everyone, herself included, that she's sure of what she's doing. He thinks she's really happy.

"*Real* maple syrup," Dink says. "This must be some announcement."

"And sparkling cider," Pablo adds. "You sure you don't want to tell us the news so we can toast?"

Dink pops a piece of cantaloupe into her mouth. "It doesn't have anything to do with having a baby, does it?"

Rick and Pablo's eyes dart to Nina. They can't believe that Dink just said this.

Nina bites one side of her lip as she tries to figure out what to say. Finally she blurts, "You are all such cow pies! I hate it that you knew first."

Pablo throws his hands in the air. "Don't blame me, it was all Dink's doing."

Rick reaches his hand across to Nina's. "We're really excited," he says in a tone similar to his father's let's-not-get-carried-away tone. "And we've decided to get married." He doesn't notice Nina's fingers fidgeting beneath his.

Dink becomes suddenly very interested in her half-eaten pile of pancakes. "Wow, you guys are making a regular family."

"Not *regular*," Nina shoots back. "That's too depressing."

Rick laughs. He loves this side of Nina. "Yeah. As long as we have Nina, we're never going to be *regular*."

"I'm being serious. I don't want to be one of those wives whose big excitement in life is pulling out her holiday apron. Or discovering a new air freshener."

"Like you *could* be," he says.

"It could happen," she says. "People slip into complacency without even knowing it. And getting married, having a baby…that's where it always begins. Suddenly married couples become all about clipping coupons and insurance…and…"

"That's not going to happen to us," Rick says, glancing uneasily at Dink and Pablo. "We're not those kinds of people."

"We need to make sure we're not," Nina says, getting up from the table and circling around to where Pablo and Dink are sitting. Avoiding Rick's questioning eyes, she gets down on one knee. "Will you be part of our family too?" she asks the two of them.

Dink pushes back from the table and crosses her arms. "Nina, *what* are you talking about?"

"Just what I said. I want you to commit to being part of our family. We need you two to keep us from being sucked into regular."

"Nina," Rick says.

"I'm serious, Rick. I have this total fear that before we both know it we're going to swept into dull."

"Well, that makes *me* feel good," Pablo says. "Dink, we're going to be the weird factor."

"You know what I mean!" Nina says slapping Pablo's arm. "I want my kid to be brought up…"

"…by a village," Dink says dryly. "We get it." Under the table, one of her knees is bouncing up and down, up and down. She feels like running.

Pablo glances at her, then back at Nina. "You know how I feel about the evil 'commit' word."

"This is different," Nina says. "You don't have to move in with us. I just want…"

"…for us to love you no matter what. I get it," Pablo says.

"No, you don't," Nina interjects. "It's not just *you* have to love *us*. We *all* have to love *each other*."

"I see," Pablo says. "But can we get days off from all this loving if one of us is being particularly bitchy?"

Nina looks to Rick. "What do you think?"

He's trying to act like he's not bothered by Nina's behavior. "Just tell her yes so we can get back to eating."

Nina levels him with her gaze. "Honey, I'm serious."

Now Rick gets it. This is no game for Nina. "O-*kay*," he says. "You can have days off." Even though he says this, the whole notion of opening up our family—*his* family—to her friends troubles him. But I'm thrilled by the turn of events. They'd be such good influences on me. Especially when I reach puberty. Now if they'd just say yes.

"Please," Nina pleads.

Pablo sighs, then shrugs. "Fine by me."

"Dink?"

Dink fiddles with her fork and doesn't answer.

"Come on!" Pablo urges. "I'm hungry."

Dink throws her head back in exaggerated exasperation, and when she speaks her voice comes out forced, as if she wants everyone to believe this is a fun game for her. "Okay! I promise. But do I have to love Pablo till I die too?"

Everyone laughs, except Pablo, who grumbles, "Trust me, if I'd realized you came with the package, I would have reconsidered." At which point Dink punches him in the arm. "Ow! What did I do to deserve that?" he says.

Nina reaches across the table to her glass of sparkling cider and holds it in the air. "To Uncle Pablo and Aunt Dink."

Rick raises his glass halfheartedly.

Dink gets up from the table. "Who needs more coffee?"

"Wish I could," Nina says going back to her place at the table. "But I need to start taking care of myself."

Pablo cuts a hunk of his lukewarm pancakes. "It's frightening to think of some little tyke calling you two Mom and Dad."

Nina laughs. "Hey. What's that supposed to mean?"

In the kitchen, Dink's eyes are glistening with tears. I know I should be sad for her, but I'm not. She's going to be part of my family and I'm glad.

❖

It's night. Nina and Rick are sleeping and I'm worrying about Nina's use of the word "regular," how she wants Dink and Pablo to keep her and Rick from slipping into "regular." I mean, what *is* regular? And who gets to decide what's regular? One thing's for sure, if you're *not* regular you get made fun of at school and have things written about you on the locker room walls…

The phone rings. Nina picks up on the third ring. "Hello?" All she can hear is tinny music on the other end of the line. "Hello?" she says again. She's answered by a dial tone.

"Who was it?" Rick asks groggily.

"Wrong number, I guess." She slides back into the warm bed, curling up next to him, and is asleep in seconds.

I'm not that easily appeased and trace the call to a seedy bar in the industrial district. The windows are covered in plywood and there's a broken neon martini glass hanging precariously above the door. Underneath is a newer, blinking sign that reads: THE OFFICE. I slip inside and find Dink, super drunk, making another call. This time she dials home.

❖

It takes a while for Pablo to pick up and a little longer for him to figure out it's her. He was right in the middle of an erotic dream about a dressage competition—beautiful young men in tight riding pants snapping leather crops across the buttocks of muscular horses…

He flops back onto his pillow. "Fuck, Dink. What time is it?" He flicks on his bedside light to see the clock: 2:00 a.m. "Where *are* you?"

"At The Office," she slurs.

"Isn't it a little late to be pushing words around?"

"Not that office. The other one. But he's trying to kick me out."

At first, Pablo doesn't understand what she means. Then he does. No one he knows would venture into that part of town at night, let alone into the sleazy bar. "Sweet Jesus."

"Who?"

"Just stay where you are."

"He wants to kick me—"

"I'm sure he's trying to close. Just stay where you are. I'm coming to get you." After some persuasion, he gets her to hand the bartender her phone. The bartender says he'll be there another hour cleaning up. Pablo promises to make it worth his while if he lets Dink stay inside. The bartender agrees, reluctantly, warning Pablo that as soon as he's done, he's leaving.

Pablo starts sliding into his clothes while simultaneously calling for a taxi.

Meanwhile, the bartender hands Dink's phone back to her.

"Thanks, mister. Think I could have a drink while I wait?"

The bartender, a rawboned man with scary bloodshot eyes and a nasty scar cutting through one of his eyebrows, shakes his head. "No more for you, missy."

❖

Twenty minutes later, Pablo asks the taxi to wait outside, then knocks on the doors at The Office. Dink is out cold, her face pressed flat against a grimy tabletop. Pablo hands the bartender a ten-dollar bill. "Thank you…sir."

"Just get her out of here," the bartender grumbles, pocketing the bill.

Pablo shakes Dink awake. "Come on, Dink."

"Pablo…"

He heaves her up from the table. "Time to go."

They push through the doors out into the quiet night. A couple of sleazy-looking men on the street corner give them a sideways glance.

"Where are we?" Dink asks, stumbling into Pablo.

"I was sleeping, and you're shitfaced."

Dink pukes on the side of the taxi.

"Shit!" the taxi driver says.

"I'm sorry," Pablo says.

"Your sorry dudn't do shit for me, buster, and it *sure* ain't gonna clean that shit up. Now pay up. I'm not letting her puke on my seats."

"You can't leave us here…"

"Like hell I can't. Now pay up!"

Pablo digs into his pocket for the cash and tosses it on the seat, then watches mournfully as the taxi pulls away from the curb. He turns and glares at Dink. "Jesus, Dink!"

She wipes her mouth with the back of her hand. "Sorry, Pablo. I didn't mean to…"

He stops her words with a lifted hand. "Let's go find you a cup of coffee."

They make their way to Ruby's, a red vinyl and chrome all-night diner, and choose a booth by the window. The place is empty. Pablo tries not to think about the workday ahead and focuses on Dink trying to light her smoke. The match circles her cigarette like an airplane awaiting the go-ahead to land. It burns down to her fingertips. "Fuck!" she says, shaking out the flame. She drops the match onto the scalloped-edged paper placemat and sucks her singed fingertip.

"You know you can't smoke in here," he says.

"Says who?"

Pablo picks up the pack of matches before she can try again. "Says the state."

"I just can't do it," she says.

"Right. It's against the law."

"That's not what I mean."

Pablo places his elbows on the table. "Dink, you're going to have to catch me up. I'm just now arriving into your little nightmare."

The big-haired waitress with saggy skin brings two coffees without even being asked. "You wanna look at a menu?"

Pablo wills the waitress not to blink. He's afraid her left Diana Ross–eyelash, peeling up at the corner, will drop into his coffee. "This will do, thanks," he says.

She shrugs and sashays her droopy butt back behind the counter.

"Talk to me, Dink."

Dink gazes into her coffee cup. "It's bad, Pablo."

"Try."

"I can't do…whatever the hell it was we promised Nina and Rick we'd do today." She forces herself to look into his dark eyes and takes a long deep breath. "I'm in love with Nina."

The right side of Pablo's mouth tips up in a grin. "You're just now figuring that out?"

Dink looks into her mug and swirls the coffee inside it. "What's that supposed to mean?"

"It's just…"

"I don't *want* to be a lesbian, all right? My *mom* is a lesbian."

"I know. You've told everyone who will listen about your mom and Ms. Bobbi the gym teacher."

Dink rubs her temples with her thumbs. "Because it's fucking traumatic."

"Your mom being a lesbian?"

"Her taking it from me."

"Dink, that's impossible."

"You don't know my mom. Or Ms. Bobbi, dyke counselor from hell."

"Di-*ink*."

"Pa-*blo*."

"People can't take your sexuality away from you."

Dink glares at him. "You think I don't know that?"

"Then what…"

"I'm a basket case, all right? A total fucking nutbag."

Pablo smiles. "That, I knew."

"And I *like* eating meat. In fact, I'm going to order a burger right now." Dink stands, looking around for the waitress. "A *double* burger. Rare! No. Make that two! Three!" She topples back into her seat and says these next words as if she were making a campaign speech, raising her voice and pointing her finger in the air. "And I see *nothing* wrong with using products that have been tested on animals. That's what they're there for. And I have *no* intention of driving a Subaru wagon, or…"

Pablo takes a hold of Dink's pointing finger.

She stops talking.

"You've made your point," he says gently.

Dink drops her face into her hands. "I'm a total fuckup, aren't I?"

He waves off the waitress, then says, "No more than the rest of us."

She peeks up at him through her fingers.

He pushes her coffee cup toward her. "Drink up. We have a long walk."

She takes a swig. "It tastes like embalming fluid."

Pablo does his Jewish mother imitation: "You want I should have brought you to a fancier place?"

Dink tries to smile but all emotion drains from her face. "I don't know if I can do whatever the hell it was we promised to do today."

"People do all kinds of things they think they can't."

"Fuck you."

"Just trying to be helpful. Anyway, I'm glad to know that you're ready to experience the more carnal of the spirit's appetites. You've been so…asexual since we met."

"Fuck you twice."

"Shall we go for a third?"

"Pablo, this hurts like hell."

"I know, sweetie."

The two gaze into each other's eyes. "Welcome to the other team," Pablo says, holding up his coffee to toast.

Dink looks at her empty mug. "Mine's shot."

"Fake it," he says.

Dink laughs bitterly, then lifts her empty mug. "To faking it."

As they make their way out into the night, Pablo asks, "How long have you known?"

Dink pauses to tap a smoke out of the pack. "My whole life. Fuck. As a kid I wanted to be a boy."

"That's not unusual," he says.

It's not? I scan Dink's brain to find out if she knows what he's talking about. She does. He's talking about girls who are known as tomboys. I'm going to have to look into this.

Dink lights her smoke. She's moved on from tomboys to thinking about what Nina said about her and Pablo keeping them from becoming regular. It grates at her. "Can we just quit with all the analyzing and walk?"

Walk? I feel like zipping through the universe at top speed! Auntie Dink and I are going to have so much in common!

I wonder if she still wishes she were a boy?

I check, but it's difficult to get an accurate read. Her feelings about identity and gender are too knotted up with feelings about not wanting to be like her mom. But who cares? Having Dink in my family is going to be great. She'll understand me. Be able to clue my parents into my issues…

…if they're still talking to her.

If Rick doesn't decide to hate her when he figures out she's in love with Nina. What if he says they're not allowed to be friends anymore? Or that she's kicked out of the family? That would make Dink hate him, wouldn't it? It might even make Dink hate Nina. And then Nina would hate Dink back. And Rick would already hate Dink. That would be catastrophic. I need Dink in my family. What if I'm a tomboy? Who will be my role model?

CHAPTER SEVENTEEN

Yesterday, I was confirmed by the clinic so today Nina's going to tell her family about me. I'm a nervous wreck. Mostly because Nina is. She's been sitting by the phone for fifteen minutes trying to muster the courage to call her folks. Rick is preoccupying himself in the bathroom playing his sax. He has the door shut and has told Nina to knock when she's ready to make the call.

Why is Nina so nervous? I'm just a baby.

Or will be soon.

Now I'm not much more than a blob of cells. In truth, I look a little like a piece of chewed gum. But hey, looks aren't everything.

She stares at the phone, afraid Iris and Harvey are going to tell her she's not *allowed* to have me, or that she's stupid to have me. Which in the first case, they can't do. I checked. And in the second case, who cares? They're not the ones who'll be bringing me up. She knows all this too, but still she worries. And this makes me worry. If she were sure about me, would she be having these thoughts? What if she changes her mind? What if they *make* her change her mind?

Nina picks up the receiver. "Honey? I'm going to do it now!"

"Did you say something?"

"I'm calling! Could you quit for a minute?"

Rick comes into the room with his sax around his neck. "You sure you're ready?"

"Ready as I'll ever be." She dials her parents' number, praying her dad will be the one to pick up. Rick hovers behind her. Nina's plan is to catch them right after dinner when everyone will be relaxed.

Iris answers. "Yes?" She sounds annoyed.

"Mom?"

"If it isn't our long-lost daughter," Iris says coolly.

"What's up?" Nina chirps. She mouths the word "Mom" to Rick. He rolls his eyes.

I zip over to the Kalinas' for a quick peek.

"Well, we saw Hester's school musical this afternoon, *South Pacific*. They did a great job." Iris brings the phone to the table so she can continue to eat while she talks. "Hester played an islander."

"Hi, Nina!" Hester yells, and, with her mouth full, begins singing a song about happy talking.

Charlotte reprimands, "Don't talk with your mouth full, Hester!"

"I'm not talking, I'm *singing*!" Hester says, then continues warbling.

"I have some news," Nina blurts.

Hester punches the lyrics about having a dream.

"Hush, Hessie!" Iris says, cupping her free ear with her hand. "We're in the middle of dinner."

But Hester won't pipe down. She wants to get to the line about dreams coming true.

Iris glares at Harvey, who signals Hester to be quiet by putting his finger to his lips.

Hester turns her singing into humming.

Iris continues, "Is this important?"

I zip back to Nina. She glances at Rick for encouragement. He's massaging his hand and doesn't notice. She takes a deep breath. "I'm getting married."

"What?"

Uh-oh. Better head back over to the Kalinas'.

Harvey's just looked up from his plate. Hester has stopped singing.

"Rick and I—"

"I can't believe what I'm hearing."

Charlotte drops her fork. "What did she do now?"

Iris raises her palm to silence Charlotte. "Honestly, Nina. You just graduated. You have your whole life ahead of you."

By now all the Kalinas are at full attention. Iris covers the phone with her hand and whispers, "She and Rick are getting married."

"I don't know what the big deal is," Nina says. "*You're* married. Besides, we're in love."

Iris centers herself by taking a breath. "You're not pregnant, are you?"

"Mom!"

"Well, are you?"

"You always—"

"You're not answering my question."

"Can't you just be happy for me?"

"This is not about *me* being happy or not. This is about *your* choices."

"That's just it, Mom! They're *my* choices. Not yours. This is *my* life."

Iris holds the phone out to Harvey. "Talk to your daughter. We're having one of our meltdowns."

Harvey takes the phone. "Nina?"

"Dad…"

"Is everything okay?"

"I hate her."

"She's just surprised, honey. We all are. This is happening pretty quickly."

Iris gets up from the table and grabs her Salem Lights from the kitchen counter. Her lighter, almost out of fluid, goes *Chik! Chik! Chik!* before igniting. She stands in the doorway, her arms crossed. "Ask her if she's pregnant."

Charlotte wants Iris to look in her direction so they can connect in mutual disgust, but Iris doesn't.

Harvey pushes his plate of lasagna forward and puts his elbows on the table. "Honey?" he says into the receiver. "This is pretty exciting. Rick's a great guy…"

I can feel Nina waiting for the "but."

"Any reason for the rush?" he asks, using his pediatrician voice, the one he uses to coax sensitive information from young mothers.

There's a pause on the line. "I'm pregnant."

Harvey sighs deeply and nods, affirming his wife's suspicions.

Iris turns her back and exhales smoke into the kitchen.

"She's pregnant!" Charlotte whispers to Hester as if Hester hadn't been right there witnessing the whole exchange.

"You know you have choices," Harvey says.

"I know, Dad. Mom works at Planned Parenthood, remember?"

Harvey brings his fingers to his forehead, wishing he could massage his brain. "Nina…"

"Dad, I know what I'm doing," she says, her resolve to have me actually being strengthened by her family's reaction. "I've thought about it a lot," she adds. "And I really want this baby. We both do." There's a pause on the line while she waits for her dad to say something. "Are you still there?" she asks.

"Of course I am."

"I've already been to a doctor."

"You have?"

"Yes."

"What does he say?"

"She."

"She, then. What does she say?"

"That I'm pregnant."

Harvey looks at a complicated Kandinsky print hanging on the wall, all chaotic lines and color, and remembers the day Iris brought it home saying it reminded her of their life since the kids. He takes a sip of wine and focuses on a squiggle in the left-hand corner. "Well then, I guess I'm going to be a grandfather."

I can hear Nina exhale.

"Is Rick there?" he asks.

"Yes."

"Could I have a word with him?"

As the phone switches hands, I worry that Harvey is going to try to talk Rick out of having me.

"Sir?" Rick says.

"Son," Harvey says. "This is a big responsibility."

"Yes, sir."

"Are you on board with this? No one will think less of you if you—"

"I love your daughter very much and we've thought about this a lot. It's something we really want to do…together. I think we're mature enough—"

Rick, all the man needs is a yes or a no.

Thankfully, Harvey interrupts. "I'm going to trust you, Rick."

"Thank you, sir."

"Have you told your folks?"

"Not yet. We thought we should tell you first. But I plan to."

"Let me know if I can help in any way. I mean that."

"Thank you, sir…Thank you…I'll make you proud…I will… Here's Nina."

The sound of the phone transferring hands.

"Dad?"

"Yes, pumpkin."

"I love you."

"I love you too."

"I think this is good."

Harvey wants to agree, but can't quite get himself to. "I think your mother would like to say a few more words to you."

Iris stubs out her smoke and shakes her head *no!* but he holds the phone firmly in her direction. She takes it. "Nina?"

"Mom."

"You can still have a career if you put your mind to it."

"Is that all you have to say to me?"

"I just don't want you to lose sight of your options."

"Aren't you happy for me?"

Iris is wondering how she can communicate so clearly with her clients at Planned Parenthood when she can't even make it through two sentences with her own daughter. She glances at Harvey for help. He lifts his wineglass and silently toasts her. She turns her attention back to the phone. "Do you have a date for the wedding?"

"August twenty-sixth. It's a Saturday."

"How can I help?"

Nina's voice comes out sounding flat. "We want to do it ourselves. Since it's about *us*. *Our* love."

Iris's conscience tells her she should put up a fight and say she *wants* to help like most mothers would. Instead, she makes a mental note to send money.

After hanging up the phone, Hester, who's been tuned into the conversation like a satellite dish, says, "Nina's pregnant?" A huge grin lights up her freckled face. "Cool! I can't wait to tell the kids at school I'm going to be an aunt."

At least *somebody's* happy.

Hopefully, it will go better with the Hales.

❖

Since Rick still isn't speaking to his dad, and has "no intention of starting now" he can't very well tell Richard about me, or the wedding. "I'll tell Mom and she'll tell him," he says to Nina that night, his mouth full of toast and hummus. Rick's sure this is the best way to go, because it's been so successful in the past—like when he quit the football team so he'd have more time with his music and when he put a dent in the family car.

"So invite her over for lunch or something," Nina says.

"Here?" he says.

"Why not?" she says. "We can tell her together."

Rick has lots of reasons why not, but is unable to form any of them into clear thoughts much less words, so he says, "Okay."

Two days later, faced with his mother standing at his door, her arms wrapped around two huge Bed Bath & Beyond sacks, he wonders how he got talked into this.

"Mom, this is Nina. Nina, my mom."

He doesn't kiss his mom or ask to take her bags. He's way too nervous.

"Please, call me Dorothy," Dorothy says, entering the apartment.

The phone rings. "I should get that. It's probably Jack," Rick says and races to the bedroom.

Nina glares at Rick's retreating figure, then turns toward Dorothy.

The two smile at each other. It's awkward that Rick has left them alone together, so this is what they do: tacitly agree to pretend that *this* is their first meeting and that the night of the flag-ripping fight never happened.

"Welcome," Nina says and leads Dorothy into the living room. All she can think about is me. *Can Dorothy tell?* she wonders, which of course she knows she can't. She tugs at her T-shirt anyway.

"I've brought you a few things, since you're starting up a new home." Dorothy thrusts the bags toward Nina. "I wasn't quite sure what you needed. Feel free to exchange what doesn't work. You won't hurt my feelings."

"Thank you! Um…But why don't we wait for Rick?" Nina places the bags on the couch. "Have a seat."

Dorothy chooses the armchair, noting as she sits that stuffing is peeking out on one side.

Nina sits cross-legged on the couch. She too, notices the stuffing peeking out of Dorothy's chair and wishes she'd thought to throw a blanket over it. "Rick's cooking. He really wants to impress you."

Dorothy cranes her neck around. "What a sweet apartment."

"Well, we're still fixing it up."

The two of them listen to Rick's phone conversation for a moment. He's talking about the schedule at work.

Nina smiles. "Sorry. He's been expecting this call all morning."

Dorothy smiles back. "Speaking of fixing up your apartment…" She gestures toward the bag.

Nina glances toward the bedroom, praying Rick is almost done.

He shrugs apologetically.

She turns back to Dorothy and tentatively reaches into one of the bags, pulling out a set of flatware. "What a perfect gift! We've only got two spoons."

Dorothy removes the fringed throw pillow from behind her back and folds her hands on top of it. "I thought it might be useful." She notices an empty ashtray on the table and wonders if Nina smokes.

Nina reaches in again and this time comes up with a set of gold towels. A third reach produces another. "Dorothy, this is too much," she says. She's worried Dorothy's going to regret the gifts once she's heard the news. "But, I mean, we do need them. And the color is perfect. Wait till you see the bathroom."

Nina glances through the doorway at Rick again.

He gestures two more minutes.

"And this last thing," Dorothy says, "well, *any* of the things really, please feel free to exchange."

Nina reaches into the other, larger, sack and pulls out a Bed in a Bag. "Oh, Dorothy. This really is too much. But it's beautiful! The sheets are such a pretty color green. And this quilt…I love it! Rick will too, I'm sure."

Finally, Rick gets off the phone. He kisses Dorothy on the cheek. "Sorry, Mom. I had to take that."

"Rick, you need to see what your mom gave us." Nina pulls a pillow sham from the bag. "And it's the right size. How did you know?"

Dorothy squeezes Rick's hand. "A little bird told me."

Rick smiles. "Thanks, Mom. It's all great." He picks up the

flatware. "Especially this. I was going to have to use the wooden spoon to eat my soup."

Nina and Dorothy laugh.

"So," Rick says. "I should check on lunch."

Nina stands. "I'll do it."

"I *got* it," he says.

Nina looks apologetically at Dorothy. "I guess we're both a little nervous."

I'll say. The two of them are acting like total dorks. Here she brought them all these presents and is trying to be so nice and all they can do is run for the kitchen. Fortunately, the lunch is ready. Actually, the soup has boiled down a bit, but Rick adds a glass of hot water. He pulls bowls from the cabinet. "It's ready when you are," Rick says.

Nina and Dorothy move to the table and sit.

Rick brings out a cookie sheet with three bowls of soup balanced on top. Dorothy is amazed to see this new side of her son. "Did you make this?"

"Yup," he says, even though all he did was heat up what was in a can. "And there's sandwiches too."

Dorothy's even more impressed that he managed to slather mayonnaise on bread and stuff it with deli roast beef and Swiss cheese. Personally, I think he should have at least added lettuce or tomato. It is a special occasion.

The conversation that follows is downright boring. They cover the weather, a few basics about Nina and her family, and *TV shows*. I mean, there are important things at stake here, gang. *Life*-changing things. But they blah blah all the way through the limp sandwiches and lukewarm chicken noodle soup as if it's another humdrum day.

Just when I think we're going to spend the whole visit hobbling along on trivia, Rick goes back to the kitchen for the store-bought shortbread. Nina excuses herself to Dorothy by saying she's going to put on some water for tea and follows him.

The kitchen, separated from the dining area by a tall counter, gives them little privacy, but since Dorothy's back is to the kitchen, Nina is able to mouth the words "Tell her" without Dorothy knowing.

Rick, who's brushing off his plate so he can use it to put the cookies on, mouths back, "I'm going to."

They return to the dining area all smiles. Rick places the cookies on the table.

"Tea will be ready in a minute," Nina says.

"We're getting married," Rick says.

Dorothy's face freezes. "Oh?" she says. And it comes out sounding as if they've just told her that they're purchasing a new chair, which is not her intention. The news just caught her off guard.

"And, uh," Rick stammers, "we're pregnant."

For two whole seconds nothing happens, then Dorothy's eyes fill with tears, and, to her horror, a lone sob lurches out. She slaps her hand over her mouth to keep any others back, but all this does is trap the rest of the sobs in the palm of her hand, making them sound like muffled squeaks.

Nina and Rick don't know what to say, or do. Nina nibbles a hangnail. Rick tries to assess if his mother is in need of some kind of medical assistance. "It's okay, Mom. Everything's fine," he finally says.

Nina gives him a little shove.

He gets up and walks over to Dorothy, handing her a napkin to blow her nose.

She does. "I'm so sorry…I just…I…well…How can I help with the wedding?"

That's it? I think. How can she help with the *wedding*? What about the baby? What about me?

Nina rolls dramatically off her chair and sprawls out flat on the floor. "I'm sooooo relieved!"

Dorothy laughs and wipes her eyes. "You've just told me I'm going to be a grandmother! How could I *not* be happy?"

Okay, so she's acknowledging me, but she's not telling the complete truth. She's worried that I'm making them "rush into things."

Nina scrambles up from the floor. "Wait till you meet *my* mom. Then you'll know why I was worried."

Dorothy likes being the preferred mother and chooses to keep her reservations to herself. And so they go on this way all lighthearted and carefree, passing around hugs like hors d'oeuvres until, over tea, Rick says the inevitable. "What do we do about Dad?"

Dorothy stiffens.

Nina places her teacup down, clipping the saucer.

Dorothy feels a twinge of guilt, as if *she* is somehow responsible for their fight. "Do you want me to tell him?" Of course Rick says yes, and with that the three of them form an alliance of sorts, which, again, makes Dorothy feel closer to her son, and now Nina too. When it comes time for her to leave, she asks Rick if Mrs. Hartman has gotten hold of him about Howie's funeral. "It's a shame they've had to put it off for so long. They've been waiting for his older brother, Tom. He's in some remote outpost and they had trouble bringing him home."

"I'll be there," Rick says, hugging her. Then he puts his arm around Nina, the first bit of affection he's shown her since his mom arrived.

Dorothy smiles before making her way down the hallway to the stairwell.

Nina whispers, "I adore her!"

Rick kisses Nina's head. "She's a sweetie, all right."

I couldn't agree more. I can already tell she's going to be my favorite grandmother.

❖

The next day I decide to celebrate the beginnings of my brand-new eyes by accompanying Rick to work. Jack's Tires is full of all kinds of terrific things to look at. Cars, for one thing. I like cars—a lot. And tools are cool too—especially the air compressor. Bang! Bang! Bang! When I grow up I want to be good at fixing things like my dad. Maybe I'll even get to wear coveralls. A green pair of coveralls will look really good with my hazel eyes.

My eyes are going to be one of my best features.

Right after Rick's and my morning break, Richard Hale shows up. Rick is surprised when he sees his dad walk through the open garage door. I am too, so I do a quick scan, which reveals that this morning, after eating his two-minute egg and slice of twice-toasted bread—which Dorothy's boycott of the kitchen has forced him to learn to make for himself—he decided to forgive his son for ripping up the flag.

"What are you doing here?" Rick asks casually, although he thinks he knows the answer: Dorothy told him about me.

"We need to talk," Richard says.

Rick picks up a tire and brings it over to the tank of water to check it for leaks. "So, you're not mad, then?"

"Well, I was, but I've had some time to think about it."

"I know what I'm doing."

"I want to believe that."

"And she's a wonderful woman, Dad. You're going to like her."

"Who's that, son?"

The tire slips from Rick's hands into the tank, splashing both of them.

"Whoa Nelly!" Richard jokes. "I didn't come here for a bath!"

Rick bends down, hoping to appear intent on finding a leak. This also gives him time to think.

"There it is, son."

"What?" Rick curses himself for being so jumpy.

"The leak. There it is!" Richard points to a little line of bubbles shooting to the surface of the water.

Rick pulls the tire out, digs in his pocket for a piece of wax stick, and marks the spot. "Mom didn't tell you."

"Tell me what, son?" Richard reaches toward the tire. "Here, let me give you a hand."

Rick jerks the tire away. "I can do it! It's my job." He looks around to see if Chad, his coworker, is watching, but Chad is in the office writing up an invoice. Richard follows Rick over to the repair area where Rick pries the tire off the rim and prepares to grind the weakened spot for a patch. "I'm getting married," he says, then, flips on the grinder.

"What?" Richard yells over the gnashing sound.

Rick turns off the grinder, leaving nothing but the sound of static from the garage radio. "I'm getting married."

Richard braces himself against the workbench. He's always assumed he'd know the girl, that her family and his would be playing croquet or something out in the backyard, that he and the girl's father would give each other covert nods of approval while the two lovebirds whacked balls around on his green lawn.

"Her name is Nina," Rick says.

"Well! This is sudden." Richard watches him apply rubber adhesive to the inside of the puncture, the whole time coaching himself to stay light, cheerful. "What's it going to cost me?"

"Don't worry, Dad. We have it under control."

"Just kidding! I mean, that's her family's responsibility, right? They've got to *pay* to take my son from me!"

Rick attempts a smile as he applies a patch onto the worn tire. "It's the end of August. On a Saturday."

I wait for him to mention me, which he's considering, but thinks,

Why should I? He'll just throw a fit. Then something clicks inside him. Why *shouldn't* I? It's *my* life. *My* baby. He resolves that from this point forward, no matter the circumstance, he will not apologize for me—ever. "And we're going to have a baby."

Richard pushes away from the workbench. *"What?"*

"Nina's pregnant."

"Oh, no. Not that!" Richard moans. "Weren't you careful?"

"Dad…"

"You sure it's even yours? There are a lot of women who will use you—"

"Stop, Dad. Just stop."

"I'm just saying—"

"It's not true."

"How do you know? Girls these days are—"

"Look! You're invited to the wedding. Come or don't come. I don't care!"

An ache flashes across Richard's face. "You don't *care*?"

"Dad, I didn't mean—"

"You don't *care*?"

"Dad!"

"Say no more, son, I understand. You don't want your old man at your wedding."

"I didn't say that."

"Yes, you did, son. Yes, you did. In so many words that is *exactly* what you said. And believe me, I will remember it for the rest of my life."

Rick lets the tire drop to the floor. It spins around on its rim a few times before settling.

"Don't forget to put air in that tire," Richard says before walking out the door.

Rick shoves the tire with his foot, sending it skidding across the cement floor.

Chad enters the garage. "What's going on, Rick?"

"Nothing," Rick replies, as empty as one of his musical staffs with no notes. "Absolutely nothing."

Chapter Eighteen

We're outside at a funeral, which has me thinking about how brief a life is. Howie, whose body was blown to smithereens by someone he didn't even know, has gotten all the touching he's ever going to get. This brings me to the obvious question: how much am I going to get? Nina's been on all these Internet maternity sites and they keep stressing how fragile a mother and child's relationship is in the first trimester. Lots of babies never make it.

Well, not lots, but quite a few.

More than makes *me* comfortable.

When did evaporation, or death as they call it, start spooking me out so much? I know I'll just get sucked back to The Known, and that's a good thing, right? Yet ever since I dripped out, I've developed this gnawing fear of evaporation—and it's only gotten worse since I started splitting cells.

Scanning the thoughts of people here at the funeral, I see that they're even more scared than me.

Nina and Rick are standing under a maple tree a little way off from the other people. Seven reservists, pinched into uniforms, are standing in formation. They feel lucky not to be the one in the coffin. Most have come close.

Nina takes Rick's arm and whispers, "You should say hello to your parents."

"I'm here for Howie," he grumbles. "Not them." He looks around at people he's known for years: old high school friends, shopping clerks, as well as some of Howie's teenage guitar students. Rick is thinking:

None of them knew Howie the way I did. None of them were Howie's best friend. And that asshole reverend, who never even met Howie, is going on and on about Howie's bravery, his love for his country... Rick whispers to Nina, "This is so full of shit."

Nina squeezes his hand, but she can't take her eyes off Howie's mom, Mrs. Hartman. She looks to Nina like the walking dead, her eyes lifeless as marbles, her hands gripping her collar as if protecting herself from a chill on this hot day. A fly lands on Mrs. Hartman's cheek. She doesn't seem to feel it.

Nina places her free hand on her belly and thinks about her responsibility to keep me safe.

Thanks, I want to say. *Now would you quit worrying? It's making your heart race.*

The seven reservists step into formation and point their guns in the air. The first shot crashes into the silent afternoon, flushing a flock of blackbirds from a nearby tree. A baby begins to cry. His mother jiggles him up and down and whispers, "It's okay, sweetie. No one's gonna hurt you. Mama's right here." Then two reservists take the flag from the coffin, fold it, and hand it to Howie's older brother, Thomas. Wearing full military dress, he takes a few steps toward Mrs. Hartman to present the flag to her.

"This flag is presented on behalf of a grateful nation..." he says, his voice cracking. As he stumbles through the speech, tears streaking his face, he stands tall. He thinks this will make his mother proud, but pride isn't what she's feeling. She's wondering how she will survive the next few minutes, the next few hours. And then the years.

Thomas hands her the flag. She passes it to a woman next to her so her arms are free to do what they want to do, embrace her only living son. She pulls him to her, hugging him tightly, one hand on the back of his neck where the hair is shorn so short, like when he was a little boy. His muscles loosen, and he begins to cry. They hold one another like this for several minutes, mother and son. They don't care that the reservists are ready to go home and get out of their uniforms. They just want to feel one another's breathing.

I can't wait until Nina and I get to hug like this.

❖

Tonight, Rick, Nina, Dink, and Pablo are in the lobby of a small local theater. They've just seen a play called *Our Town*. Lottie Yang, who worked on the show as a dresser, scored them four comp seats. Nina wants to wait around and congratulate her, maybe get a chance to meet a few of the actors. Rick wants to leave. The third act, the playwright's morose interpretation of evaporation, was difficult for him to sit through.

Lottie enters the lobby dressed in a gold lamé miniskirt, black halter top, and four-inch heels. "Hey, you guys! Want to come to the cast party?"

Of course Nina does. She thinks she can make some connections. Pablo wants to go too.

"Think I'll pass," Dink says.

Nina walks over to the doorway where Rick is waiting. "Hey, sweetie, we just got invited to the cast party."

He shoves his hands in his pockets. "I'm not really in the mood."

She fiddles with his collar. "Please?"

"Why do you need me there?"

"It will be fun."

"For you."

"It might make you feel better to—"

Rick raises his palm. "Nina, stop." He instantly regrets sounding so harsh and takes her hands in his. "You go. And take the car. I'll walk."

"You sure?"

"Positive."

This means Rick and Dink are going to have to walk home together. Wonder how that's going to work out?

They walk side by side, not saying much, Dink, because she's unsure how to act around Rick now that she's admitted to being in love with his fiancée; and Rick, because he's starting to question what he's doing with his life.

Dink lights up a smoke and starts talking, and once she starts she can't seem to stop. "Two intermissions is a travesty. Who wants to have to be all sociable twice? And they didn't have enough stalls in the women's restroom; the lines were a joke. You don't know how lucky you guys are…"

Dink's prattle reminds Rick of a night when he was hanging out with Howie at Chuck's Pizza Joint after Rick had had a huge fight with his dad. Howie was going on about how the restaurant got the Parmesan cheese into the shakers when the holes weren't big enough. Rick knew that Howie was talking just to keep things light and wonders if this is what Dink is up to now, if his mood is that obvious. But really all Dink is trying to do is pretend she's not feeling her feelings.

"I've got a joint," she says. "Want to veer through the park?" Smoking pot always helps her when she doesn't like what she's feeling.

"Why not?" Rick says, seeing as he's not too happy with what he's feeling either.

The park is empty, except for a few homeless people sleeping on benches. They stop at a secluded spot on a small bridge that runs over a dry gulch. Dink fires up the joint, and they smoke in silence—a loud silence. Both of their minds are churning with things they want to say. Dink's is spitting out things like: *Don't worry! I'm not going to take your precious Nina away from you. I don't even want to be in love with her. Okay?* While Rick's is coughing up: *I don't know if Nina and I are right for each other. She can be so self-centered. Maybe what we're doing isn't such a good idea after all.*

As for me, I want them to work this out. I need Dink in my life. And I need Rick too. I hope they're careful with their words.

"How long have you and Nina known each other?" Rick finally asks.

"Since freshman year," Dink says, remembering the first time she laid eyes on her. Nina was stepping into a pool of light on the stage, which she herself was providing with the follow spot. "So, you guys are getting married," she says.

"Yup."

Dink takes a final hit, then pockets the roach without asking Rick if he wants more. "You realize dealing with Nina can be tricky."

Rick laughs. "Tell me something I don't already know."

Dink chuckles appreciatively.

The pot seems to be working. She's not feeling quite as wary.

"Do you know anything about becoming a firefighter?" Rick asks as they begin walking.

"Nope. But you'd look good in one of those trucks."

"You think?"

"Definitely."

Dink is wishing she didn't like Rick. It would make things so much easier. "So, who's your best man going to be?"

Rick groans. "I've no idea. Nina keeps telling me I have to pick someone, but whoever I pick will just be a stand-in for Howie."

Dink considers this for a moment, then says, "So get a stand-in. That guy you work with…"

"Chad?"

"Is he the blond dude?"

"Yeah. But no way. Chad is a moron."

"Somebody else, then."

"There *is* nobody else."

"What you're saying is there's no other Howie. But you don't need a Howie. You just need someone to play the *part* of Howie. You know, wear his jacket or something, so everyone will know. You can even put it in the program. Like a tribute."

"Like acting."

"More like a proxy."

Rick is silent for a few seconds. "You want to do it?"

Dink's stomach lurches. "Me?"

"You said it could be anybody. Why not you?"

I want to scream: *Because she's in love with Nina, that's why!* This will screw things up for sure. But the thought of being his best man is just appalling enough to intrigue Dink. Especially since she's higher than a kite. "You serious?" she asks.

"Why the hell not?"

"Because it'll trip Nina out, that's why."

"So?" Rick says. "You'll be *my* best man."

It isn't until Dink is alone in her flat that she realizes how stupid the idea is. She takes a swig from a bottle of cheap whiskey, then whacks her head with the heel of her hand. *What was I thinking?*

My question exactly. Although I am intrigued by a girl getting to be something called best man, and think it's cool my dad would ask a girl to perform this function—Maybe he's more open-minded than I thought?—the whole thing could backfire horribly.

Chapter Nineteen

Nina is sleeping. Rick is getting ready to go to work. Coffee's brewing and the new TV is on without the sound. He leans against the sink so he can see into the living room where the TV is. He picked it up at a yard sale this past weekend and loves it. Having his own TV in his own house makes him feel like the master of his world.

He pours a bowl of cereal.

Nina shuffles into the kitchen. She's not too big on the new TV. She thinks it will squelch his creativity.

She pours herself a cup of coffee.

"Morning," Rick says, annoyed that she's poured herself coffee before it's fully brewed because now his cup won't be as strong. "Should you be drinking that?"

"Just a few sips, so I won't get a headache."

The news anchors on the TV laugh silently.

Figuring there's no point in waiting now, he pours himself a cup of weak coffee.

Nina perches on the one kitchen stool. She's a tad queasy.

"How was the party last night?" he asks.

She nods. "Typical. Actors wanting to talk about their performances."

Rick pours milk into his cereal. "Well, you might be interested to know I now have a best man."

This surprises Nina. Who could he have found between last night and now? "Really? Who?"

"Howie."

Nina searches his face trying to figure out what he's talking about. "Howie?" she says finally.

"Yeah. Dink's going to stand in for him." When Nina doesn't say anything, he asks, "Does it bother you?"

Nina crosses her arms and legs at the same time. "Not really. It just seems kind of—"

"What?"

"I don't know. Like…well, why does it have to be Dink?"

"Why not?"

"Dink's my friend. The best man should be yours."

Rick shoves the cereal box into the cabinet without properly closing it. "My best friend is dead, Nina."

She has to keep herself from rolling her eyes. She's tired of hearing about his dead friend. "I know, but—"

He turns toward her, his face taut. "Can we talk about this later? I've got to get to work."

"You're the one who brought it up."

"I thought you'd be happy, okay?"

"I am happy. I just think—"

"I *said* let's talk about it later!" Rick stomps off to the bathroom, leaving his cereal to go soggy.

"I just think we need to communicate about these things," she yells after him. Then she gets up and snaps off the TV. On her way back to the kitchen she plumps a throw pillow that doesn't need plumping.

Nina feels that Rick isn't taking their wedding seriously. Another thing bothering her is that Iris guilt-tripped her into asking Charlotte to be maid of honor. Why should she be stuck with her sister while Rick gets her best friend?

I wish she'd go into the bathroom and put her arms around him. Maybe then he wouldn't feel like punching the mirror.

He leaves for work in a stony silence.

She dials Dink.

"Did you say you'd be Rick's best man?"

"Nina, this is a bad time. I'm late for work."

"Just tell me, did you?"

"I said I'd stand in for Howie."

"What if I want you as one of my bridesmaids?"

"Well, you missed the boat. Maybe you can talk Pablo into it."

"I'm being serious."

"So am I. Look, I gotta go. Bye."

"Dink!"

"What?"

"You're my best friend…"

There's a long pause on Dink's end. "Yeah, Nina, I know. Now I really do have to go. I can't be late one more time this week."

After hanging up, Nina dials Lottie Yang, who responds to the news by saying, "But that is so gender-bendingly cool."

"You think?"

"God, yes. Most weddings are so boring. I mean if you view them as a theatrical event, you're doomed from the get-go. I mean, everybody knows how it's going to end. So why not make the getting there interesting? Shake it up a little."

This gets Nina's mind whirling. Why *not* do something different?

After a whole day of thinking it over, she assaults Rick with enthusiasm when he gets home. "Having Dink as your best man was such a great idea! And it will be just the tip of the iceberg! I think we should make our wedding really different, more of a theatrical event. Maybe even a little pagan."

Rick, having thought about their fight all day and deciding it was more important to make Nina happy than have Dink as his best man, is now totally confused. "Whatever you want is fine with me," he says.

❖

Nina's St. Theresa's theater friends are all at the apartment drinking wine—except Nina, who's nibbling on the carrot sticks and hummus. It's four days after she decided it's okay for Dink to be Rick's best man and now she wants her friends to help her produce her super-creative wedding ritual. It's obvious she's forgotten all about her and Rick's promise to communicate their plans to one another; she's taken the event over, lock, stock, and barrel. The only one of the original *Endgame* group not here is Dink. Nina invited her, but Dink said, "Hey, I've flipped over to the other side. I'm the best man now." Which is fine by me. Now that she's admitted to herself that she's in love with Nina, she gets all weird whenever she's around her.

Missy is currently sitting next to Nina on the couch and has just taken a cube of Havarti off the plate of cheese and apple slices. "I'm so happy for you and Rick. I knew right away you'd be perfect for each other! In fact, that night when he fainted, I invited him to the dance because I had this feeling you two might like each other."

I wait to see if any of Nina's friends have the guts to tell Missy she's full of it.

Apparently not. History is rewriting itself before my very eyes.

But I can live with this. What I can't live with is that Nina still hasn't told her friends about me. She's been trying to get up her nerve since they got here and I *think* she's just about ready, but then I've thought this for the last half hour. She drums her fingers on her cup. "Um, you guys? There's something you don't know…"

"Ooo!" Missy says. "A secret."

Everyone turns to listen.

Come on, Nina. You can do it.

She wrinkles her nose, then spits it out. "I'm pregnant."

To my utter disappointment, they all just sit there looking dumbstruck.

Lottie places her plate of hummus and carrot sticks on the coffee table and pushes back her ragged jet-black bangs so she can get a good look at Nina. "Why didn't you tell us before?"

"I don't know." She draws in a short breath. "I guess because I thought you'd think the baby was the only reason I'm getting married."

So what if it is? I think. *What's wrong with that?*

Lottie rests her elbows on her knees and folds her delicate, ring-covered fingers. "Is it?"

"Is it what?" Nina asks defensively.

"The reason for this wedding?"

"No! I love Rick—adore him! And he's going to make a really great dad."

"And you *want* this baby."

"I do. I really do."

As Lottie searches Nina's eyes for any smidgen of doubt, I think how lucky I am that Nina's such a good actress. Even Lottie, a sharp judge of character, doesn't spot the gazillion uncertainties Nina's having. She just slaps her designer denim–covered thighs and says, "Well then, I guess we're going to have a baby!"

Everybody whoops, then they all hug Nina. "Congratulations!" "How exciting!" "How far along are you?" they say.

At least I'm not a secret anymore. What a relief. Even if they are all thinking, *Glad it's not me!* and *She should have been more careful.* For some reason they all believe it's okay to have *sex* before you're married, but getting *pregnant* before you're married is, well, not okay.

Nina confides how difficult her mom is being. "She's acting like I'm throwing my life away. Like having a baby is going to keep me from doing anything else."

"That's horrible," Rhonda says.

"I'll say," another chubby one chimes in, even though she thinks Iris is right.

Fortunately, their reservations don't stop them from planning the wedding. There's nothing theater people love more than putting on a show. And these girls haven't done a show together since St. Theresa's.

They decide that Juniper, who works for her mom's catering business, will oversee the food; Missy will check out what it takes to use the small amphitheater at Slater Park; and Lottie will supervise the look of the event.

"I'm sure Pablo will help with flowers," Nina says, popping a piece of organic chocolate in her mouth. She couldn't be happier.

I should be too. Instead I find myself feeling kind of sorry for Nina, a kind of sorry that hurts so much I can barely stand it. I want to scream at them all, *Don't blame her, blame me! I foisted myself on her. I put her in this position.*

But of course I can't.

And wouldn't.

I don't want people to not like me.

A couple of bottles of wine later, they're starting to get creative.

"If we really want to screw with people's expectations, we should call it something besides a wedding," Lottie says.

Missy snaps her fingers. "A commitment ceremony!"

"Too gay," Rhonda says.

"Ceremony of Love?" Juniper says.

"Too Hallmark," Nina says.

Lottie jumps out of her chair, sloshing wine on her jeans. "A Love Happening!"

Everyone takes a moment to try this on, their faces screwed into expressions of deep thought. "Like the happenings in the seventies?" Missy finally asks. "That we studied in theater history?"

Lottie blots her jeans with a napkin. "Exactly."

Nina nods her head cautiously. "I like…the sound of it. It has an organic ring…like how love just spontaneously, well, *happens*."

Well, duh. Like how babies spontaneously, well, happen? Like how life spontaneously, well, happens? But is this a good theme for a wedding? Aren't weddings supposed to be about commitment? Give the impression that the participants have given the whole contract a bit of thought?

Nobody thinks of this, though. They just grab their wineglasses and jump on the Happening bandwagon, changing the names of *everything*. The bridesmaids become Sisters in Solidarity. Charlotte's role changes from Maid of Honor to She Who Bears Witness. Lottie sketches costumes on the back of a napkin while Juniper works on the menu.

It's Rhonda who finally notices how late it's getting. "What time does Rick get home?"

"He's working late tonight."

"What time *is* it?" Lottie asks looking up from her drawing.

"Going on six."

Lottie shoots up from the couch. "Shit! I've got a production meeting." She begins clearing the plates.

Missy joins Lottie. "So Rick couldn't find a guy to be his best man?"

"If Dink were a *guy* it wouldn't be so cool," Rhonda says from the living room.

"She's going to look *hot* in men's clothing," Lottie says. "She has the build for it."

They make a date to meet again and then everyone gets their stuff to go.

"We are so damn creative!" Lottie says.

Missy throws her hands in the air and wags her pinkies. "The Sisssstahs in Solidarity!"

Everyone stares.

"What the hell was that?" Nina says, stifling a laugh.

"I don't know. I just thought we needed, like, a secret handshake or something."

"But, Sisssstahs?" Nina wags her pinkies condescendingly. "You've got to be kidding."

Lottie walks over to Rhonda. "Hey, Sissstah." She wags her pinkies. "How's it going?"

"Pretty good, Sissstah," Rhonda says, wagging hers back. "How about you?"

And even though they're all acting like it's stupid, they keep doing it. It's all Sisssstah this and Sisssstah that until pretty soon they're all saying good-bye by wagging their pinkies. "See you, Sisssstah!" "Bye, Sisssstah!" When Nina finally closes the door, she's sure the Love Happening is going to be the most inspired thing she's ever done. She imagines her family marveling at her imagination, her cool friends, her artistic wedding.

So why aren't I happier? I mean if she's happy, shouldn't I be? The thing is, I can't get her friends' thoughts out of my mind. How all of them, even if they are calling themselves the Sisters in Solidarity, are harboring judgment. I get that weird new feeling again. It's kind of like hurt and kind of like love. I guess it's what it means to feel compassion for someone.

Chapter Twenty

I'm trying not to take it personally, but my arrival onto the scene seems to be stirring up everybody's unresolved issues. Honestly, I've a mind to scream to them all: *You think you showed any more sense than I did when you were a Floating Soul? You think you were patient and chose the perfect family? Chose the perfect timing?* No way. You took whatever you could get. We all did. It's what we Floating Souls do. And if we happen to strike it lucky and get born into a family that is already planning to have us, has already decorated our room with little duckies and butterflies, well, lucky for us.

Once born, people get such a lofty sense of entitlement. Like they're some kind of gift to the world.

Take today, for instance.

I'm hanging with Nina and Pablo. He's been acting distant with her for the last few weeks, hasn't been returning her phone calls and things like that. Then today, when he did manage to actually pick up the phone and Nina suggested they get together, he said she could "tag along with him" while he goes shoe shopping. Turns out he's been promoted to assistant manager of the flower store and he wants to celebrate by buying shoes he can't afford. So now we're at this upscale shoe store, McNeely's, and they're waiting for the snobby salesman to return with a pair of what I think are a hideous pair of Italian loafers. But Pablo likes them. Meanwhile, Nina's trying to think of something to say to pull Pablo out of his brood. "I think the salesman is gay," she whispers.

"And what gave you your first clue?"

"Well, he just seems…"

"I was kidding, Nina. Of *course* he's gay."

"Sorry." She's not quite sure what she's apologizing for and scrutinizes the store to mask her confusion. *A pair of these shoes would eat up Rick's entire paycheck*, she thinks.

The salesman flounces back. "I hope I didn't keep you waiting too long," he says, opening the box with a flourish. He places the shoes in front of Pablo's socked feet, then, with a flick of a wrist pulls a shoehorn from his back pocket. "You will find them a bit stiff at first, but I can assure you this leather will learn your foot. Before long, they'll be as comfortable as slippers."

"They look nice," Nina says, but neither man acts as if he's heard her. She gets up and begins to wander the small store. The squishy wall-to-wall carpet is dotted with ankle-high mirrors; each shoe is displayed as though it's a piece of art. She picks up a ladies' red pump and lets her eyes rest on it while her mind tries to figure out why Pablo has been so cold to her.

She puts the shoe down and focuses on her own scuffed sandals in one of the low shoe mirrors, then, realizing the store has gotten quiet, looks up. Pablo is sitting by himself squeezing a shoe as if checking its ripeness. She walks over. "Are you mad at me?"

"Neen…"

The salesman swooshes back in. "A tragedy! The last pair in your size apparently went out yesterday. It was not on my shift, I might add, and my coworker was remiss in not letting me know. Still, I must offer my apologies. It is not my modus operandi to offer what I cannot provide."

Nina turns away while the salesman tries to interest Pablo in yet another ugly pair of shoes. As she listens to their tedious interactions, she wishes she hadn't come. Pablo, she's sure, no longer likes her.

When Pablo is finally ready to leave, he prepares to do so empty-handed.

"We do have a European shipment coming in next week. Can I give you a call?" the salesman says.

Pablo pulls a gold-embossed card from his blazer and the salesman produces a pen. Pablo writes his home phone number on the card and hands it back. "I look forward to hearing from you."

The salesman puts the card in his breast pocket. "I'll be in touch."

Pablo flashes the salesman a flirtatious smile and heads for the door. Nina has to scamper to keep up. "Did you just make a date? Was that a date?"

"He's calling me about shoes."

"I saw the way he looked at you. You guys made a date."

"He has to call before we make a date."

"Oh, he'll call. I think his modus operandi was getting a little aroused."

Pablo laughs. "That could be fun—for a night or two."

Nina is relieved that he seems to be lightening up.

They stand on the busy corner trying to hail a taxi. Nina fiddles with her bracelets. "So, why are you being all weird with me lately?"

Pablo stiffens. "I don't know what you're talking about."

"Ever since Rick and I decided to get married, you've been weird, like it's going to be some kind of burden to even attend."

"I said I'll do your flowers, what else do you want?"

"Are you jealous of Rick?"

"Nina, please."

"I'm just trying to figure out what's going on."

Pablo reaches out his hand to hail a passing taxi. It speeds by. "Shit!"

"We'd love it if you'd be in our weddi—Love Happening."

Pablo places his hands on her shoulders. "Shall I spell this out for you?"

Nina steps back, freeing her shoulders from his grip. "I guess you're going to have to."

"Nina, a gay person having to go to a wedding is kind of like…a Chassidic Jew being forced to sit on Santa's lap."

"You don't need to be so condescending."

"I don't even get to *kiss* a guy in public, let alone invite all our family and friends to come and watch us do it. Weddings are for straight people, Nina, not gay ones."

"What about commitment ceremonies?"

"Please."

"I'm serious."

"I know, sweetie, that's the problem." Pablo leans against the lamppost with his arms crossed and sighs. "Do you think my good Catholic mother would come to my commitment ceremony? Or any of my sisters?"

"But does that mean—"

"Look. I'm sorry. It's not your fault the world is the way it is. But, it is what it is."

Nina wants to point out that gays can get married in Massachusetts, but even she knows this is trivializing his point. A taxi drives by unnoticed. She focuses on a weed forcing its way through a crack in the cement. "So you're not mad at me per se, but heterosexuals in general?"

"Weddings just kind of bring it up, okay?"

"Would you quit calling it a wedding?'

"Love Happening. Whatever."

"Well, do you even want to come?"

"Of course I'll come. And I'll do the flowers like I said. I do flowers for weddings all the time."

Nina kicks the weed. "So you want to go look for more shoes?"

"I'm not in the mood anymore. Let's go find some chocolate."

She smiles as if she's not hurt, but I can tell she is. She wants Pablo to be happy for her. She's doing what you're supposed to do if you get pregnant. She's following the rules; she's getting married. *Is it my fault the rules are unfair?* she thinks.

Personally, I find her inability to understand Pablo's predicament worrisome. How's she going to deal with my needs if she can't understand something as simple as a person feeling left out?

❖

Okay, so I've decided it's not *me* that's causing everyone's issues to surface, but this *Love Happening*. Why do they have to get married anyway? I really don't see the point of this whole ritual.

I remind myself that Nina and Rick's marriage will make things like future Parent/Teacher Nights and filling out doctor forms much easier—but honestly, it's creating so much conflict, I'm starting to wonder if it's worth it.

At the moment, Rick and Nina are on the verge of yet another argument. She's just shown him Lottie's first costume sketches and he's looking aghast at the one he's supposed to wear: flowing pants and a tunic number. "You're joking, right?"

Fortunately, I can sit this one out—unlike when I become a baby, then I'll have to put up with *all* their fights—but for now I can vamoose. And vamoose I will. I decide to visit Richard Hale, see if he's finally warming up to the idea of me. Last I saw him, he was ranting to Dorothy about how I was making his son a "slave" to "some girl."

I discover him outside White's Insurance where he works, fumbling for his keys. He's sure he had them when he got off the commuter train and can't figure out where they've gone. In his mind it's all Dorothy's fault.

Lately, Dorothy has been driving him crazy. In the past she always had his coffee, two-minute egg, and twice-toasted toast ready the moment he descended the stairs. Now, though, she often sleeps in, or he'll find her in the dining room hunched over a tablet writing as if she's been up since sunrise, her hand moving across the page like a figure skater. But *never* is there any breakfast and only once in a while any coffee. On the mornings he finds her at the table, he says in a chipper voice, "Good morning!" in hopes that his pleasant demeanor will inspire her to hop to it.

"Morning," she'll reply, her head never rising from the page.

He's tried being understanding and has dropped, what he considers to be, delicate hints. "Would you look at that? No coffee," is one of his favorites.

"Oh, did I drink it all?" she'll say absentmindedly. "Guess you'll have to start a new pot." One day, she simply said, "I've decided to stop drinking coffee." Then two days later, he noticed, she'd started up again.

Which was why he's been coming in to work early. Josie, the receptionist, *always* has a fresh pot brewed. Now if he could just find his goddamned keys.

"Hey, Mr. Hale, you having a little problem?" Josie asks, opening the door from the inside. As usual, she's all smiles.

"Just can't seem to find my godd—" His keys slide from his folded newspaper to the ground. "Ha! Right where I left 'em!" With great effort, he returns Josie's smile, but it comes out more like a grimace. He hates having to deal with anyone before his first cup of coffee. Also nudging his ulcer is the thought that Josie might have guessed his marriage is struggling. He worries about gossip.

He picks up his keys, grunting as he bends, and heads for the conference room, planning to grab a cup of coffee and a pack of vending-machine peanut butter crackers before escaping to his cramped office. But today there's a stranger in the conference room. A clean-cut, young guy with his briefcase open and ready to go. "Howdy!" the stranger says, "And who might you be?"

Richard tries to focus through the fog in his brain. "I work here."

The stranger laughs, too loudly, revealing a mouth crowded with massive white teeth. "Well, I hope you work here. It's before hours."

"I'm Richard Hale." He wishes the stranger weren't between him and the coffee.

"Ah! Well, let me just give you your name tag, Richard Hale. My name is Stew Snodgrass. I'm from Main. I'm here for this morning's briefings."

Richard sticks himself in the chest as he tries to pin the plastic name tag onto his shirt. "Aren't you a little early?" he asks while simultaneously noticing the Snodgrass guy isn't wearing a name tag.

Snodgrass flashes his piano-key teeth again. "You are too! I like that in a guy! I'll put in a good word for you to Stan down at Main."

Richard observes the attention Stew gives to his boss's first name, and thinks, *So this little faggot thinks he has one up, does he?* He sidesteps Snodgrass to get to the coffeepot and pours a full cup. He's trying to look like he doesn't need it—like he doesn't need anything—especially from the likes of this kid, but, before he even has a chance to rip open the little bag of sugar, Snodgrass butts in, "So, you're a coffee drinker!"

Yes, I'm a goddamn coffee drinker! he thinks, and is just about to excuse himself when Tate Mueller saunters in.

"Hey, hey, hey! It's another beautiful day for making a buck!" Tate's picture is hanging on the wall with the caption INSURANCE DEALER OF THE YEAR underneath. Tate takes in the new guy. "Who the hell are you?"

Richard is glad that for once he's a step ahead of Tate. "This is—"

Snodgrass thrusts his hand forward. "Stew. Stew Snodgrass." Again, the teeth.

"He's from Main," Richard says. "And now if you'll excuse me…" He's given up on the idea of the peanut butter crackers. There's no way he's going to socialize with these bozos during his first cup of coffee. He picks up his briefcase and does a silent prayer that he'll still be able to take a decent dump. Sometimes, if he gets too wound up in the morning, he stays backed up all day.

"Hang on, mister! Not so fast!" Tate says, giving him a look he can't read. "You've been holding out on us!"

Now what? Richard stares at Tate, hoping for a clue.

"*Dolly* ran into your *wife* yesterday…?" Tate says this as if it's supposed to explain something.

Out of the corner of his eye, Richard checks out Snodgrass. "And?" he prods, unsure he wants to know what Dorothy has to say about him these days.

"And you have some special *news*? Coming this *summer*?"

Richard is completely blank.

"Your boy? He's…"

The penny finally drops.

"Getting married!" Richard blurts.

"You dog, you! You didn't tell us. Who's the lucky girl?"

Richard's ears go hot. He can't for the life of him remember Nina's name. "Uh. They met at school."

"Dolly says she's a *St. Theresa's girl*."

"Uh, yeah. She is."

"Well, that boy of yours must have some pretty slick moves."

What the hell does that mean? Richard wonders. Unfortunately for him, his face betrays his ignorance, because Mueller delivers his next line like a stand-up comedian. "It's an *all girl* school!"

Snodgrass sniggers.

Who does Tate think he is? Richard thinks. *Fucking Robin Williams?* Then Richard does something that surprises even him. "She's a nice girl," he says, "And we're very excited about the wedding." He picks up his newspaper. "And now, if you'll excuse me, some of us have work to do."

Personally, I think he's already done a lot this morning: He's admitted to himself his son is getting married. Surely that's worth a few insurance policies. But him using the faggot word, even if it was only in his head, has me worried sick. What if I turn out to be gay? Will I have a grandfather who hates me?

❖

Later in the evening, Richard is sitting on the couch gazing over the sports section while Dorothy, in the rocker, pulls a stray thread from a length of red and purple velvet. As for me, I'm hoping that Richard's acknowledgment of the wedding will bring these two together.

"So," Richard says. He's trying to sound light and not stir things up. "When do we get to meet the bride-to-be?"

Dorothy scrutinizes him as if he's an impossible knot of thread.

He folds the sports section in two. "What? I just wanted to know—"

"I heard what you said."

"Well?"

"I've met her. I spent Monday afternoon with her planning the rehearsal dinner. She's delightful."

"What's that supposed to mean? Just because you and that girl—"

"Her name is Nina."

"Just because you and *that girl* have been plotting this whole thing behind everyone's back."

"Why don't you ask your son when you can meet her?"

"He said he doesn't want me at the wedding."

"I'm sure he didn't mean that."

"You should have heard him!"

Dorothy puts down the bolt of velvet and folds her hands. "We are hosting the rehearsal dinner the night before the wedding. At that time you will meet Nina and her family. Some of Rick's new friends will be here too. If you want to meet her before that time, I suggest you deign to talk to your son. I'm very busy. And now, I need to get back to my work. I want to have these curtains done before the dinner."

Richard is incredulous. *That hideous fabric is going to hang in our house?* He tosses the sports section to the floor, annoyed by the lightness of its fall. "Am I the only one who cares that our son is throwing his life away on a girl who claims she is pregnant?"

"It's not just a claim."

"Well, can't we just pay her some money and make her go away?"

His remark stuns Dorothy.

And me.

Fortunately, *I* don't have to respond. Dorothy does, though, only she can't think of any words. She stares at him for an eternal five seconds, then turns, picks up her fabric, and leaves the room.

Richard drops his head into his hands. "I'm sorry, Dorothy," he whispers. "I am *so* sorry." He's picturing her on their wedding day. She wore a full gown to hide the fact that she was showing.

Wow.

Rick and I both attached to our parents before they were ready for us. Does he know this? Does he know that, like me, his arrival was... unplanned? I zip back to Delight Street and find him stirring a can of tuna into a pot of macaroni and cheese. A quick scan of his brain reveals no memory of the shotgun wedding he caused.

I guess Forgetting does have its advantages.

He brings Nina a bowl of his concoction. She's in bed and feeling all lovey-dovey. "I'll talk to Lottie about the costume. You need to feel comfortable."

He climbs in next to her. "It doesn't matter. I'll do whatever makes you happy."

"It does matter. It's our day."

They kiss once, place their bowls on the mismatched nightstands, then dive in for more extensive kissing.

Having no desire to watch their version of making up, I head to the Kalinas to see how they're doing with the whole wedding/baby thing.

❖

Iris is standing in her dining room surrounded by paper. There's a box of mailers to collate and fold, a stack of envelopes to be stamped, another stack to be addressed, and still more to be sealed. I'm the last thing on her mind.

"What made me think I could get this done by tomorrow?" she mutters to herself and moves over to the seal-and-stamp pile. Picking up an envelope, she thinks, *It's absurd I'm even doing this. I should be working on one of the grants or making calls about the open house.* She runs its adhesive flap across a sponge. *A volunteer should be doing this.* She folds it over, sticks it with a stamp, and throws it into the to-be-addressed pile. *I devalue myself when I take this stuff home.* She picks up another envelope. *I'm Executive Director, for God's sake!*

Sponge, fold, stick, and toss. She presses her thumbs into her temples. A migraine is coming on and the sound of Charlotte's food processor from the kitchen isn't helping.

Hester slams through the door in soccer shorts. "We creamed 'em!"

Iris winces. "Oh, did you have a game today?"

"Why do you think I'm home so late?"

"Right. I wasn't thinking."

"I scored, Mom! My first goal!"

"Good for you," Iris says. She wishes she could sound more enthusiastic, but her head is pounding. "Now why don't you wash up for supper? Charlotte is making us—"

"Another of her casseroles," Hester groans. "Puke-o-rama."

The sound of the door again. "I'm ho-oome!"

Hester runs to meet Harvey. "Dad! I scored my first goal today!"

He ruffles her hair. "That's great, pumpkin! Pretty soon, they'll be moving you to center."

At least *he's* happy for Hester.

"Oh, and get ready. Charlotte's making us *another* casserole."

Harvey chuckles. "More 'mystery' ingredients?"

Hester makes a gagging sound, but when the phone rings she recovers instantly, yelling, "I'll get it!" and charging up the stairs.

Harvey enters the dining room. "And how is my love?"

"Tortured. This all has to be done by tomorrow."

He picks up one of the mailers. "Looks good. I'd give money, if I hadn't already."

"Thanks. Only a measly three hundred to go."

Harvey comes up from behind and wraps his arms around her. "Maybe after dinner we can all pitch in."

Iris leans into him, closes her eyes, and feels her migraine begin to ease.

Charlotte bursts through the kitchen door. "Mom! Dinner is going to be ready in ten minutes! Where am I supposed to put it?"

Iris doesn't even bother to open her eyes. "How about we eat out on the porch tonight?"

"Ugh!" Charlotte pushes back through the swinging door.

"How did this happen?" Iris complains. "One of my daughters is barefoot and pregnant and another is obsessed with casseroles."

Great. Iris thinks I've turned Nina into a baby-making dolt. If I could, I'd yell, *Just because you don't cherish your kids doesn't mean Nina won't cherish me!*

Thankfully, Harvey comes to my defense. "I would hardly call Nina barefoot and pregnant."

"You know what I mean. She's just out of college, she hasn't even given herself a chance."

To what? Fold and stamp mailers?

"Speaking of…" Harvey says. "Nina called me at the office today."

"To complain about her evil mother, I'm sure."

"She *is* hurt." Harvey doesn't mention that he's hurt too. Nina told him that, due to the "untraditional nature of the wedding," he wouldn't be giving her away. "The practice is archaic," she said. "Developed when daughters were thought of as property."

I knew she should have waited and told her dad in person, but noooooo, she had to do it over the phone and hurt his feelings. I'll probably get blamed for this too, like it's my fault that pregnancy requires a wedding.

Harvey massages Iris's tight shoulders.

"What does she want from me?" Iris moans. "She barely calls, plans her wedding without even talking to us, when I do talk to her, she acts as though she can't wait to get off the phone…"

Harvey works on a particularly tight spot. "You raised her to be independent."

Iris rolls her head forward. "It's so ironic. Asserting her independence by getting married and having a baby."

Your point? I think.

Hester enters the dining room with a handful of mail.

"Don't mix those up with these," Iris barks.

"Will you chill?" Hester says. "I just wanted to see if my temporary tattoos came."

Ignoring Hester's smart remark, Iris continues to Harvey. "I made sure Charlotte and Nina had birth control at sixteen."

"Things happen," Harvey says.

"They don't *have* to happen."

"She really wants this baby, Iris, you're going to have to make peace with it."

"Dinnnnnner!" Charlotte wails.

Iris takes a deep breath and steps out of her husband's arms.

Hester acts like she didn't even hear Charlotte. "Yeah, Mom, give Nina a break."

I couldn't agree more. Just because Iris thinks her daughters are getting in the way of *her* life doesn't mean Nina's going to feel that way. I bet Nina's going to be the kind of mother who drives me to my soccer game and then sticks around to cheer me on. Hell, having me will probably quell her self-centered fantasy to become the next Meryl Streep.

It could happen.

I decide to check back in with the grandmother who I know will love me, Dorothy Hale. I find her sitting in the driver's seat of the family station wagon. It's parked in the garage and it's dark. She's wondering how long she's been there, but has no way of knowing. When she charged out of the living room and through the kitchen door to the garage, a length of velvet still under her arm, she didn't know where she planned on going. She just had to get away from Richard. Now, sitting at the wheel, she realizes she forgot her car keys. Unwilling to go back inside, she sits in the gloomy garage, alone, wondering if this is what it feels like to be dead. Bundled in a casket with no alternatives. *Does it ever occur to him*, she thinks, *that my life hasn't gone as planned either? Does he really believe that the last twenty-four years of propping up this marriage are what I dreamed of as a girl?*

Dorothy tries to imagine Rick as a father—a husband—but she can't. *He's too young.* Her mind skips to the day she spent with Nina one week ago. Nina invited her for lunch and made what Dorothy thought was an interesting rice dish, although the rice wasn't fully cooked. Of course, Dorothy didn't say so, and focused instead on the spices Nina used. Their names sounded to her like railway stops on a trip through the Orient: Saffron, Cayenne, Cumin, Cardamom…

She and Nina got together under the guise of planning the rehearsal dinner, but spent most of the day just talking. Nina had so many questions about giving birth. One time she even said, "I figure since you did such a good job with Rick, you must really know how to do this." Dorothy was amused. Still is, as she sits in this dark garage. She doesn't think of Rick as being a product of her labor; she believes he came to her perfect, like a seed, everything there from the start. All she had to do was keep the soil fertile, cut back what might obstruct sunlight, and water.

She takes the steering wheel in her hands and imagines driving away, fast, just a suitcase in the back, down roads she's never been, staying in roadside motels, eating at truck stops and small cafes… *Soon*, she tells herself, *soon. First I have a wedding and the birth of my grandchild to attend to.*

Wait. She can't leave. She's going to be my favorite grandmother. She's going to be the one to bake me cupcakes and read me stories about trains.

She considers going back into the house and slipping between the sheets next to Richard, but can't make herself do it. Some nights, just the sound of his breathing is enough to make her want to pound his chest with her fists.

I wonder what would happen if Dorothy actually did this? Maybe it would break through the wall around Richard's heart and he'd remember the girl he fell head over heels for, beautiful Dorothy, before she became a wife.

She gets out of the car, pulls a picnic blanket from a closet in the garage and makes a pillow by stuffing laundry into a pillowcase, then lays the backseat of the SUV down and creates a bed. Lying on her back with her knees bent up, she looks out the rear window and remembers riding this way as a child. How she watched the treetops, clouds, and rooftops go by, trying to figure out the route by landmarks in the sky. But tonight as she looks into the dark garage, all shadows, and shadows of shadows, she can't find a landmark anywhere.

When I arrive, *if* I arrive, I hope that Nina and Rick think *I'm* perfect.

And that Nina never has to sleep in a garage.

CHAPTER TWENTY-ONE

Only six months and two weeks until my due date. My organs are all in place, my toes and fingers are adorable, but my head is gigantic—monstrous! Presumably, the rest of my body will catch up, but can there possibly be enough time?

On top of this, the turbulence this Love Happening is causing is getting out of hand. Nina and Pablo are still feeling estranged; Dorothy Hale has all but moved out to the garage, storing pillows and blankets in the backseat of the car—she even put her toothbrush by the utility sink; Richard, bent out of shape because nobody in his family seems to give a good goddamn what he thinks about anything, has taken to talking to himself as he tramps around his house, saying things like: "Lookie here, we're all out of scotch! Is someone going to get the scotch? No? Well, I guess I'll have to go get the scotch myself!" Iris Kalina is still hoping she can get Nina to change her mind; Harvey Kalina is performing the Herculean task of keeping his hurt feelings as far from his logical mind as possible; Charlotte is sleeping poorly, because she agreed to take part in the Love Happening when she thought it was going to be a normal wedding, and, when she does manage to sleep, her dreams are filled with the myriad possible humiliations that Nina could inflict upon her; the Sisters in Solidarity are all being outwardly supportive while quietly questioning Nina's choice; Rick isn't speaking to Richard; Nina is barely speaking to Iris; and Dink, bless her heart, is to be the best man in a wedding where she's in love with the bride! What a mess.

The only ones who seem even remotely happy about my forthcoming arrival are Dorothy and Hester. In her Girl Scout troop, Hester is making me an Indian necklace. Today, for a few dismal hours,

I convince myself that the whole reason for my life-to-be is Hester's leather and bead project. It's a bleak thought.

❖

Friday night. Rick is coming home from a long day of changing tires. His body is tired and his mood grumpy. When he gets out of his car, he sees two familiar figures hunched over, examining something at the base of a tree. One is wearing a Hawaiian hibiscus-covered muumuu cinched at the waist by a rainbow belt, and a baseball cap with a daisy appliqué stitched over the team emblem. The other has on a purple rhinestone collar. Rick wishes he didn't have to make conversation. He's worried about the rent this month and has planned to talk to Viola about working off a portion. *Just not now*, he thinks. "Hey, Viola. Hey, Franklin," he says.

Viola looks up from what Rick now identifies as a squashed candy wrapper. "Why hello, Rick. Don't mind us. We're treasure hunting."

"Just wanted you to know I've got the bathroom all re-caulked and the curtain rods back up."

"Nina showed me," she says. "You did a bang-up job. And I noticed you took the *oomph!* out of the door too."

"Oh yeah. That was easy." Rick focuses on Franklin, who's now frantically trying to bury the candy wrapper. Should he say something about the rent?

"I can't tell you how glad we are to have you in the building. And tell Nina I got the invitation to the Love Happening. It's delightful! Those pressed flowers tucked inside were such a lovely touch. And of course Franklin's thrilled that you're having it outdoors. You know how he hates being excluded."

Rick draws his attention from Franklin's high-powered paws. "So you're both coming?"

"We wouldn't miss it. And now, I'm sure you have more important things to do on this beautiful summer evening than talk with an old lady and her dog. Besides, Franklin and I are late for a date with a friend. But it's so hard not to take in the sights. Oh, but before we go, I wanted to ask if you'd be up for painting the foyer. It's such a dingy gray. I was thinking maybe a nice lilac."

Rick is so happy about this opportunity to work he could almost drop to his knees next to Franklin. "Sure. I'll jump on it this weekend."

"That would be ducky! Come by my apartment tomorrow and we'll make arrangements."

Before Rick can thank her, Viola lightly slaps her hands against her thighs. "Come on, Franklin. Mrs. Tan awaits." As they toddle off, Viola says over her shoulder, "And whatever you do, don't skimp! Life is too short for skimping!"

Click! Click! Click! Click! go Franklin's toenails down the street.

Rick, feeling a surge of energy, pushes through the door into the apartment and starts to race up the stairs to tell Nina the good news. Then he remembers to check out a small bulletin board for tenant communication by the stairwell. Along with the usual notes about upcoming events and things for sale, there's one that reads: WE'RE MOVING! THANKS FOR EVERYTHING! It's signed simply 2C. *They must be the couple below us*, he thinks, taking the stairs two at a time. *I never really got to know them.* Sad to be losing something he barely knew he had, he makes a point to get to know the new neighbors when they move in.

As he gets closer to his doorway he hears music. A woman named Aretha is singing about kisses being sweeter than honey. He opens the door to an empty living room blasting with sound. "Nina?" There's no response. He walks through the blaring horns and thumping tambourines to the bedroom door where he discovers Nina, oblivious to his arrival, singing with Aretha, only she's using a hairbrush for a microphone. Watching her, he feels a sudden satisfaction with his life. This is *his* home, *his* fiancée. He picks up a wine-bottle candleholder hosting a stump of green wax, flips it guitar-style under his arm and Chuck Berrys his way into the room spelling out the word R.E.S.P.E.C.T. Nina turns toward him, raises her eyebrows in acknowledgment and holds the brush out so he can sing into it with her. Once the song is over she runs into the living room to turn down the record player. *"It's a girl!"*

Just as I thought, Rick's first feeling is disappointment, but he quickly covers it up by saying, "That's great!" The thing is, he's always pictured him and me doing boy stuff together. I want to scream, *We still can, Rick! Don't give up on me yet!* But of course, I can't scream and he can't picture having a really good session of shooting hoops with a girl.

Nina is thrilled. She's already pictured me being a tiny version of her—minus all the neuroses she blames on her parents. Since the doctor's visit, she's spent the day imagining her and this tiny-version-of-her hanging out together. She pictures us like two best friends who share everything. I notice she's conveniently skipped over the first years when she's underslept, dripping breast milk, and sick of cleaning poop and spit-up.

"And there's even more good news! My parents must have had a fight!"

"Huh?"

"Look!" Nina zips over to the table and picks up two envelopes. "They both sent checks! And they both said not to tell the other one they'd done it! We're rich!" She holds the checks above her head like two bunny ears.

"Sweet."

"I say it's time to celebrate! And *I'm* taking *you* out tonight!"

Rick drops playfully to his knee and kisses her hand. "How should I dress, madam?"

"For Sweetie's Creamery," she replies, tossing an imaginary feather boa over her shoulder. "We're having banana splits for dinnah."

Forty-five minutes later, they're sitting in a pink and white ice cream parlor with a giant banana split in front of each of them. Rick is stoned.

Nina dives into her mint chocolate chip. "I've been thinking about names."

"I like the name Britney," Rick says before shoving a big bite of chocolate-smothered vanilla in his mouth.

Nina frowns. "No way. Britney Spears has ruined that name for generations to come."

Phew! With a name like Britney I'd be toast on the playground. I was thinking more along the lines of Chris or Dana. I'd even go for Josephine, which I could shorten to Jo.

"How about Ruby?" Nina says.

Rick shakes his head. "Used to have a babysitter named Ruby. She was psycho."

Nina takes another bite of ice cream, then says with her mouth full, "She needs a powerful name. I don't want to raise a girl who's scared of everything."

"How about Spanky," Rick says, laughing. "You know, from that old show they show on Nick at Nite."

"Be serious."

Rick picks a chocolate sprinkle off Nina's shirt and places it on her outstretched tongue. He's having trouble thinking of me as a girl. "What's wrong with Spanky?"

"For our baby girl?"

He shrugs. "She'd be the only Spanky in her class. You could be sure of that."

"Rick. How much pot did you smoke?"

❖

Later at home, Nina is brushing her hair in the bathroom, and I'm thinking to myself how beautiful she is, when we hear an extraordinary sound coming from the living room. It's like the earth turning, or a hundred monks chanting on a mountainside.

Nina tiptoes to the doorway. I follow. Rick is bathed in moonlight and has his saxophone pressed to his lips. He's not just doing his usual scales, either; he's inspired, playing in a way he hasn't since Howie's death.

"Come on, Spanky," Nina whispers. "Let's listen to Daddy."

In her bathrobe and sock feet, she quietly enters into the moonlit room and lies on the small throw rug. She opens her robe and spreads her bent knees wide, then places her hands on either side of her belly. She's imagining the moon caressing me like a million butterfly kisses.

My first lullaby. Me, Spanky.

We're having love.

CHAPTER TWENTY-TWO

Expecting." That's what people say Nina's doing in regard to me. It's a new concept for me, but as far as I can make out "Expecting" gives people a way to navigate through the unknown with a sense of confidence. A smiles at B on Monday, A also smiles at B on Tuesday, by Wednesday, B "expects" A to smile.

Expecting, however, has one big flaw: People change. Take Richard Hale. He's spent his whole married life tending his lawn. He's fertilized it, mowed it, edged it, aerated it, weeded it, and had lengthy conversations about its health with his neighbor. But over the past two weeks he's walked right past the same dandelion maybe two dozen times without yanking it out or poisoning the spot where it grows with a shot of herbicide. Who would have expected this? He still sees the dandelion, but now, instead of trying to outdo his neighbors, he's using his lawn to send a message to Dorothy, his son, and any-goddamned-one else who cares enough to know: "If my son doesn't want me at his goddamn wedding, I don't want his goddamn rehearsal dinner at my house! So there!"

Dorothy notices the lone dandelion too, every time she walks down the path with bags full of ingredients for Indian cuisine. *How it must pain him*, she thinks, *to let the yard appear so unkempt. No doubt why his ulcer's been acting up.*

Dorothy is also a victim of expecting, but hers has to do with Nina. Having experienced Nina's cooking, she expects the Kalinas to have similar tastes and has been testing recipes for curries, pilafs, and dishes that feature rice noodles and peanut sauce. This really did a number on Richard's expectations the other night.

At dinner, he pushed a foreign substance across his plate. "What's this?"

"Curried lentils in pineapple," Dorothy said. "Try it with some of the coconut raita. Or were you talking about the Jerusalem artichoke salad?"

"I don't know why we just don't barbeque the goddamned dinner!"

"Are you planning on coming then, dear?"

Richard raised his napkin to his lips. "I was speaking hypothetically."

"I see…well…since you, hypothetically, aren't even going to attend your son's rehearsal dinner, it doesn't make sense for me to plan the menu around your taste preferences."

It's bothering Richard no end that Dorothy's moved out of their bedroom and into Rick's vacated room. *No telling what anyone will think when they see that!* Which dovetails into a whole other set of his anxieties: Dorothy has been replacing the tan, cream, and brown plaids of their decor with reds, golds, and deep purples. Velvet curtains with large tassels now drape around what was once an unadorned bay window, and the corduroy sofa, which they bought together at Sears not three years ago, is now smothered in colorful satin pillows with fringe and tiny mirrors. This, on top of the goddamn potted jungle plants drooping off their rolltop desk and bookcases, makes Richard feel like a stranger in his own home.

And it's not just the Hales whose expectations are being messed with. Poor Dink thinks everyone expects her, as best man, to throw Rick a bachelor party. In truth, no one has given this a thought, but her need to live up to their expectations is blinding her.

She calls Pablo from work.

"Cobblestone Florists. Can I help you?"

"Pablo, we have to do a bachelor's party."

"Dink?"

"We're only three days away from the weddi…Love Happening. We gotta do it."

"I'm with a customer."

"I'm going to call Rick. Keep Thursday night open."

"Dink, this doesn't sound like a good idea. We should talk."

"I'm just going to fucking do it. I'm the best man, after all."

"Do we have to invite those clods he works with?"

"No. Just the three of us. Our house. Eight o'clock."

"You're a masochist. You know that."

"Yeah, I guess." She hangs up the phone and calls Rick.

Two days later she's bought three bottles of gin, two of vermouth, a bunch of olives, and a half-ounce of sinsemilla, and she still worries that it won't be enough to anesthetize her aching heart. Fortunately, at the bachelor party, Rick has so much on his mind, and is so high himself, that he doesn't notice that Dink is acting more like a person at a wake than a person celebrating a wedding. Indeed, Rick's so busy slamming back martinis and boasting about how happy he is that he doesn't notice much of anything.

I'm a bit disappointed in all three of them. They're beyond reasonable inebriation. Is this any way to start our new family?

Dink and Rick are slumped on opposite sides of the couch while Pablo is stretched across the armchair facing them. Dink reaches across the expanse of the couch to hand Rick his present. "In lieu of a woman jumping out of a cake," she slurs as she passes him a Lucite writing pen with a tiny woman inside. "Tip it upside down. She get's naked."

Pablo sniggers from his chair. "You need that more than he does."

Rick's so loaded he lets Pablo's words and Dink's embarrassed "Shut up!" slip right past him. He proceeds to tip the pen back and forth, back and forth. He's trying to remember the last time he saw a pen like this. Then he does. *Howie had one.*

The muscles in his face tighten. So does the back of his throat. He clutches the pen and locks his jaw to keep the surge of unexpected emotion from escaping, but a lungful of air lurches its way through and the next things he knows a bunch of short, choppy sobs follow. And it's not just about Howie, either. He's crying about the estrangement he feels from his dad, and how he's now going to be a dad—a husband. *My life is changing so fast*, he thinks. *Is this really what I want?* In his blurry state of mind, he imagines himself a man walking through sand at the edge of the sea—his past washing away one footprint at a time.

Dink and Pablo look on in shock. Bachelor parties are supposed to be all backslapping and raucous jokes, not crying.

Before I have a chance to look too far into this surge of—regret?—I notice Dink making strange little choking noises and commanding her body, *No! No!* She squeezes her eyes against the sting and presses her fists into her legs. Then she starts crying too. And while Rick is picturing footsteps in the sand, she's picturing her heart ripped in two like an unwanted valentine. She pulls up her long shirttail to cover her face.

I check in with Pablo. Surely he can pull them out of this.

He crosses his arms and raises an eyebrow. Then, to my dismay, he's ambushed by all the times his mother asked him when he was going to settle down and get married, and how, when he's brought one of his lovers to meet her, he's never had the guts to tell her they were more than friends. He too begins sobbing.

Well.

I sure didn't expect a big boo-hoo fest on the eve of the big Love Happening.

I suppose none of them did either.

I wait patiently as they snivel and sniff, running their sleeves across their snotty noses, all the while trying to pretend this isn't happening. And once they finally do manage to finish crying, the three of them are left in a super-awkward silence. Dink scratches at the eyeliner smudges on her shirttail. Pablo clears his throat, while Rick checks to see if his shoes are still tied. Confident that they are, he says, "That was weird."

"Fucking weird," Dink says.

Pablo reaches for one of Dink's smokes.

"Since when do you smoke?" asks Rick.

"Since now," Pablo says.

Dink grabs her martini and sloshes it into the air. "To fucking love!"

Rick picks up his glass. "To fucking love!"

"To love and fucking!" Pablo yells, and they all think this is the funniest thing anyone on the planet has ever said.

I find this whole display of emotion most inauspicious.

❖

At 448 Delight Street, Nina puts a novel down on the bedside table and thinks, *I suppose there's no point in me waiting up.* It bothers her that Rick and her two best friends are having fun without her. She turns off the bedside reading light and waits for her eyes to adjust to the dark, then slides her hands under her belly. "Your daddy is having a good time tonight, Spanky," she whispers.

Want details? I feel like saying.

She pulls the sheets up around her neck and closes her eyes.

She's expecting.

CHAPTER TWENTY-THREE

11:00 a.m. Only six and a half hours until the big rehearsal dinner.

I hope everybody gets along. Nina's family is planning to stop by our house before heading over to the Hales'. It will be their first time to see where we live.

If Nina's and my relationship is any indication of how things are going to go, we're in for trouble.

She's currently sprinkling cleanser on the chipped Formica of the kitchen countertop and rubbing it in with a damp sponge. The toaster, cutting board, and other stuff usually stored on the counter are scattered across the floor.

She's been cleaning for hours.

And even though her mother is miles away, Nina's talking to her. Not out loud, but in her head. *This baby is not going to ruin my life! I can still be an actress. You just wait and see. What's more, my baby is going to be allowed to say her feelings without being told she's whining. And my baby isn't going to always feel like she's not practical enough. And my baby...*

I wish she'd shut up already. She's giving me a headache.

For the gazillionth time she peeks into the bedroom to see if Rick is up yet. He's not. He's sleeping off last night's bachelor party. She puts her hands on her hips, hoping he'll "intuit" that she wants him to wake up.

He doesn't.

She checks the clock and convinces herself that he *should* be awake. "Good morning, sleepyhead!" Her voice, despite the attempt at cheerfulness, sounds annoyed.

Rick groans into the pillow. His head is spinning, "What time is it?"

"Just after eleven. Mom and them should be here by three. Don't go back to sleep."

He flops onto his back with his eyes still closed. *That's four hours I could be sleeping*, he thinks.

Nina sits on the edge of the bed. "How did it go last night?"

"Good," he croaks.

I'm glad he chooses not to tell her about the boo-hoo fest—until I realize he doesn't remember it. All his last night's gurgled-up fears about having me, and getting married, are now knotted in his right shoulder.

"I've got the apartment mostly clean," she says.

He opens his eyes. "I'll be up in a minute."

She kisses his forehead. "Thanks."

Once she's out of the room he closes his eyes again. *Will Dad show up?* Dorothy told him not to worry, that Richard wouldn't be caught dead giving up a chance to be the man of the hour. But she wasn't there that day at Jack's Tires.

"I think we should move the sofa," Nina says from the other room. She's hoping that if she can find the perfect configuration of furniture it will somehow make Iris think I'm a good idea. "When you're up, could I get some help?"

Rick sits up. A bolt of pain shoots through his shoulder and neck. He rubs it briefly and rolls his neck a few times, attributing the stiff neck and shoulder to sleeping in the wrong position. He puts his feet on the cool floor and, naked, makes his way toward the coffeepot.

"I wish I'd made those curtains," Nina says.

He pours himself a cup of coffee. "Do we have any ibuprofen?"

"In the cabinet. I was thinking about moving the couch. What do you think?"

"I like it how it is."

"It shouldn't have its back to the door like that."

"Let's move it, then."

"Do you think we should?"

"Can I take some ibuprofen and put on some clothes first?"

Think I'll give them some space.

❖

11:15. Dink is passed out on the couch. The pen with the naked lady is pressed between her cheek and a throw pillow, and she's snoring.

Across the hall Pablo's in his bed with a cup of coffee. He woke a few minutes earlier from a nightmare, and now is trying to remember it.

A bride's bouquet sailing through the air…people…his mother, two of his sisters, yelling, "Catch it! Catch it!" His father, wearing his butcher's apron, stands behind Pablo at the door of the church. Pablo can smell the unmistakable stench of his father's cologne mixed with perspiration and animal blood. The bouquet drops at Pablo's feet. It's all baby's breath and miniature pink roses. Pablo can't figure out how it could have landed at his feet. It was sailing through the air in the other direction, toward the women. Church bells clang so hard a bell falls to the ground. Nobody notices. They're all too busy clapping and laughing. Pablo tries to figure out what to do with the bouquet. He bends down to pick it up. It falls apart in his hands. His father spits and stalks off, leaving a trail of bloody footprints.

Pablo takes a sip of hot black coffee, musing at the lack of subtlety in the dream. He thinks back to his little sister's wedding: a huge affair with twelve bridesmaids all dressed in mint green satin with matching shoes, the groomsmen in white tuxes. All day his aunts and uncles elbowed him and asked when he was going to tie the knot. As usual, he did the old shrug and smile. *This time*, he thinks, *if anybody asks me, I'm going to tell them the truth.*

In the other room, Dink does a really loud snort.

"Turn over!" he yells, but she doesn't.

❖

11:25 "Hester!" Iris shouts up the stairs. "Get off the phone! We need to leave!" She turns to Harvey, who's standing in the open door. "The ride up is going to be sweltering without air-conditioning."

He takes off his glasses and cleans the lenses on his shirt. "The dealership couldn't fit us in until next week."

Charlotte charges in. "Who used my new kerchief for a rag? I was planning on wearing this!"

❖

2:45. Nina and Rick are finally finished cleaning and are perched on their couch, which, after several moves, is now back in its original place. They're waiting, he in his best pair of jeans and a new button-down shirt, she wearing a new sundress. A *Music From India* CD is turned to low. Neither one of them is really a fan of Indian music, but Nina feels it exhibits a cultured taste. Rick is clipping his fingernails into the ashtray. Nina wants him to finish so she can empty it. The imprecision of the Kalinas' arrival time, "any time between three and four," is making them both nuts.

When they get here, Nina thinks, *we can't be sitting on the couch like this. We'll look lazy. We should be caught in the middle of something, like we're too busy to give their arrival much thought.* She admires the mobile of dangling crystals that Lottie gave her and hopes her family arrives in time to see the spray of rainbows that dance around the room. Daisies, in vases made from empty peanut butter and honey jars, are sprinkled around the tiny apartment giving the place a bohemian look. She imagines her parents sitting in the living room and saying things along the line of: "We see now, you are much more extraordinary than we ever imagined! To think, we never noticed it when you lived under our roof!"

Boy, is she going to be disappointed. They're stuck in a huge traffic jam—and boiling hot. Hardly in the mood for a home and gardens tour.

❖

3:00. Dorothy Hale is bustling around the kitchen while Richard paces the house in a snit. "Smells like bloody Timbuktu in here, for crying out loud!" He flicks back a tassel that obscures his view of the front yard. He thinks Dorothy hasn't heard him, so he tries again. "Smells more like perfume than food!"

"Did you say something, dear?"

"I suppose you think serving up this fancy-schmancy food is going to impress the hell out of everyone! Well, I don't know about you, but I'm proud just to be an American Joe!"

"It's just food, dear. I'm trying something new."

❖

3:15. Pablo leaves his apartment with Dink still asleep on the couch. He writes her a note. "If I don't show up tonight, tell Nina and Rick I'm sorry." I follow him for a while, but all he's doing is walking.

❖

3:40. The *Music From India* CD is on its third run. Nina looks over at Rick, who's starting to doze on the couch. *I should put the cheese and crackers out*, she thinks. Her original plan was to do it when they got there, as if she just happened to have all the ingredients on hand. Now there won't be time. She goes to the kitchen.

❖

4:00. I can't get Pablo out of my head. He *has* to come to the dinner. If he doesn't, Nina will be upset, and, more and more, when Nina's upset so am I.

I find him sitting on a fake-leather bar stool drinking a Tom Collins. He's feeling disgusted with himself for being in a pitifully dark dive on such a beautiful day. Someone at the other end of the bar is checking him out. Pablo recognizes the guy as a Safeway cashier, even though the guy looks really different here. His hair is all slicked back and he's wearing a shirt so tight it clings to his muscles.

Pablo makes eye contact with Mr. Safeway, then shoots his drink. After putting the empty glass down on the bar, he walks back to the restroom. Mr. Safeway follows.

I sure hope they're quick.

❖

4:30. I appear in time to see Nina lunge for the ringing phone. Rick jerks into consciousness.

"Hello?"

"Honey, we're running a bit late," Iris says. "We got stuck in traffic, the car has no air-conditioning, and the motel couldn't find our reservation. Once we finally got it all worked out, we collapsed. We're just now cleaning up."

This is just like her! Nina thinks. *So self-centered! Does it ever occur to her that she might be inconveniencing anyone?*

Rick is listening to Nina talk to her mother. Her tone reminds him of a teacher sounding out syllables for an exceptionally slow second-grader. "Yes…Okay…Fine…We will be here…" He reaches for one of the crackers with cheese displayed on the blue and white china. Nina waves him away from it. He slumps back into the couch.

Nina slams the phone down.

"Running late?" Rick asks.

"They could have called earlier."

Rick reaches for her hand, but misses; she's already whisked it into an exasperated gesture. "Now they're not even going to have time to see our apartment!"

He looks around at the small one-bedroom dwelling, kitchenette separated by a short tile counter, and thinks, *There's not much to see.*

I zip over to the Kalinas.

Iris is assaulting her teeth with a toothbrush. "I'm a terrible mother," she says through a mouth of foam.

Harvey runs a comb through his thinning hair. "Honey, you're not."

"She hates me. She does. She always has. Nothing I do makes her happy."

"She's just nervous. And scared. Remember your first pregnancy."

Iris spits into the sink. "I'm going to round up the girls."

❖

5:15. Nina's just had a good cry and is splashing water on her face. The sound of the doorbell throws her into a panic. She considers rushing for the CD player to put *Music From India* back on, then thinks, *Why? Mom didn't make any effort to rush for me!* She splashes more cold water on her face. "Honey?" she calls to Rick. "Could you get that?"

Rick has just placed a stale saltine slathered with peanut butter into his mouth. *Shit!* He crams the crackers back into the box, screws the top back on the peanut butter, and throws it into the cabinet.

"Did you hear me?" Nina yells from the bathroom.

Attempting to swallow the peanut butter and cracker bits, he runs the knife under the faucet. The peanut butter sticks to his hands, the sides of the sink, the faucet.

The bell rings again.

"Honey! I'm in the bathroom!"

Rick stares at the sink. *Nina's going to kill me.* There are crumbs and watered-down Skippy all over it. He swipes it with a sponge, getting most of the crumbs, splashes some water in his mouth, takes a deep breath, and races to the door, all the while running his tongue over his teeth. He clears his throat, reminding himself not to open his mouth too wide in case there are still Skippy bits in his teeth, and flings the door open. "Welcome!"

Hester, all by herself, looks up at him. "Since we're running late, Mom said I should come up and get you. She said we can follow you over."

So much for the crackers and cheese.

CHAPTER TWENTY-FOUR

It's 5:31 and I'm at the Hales'. Everybody else is one minute late. Dorothy and Richard don't seem particularly put out, but I am. Then again, I'm just the unofficial host. The one nobody dares to mention.

Richard paces in the front room talking to himself. Dorothy is back in the kitchen. She's wearing a colorful loose-sleeved tunic over cream pants with a silver low-slung belt. It's a new outfit and different from her usual dress-up clothes, the ones she wears for church.

"Weren't you going out, dear?" she says through the kitchen doorway.

"Not on your life! This, I've gotta see. I mean, these people must be real important. I mean, they don't rate just *ordinary* food. God forbid their lips should touch a humble hamburger or T-bone."

"Would you like me to fry you up a cube steak, dear?"

"Nooooooooo. I don't want to be left out of this exotic soirée. No siree. You think I don't know my way around a goddamn sukiyaki? You think I don't know an egg roll when I see one?"

"We're having Indian food, dear. I don't think they go in for egg rolls in India."

"Very funny, Dorothy. Very goddamn funny."

Being funny is the last thing on Dorothy's mind. She wants to get her condiments correct. She pours a bag of flaked coconut into a small red bowl, spoons chutney into another, dumps crispy fried onions into another.

She's aware that Richard is expecting her to do what she always does when he says he won't go somewhere, do something, or talk to some person on account of one of his zillions of principles. She's supposed to beg, plead, and barter with him to change his mind. Then, when he finally announces that he will go, he can act as if it's against his will, all her doing. But she's not in the mood today and hasn't been for a while. That's why he's springing off the walls like a squash ball.

Personally, I'm glad he's here. At least Rick won't have to explain to the Kalinas why his dad doesn't want to meet them. This would definitely make a rotten first impression. The Kalinas would think Rick was such a loser his own dad wouldn't even come.

The doorbell rings.

Dorothy stops chopping peanuts and goes to answer it, but Richard cuts her off at the pass. "Well, okay, then. Since you insist, I'll stick around," he grumbles. "The things I do for you two!"

Three, I think.

He opens the door with a flourish and speaks as though it's the grand opening gala of a business. "Welcome to the Proud Home of the Groom!"

Dorothy smiles and wipes her hands on her apron. *The Man of the Hour has arrived*, she thinks.

I'm relieved too, even if it's not the Kalinas at the door.

"And who might you two lovely ladies be?" Richard asks, staring at what looks to him like a beautiful China doll with a blue stripe in her hair. His glance shifts to Missy, who's fiddling with one of her eyebrows.

Lottie peers over her lavender granny glasses. "I'm Lottie Yang and this is Missy Hooten. Are we the first?"

"You certainly are. I'm Rick's dad, Richard Hale."

Dorothy walks past him to greet the young women. "And I'm Dorothy. It's delightful to meet you both. Lottie, you're a costume designer, aren't you?"

"Well, I was. I'm working for an interior designer now."

"Nina says you girls are going all out on this Love Happening, that it's going to be quite a theatrical event."

Richard's face pales. *Love Happening? Theatrical event? What the hell does that mean?* Before he's finished imagining the possibilities, Dorothy has ushered the girls into the living room.

"What do you say I get you girls a drink?" he says to their backs.

"We have sangria and lassi," Dorothy says.

Lottie and Missy exchange looks. Neither of them knows what lassi is. "Um, sangria sounds good," Lottie says.

"Me too," Missy echoes.

Dorothy exits to the pantry.

Richard leans against the mantle, looking down at Lottie and Missy on the couch. "You girls the lucky bridesmaids, then?"

"Kind of," Lottie says, arranging her wire-rim glasses.

"Sisters in Solidarity. Isn't that it?" Dorothy shouts from the kitchen.

"You got it!" Missy shouts back.

Richard's eyelid twitches. *What the hell kind of wedding is this going to be, for Christ's sake?*

The doorbell rings.

Better be my son, Richard thinks, and flings the door open once again booming, "Welcome to the Proud Home of the Groom!" But it's more Sisters in Solidarity, and these barely stop for the obligatory hellos and how-do-you-dos before parting around him like a school of fish negotiating a large rock.

I feel kind of sorry for Richard, especially when the Sisters in Solidarity all wag their pinkies and hiss, "Ssssistaaaaahs!" The hair at the nape of his neck bristles. He chides himself for neglecting Rick these past months. *My boy has found his way into some abnormal company.*

Dorothy comes out and offers drinks to the new arrivals.

The doorbell rings.

This has got to be him, Richard thinks, and one more time flings the door open and bellows, "Welcome to the Proud Home of the Groom!" But this time it's Dink, and she's wearing so much black eyeliner and is so sullen looking that Richard thinks she looks like a raccoon.

After introducing herself, she peers past Richard to see who's already arrived and is bummed to see no Rick or Nina, just the Sisters of Stupidity, as she's dubbed them.

"So, can I come in?" she asks.

"Why not?" he says, finishing the thought in his mind with, *And join the rest of the loonies.*

This is totally depressing; my party is turning into a dud. Where the hell are Rick and Nina?

I find them two blocks away at a stoplight, the Kalinas' car right behind theirs. "I could kill her," Nina is saying as she adjusts the rearview mirror to look at her mother.

Rick drums his fingers on the steering wheel.

"What if your dad doesn't show?"

Rick grinds the car into first gear. "What do you want me to say?" He readjusts the mirror before heading out into the intersection.

At least they're on their way.

I return to the Hales.

Dorothy has just come out of the kitchen. "Can I get you something to drink, Dink? Sangria? Lassi?"

"Or how about a beer?" Richard adds.

Dink reconsiders her initial dislike of Richard. "Beer sounds great."

Richard beams as if he'd just scored the winning touchdown. "Coming right up," he says, then gives Dorothy a meaningful look.

Dorothy shakes her head and walks off.

Richard returns with two beers. "Budweiser to the rescue!" He hands one to Dink and pops the tab on his own. "So, you must be one of these…" he completes his sentence by shaking his pinkies in the air and hissing, "Sisssstahsssss!" But Dink hasn't seen the Sisters' secret language and looks at Richard like he's got Tourette's.

Lottie laughs. "She's not one of us. She's the best man."

Hit with an overwhelming need to speak with his wife, Richard strides off to the kitchen under the guise of getting fresheners for the girls' drinks.

I hear Rick and Nina pull into the driveway and zip out to greet them. They exchange pained smiles before getting out of the car.

"I love you no matter what," he says.

"I love you too," she says.

You'd think they were about to execute a suicide pact.

Hand in hand, they head toward the house with the Kalinas right behind.

Upon reaching the door, Rick decides on a comic entrance and pokes his head in. "Is this where the party is?" But the vision of Dink stretched out in his Dad's favorite chair gives him an instant stomachache. *No Dad.*

Too bad they weren't on time; they would have gotten to hear, "Welcome to the Proud Home of the Groom!"

Dorothy enters the living room. "Welcome. I'm Dorothy Hale."

Iris thinks Dorothy looks like a mouse in flamboyant clothes, and thinks, *I hope I'm not required to like her.* "I'm Iris," she says reaching out her hand. But Dorothy has already opened her arms to hug Iris and is now in the awkward position of having to act like she didn't. She swoops her hands together and takes Iris's one hand in both of her own. It's not very convincing.

Iris pulls her hand away and gestures to the rest of her family. "And this is Charlotte, Hester, and my husband, Harvey." Dorothy reaches out her hand to each, feeling foolish for her previous warmth. Harvey—who also thinks Dorothy looks like a mouse, but a nice mouse—tries to compensate for Iris's coolness by taking both of Dorothy's hands in his, but it's obvious from Dorothy's newfound formality that the damage is done.

"Where's Dad?" Rick blurts, then internally kicks himself for sounding so desperate.

Before Dorothy can reassure him, Richard enters through the kitchen door toting a tray of stuffed mushrooms caps. "Where's Dad? Where's Dad? You sound like a parrot, son. The Father of the Groom is present and accounted for. What's more, I have a plate of delicacies from the far corners of the earth that my dear wife has been breaking her back over." He hands the tray flamboyantly to Missy, who blushes.

"Hey, Dad."

Richard places his hand on Rick's shoulder and speaks in mock sincerity. "Son, welcome to your last night of pissing with the seat down and drinking out of the milk carton." Then he slaps Rick on the back and busts up laughing.

No one joins in.

Dorothy heads for the kitchen. "I'll get us some drinks."

"Dad," Rick says, "This is Harvey and Iris Kalina."

Richard, trying to make a comeback, gives Iris the once-over. "I see where your daughter gets all her good looks." He slaps Harvey on the shoulder. "You got yourself a real looker here, Harv. A real looker. I'll bet this little woman keeps you on your toes."

Iris's crow's feet go taut.

Rick thinks, *Please don't let him start in on his Three Things a Man Needs routine: Nice house, Fine car, Beautiful wife*, while Nina prays her mom won't jump on one of her soapboxes.

For the next half hour they all sit around sipping sangria and nibbling nuts, olives, stuffed mushroom caps, and vegetables dipped in aioli. Not at all what I expected. Where's the dancing? The music? All they're doing is talk-talk-talking, which is particularly painful because all the talk-talk-talking is pointedly staying off one important topic. Me. They listen to Hester's blow-by-blow account of her summer camp play like it's the most important thing in the world. Or, should I say, they pretend to listen. Everyone's mind is preoccupied with sizing everyone else up.

I tune in to Dink. She's watching how perfectly Nina fits beneath Rick's arm as they snuggle on the love seat. Nina's hand is fiddling with a crease in Rick's pant leg. Dink's wishing that she'd had the sense that Pablo had to ditch the whole scene.

Pablo! I'd forgotten all about him. Surely he can't still be in the bathroom with the Safeway guy. That would be…um…extreme.

I scan the room to see if anyone else has noticed his absence, and find that Nina's obsessing over it. She keeps glancing at the door, the clock. She doesn't want to have to explain the empty place setting to Dorothy, doesn't want Iris to think she has flaky friends.

His excuse better be good, that's all I have to say. As Richard Hale launches into a particularly tedious golf anecdote, and everyone sits there trying to look interested while placating themselves with hors d'oeuvres and sangria, I go in search of him.

I find him sitting on a park bench, three blocks away from the rehearsal dinner. Next to him is a bouquet of light blue delphinium and peach roses for the hostess. He's been sitting here over an hour. *Why am I making such a big deal about all this?* he's thinking. *Surely, I should be able to put my feelings aside for just two days. Besides, it's not Nina's and Rick's fault the world is the way it is.* He notices that the delphinium stalks are beginning to wilt; the tops are no longer able to hold themselves up. Being in the flower business, he can't bear this. He pries himself off the bench and begins the walk toward the party amused that something as superficial as flowers is giving him the strength to go. With each step his mind chants: *These are my friends. These are my friends.*

It makes me so sad. And I just bet that if two boys could marry, he wouldn't have had to go into the bathroom with Mr. Safeway.

When I get born, I'm going to tell Pablo that I think it's stupid that there's one set of rules for girls and boys who love each other and a whole other set for boys who love boys and girls who love girls. Maybe I'll even work at changing the rules, get all political. For all I know—

But wait, here we are, ringing the doorbell.

Nina answers. "Pablo! You made it." She looks so happy to see him that he feels guilty for being so late. He smiles a smile that's obviously trying to cover up his insecurity and says, "I wouldn't miss this for the world."

She takes his hand and tows him into the room. "Look who's here!"

"My apologies to all," he says addressing the room as if they're his constituents, "but the flower business rests for no one." He then presents the bouquet to Dorothy Hale. "For you, Madame." The white tissue paper and blue satin ribbon with a peach rosebud tucked in the knot doesn't disguise the fact that the delphinium are wilted at the tips.

Dorothy blushes. No one ever gives her flowers.

Richard Hale, thrilled that Rick has at least one male friend, stands up to greet Pablo. "At last!" he says. "I was starting to wonder if my son was some kind of pansy."

No one laughs.

Pablo's jaw tightens. He's determined not do the old shrug and smile, but can't very well say: *Actually, I am a pansy, Mr. Hale.* He reminds himself that this is Nina and Rick's day and he shouldn't upstage them. A rascally smile breaks across his face. "Oh, I can assure you, sir, your son is no pansy. Believe me, I know a pansy when I see one."

Richard pops an olive in his mouth. He can't figure out why Rick's friends laugh at Pablo's statement.

"We're just about to eat," Dorothy says, "but could I get you some sangria? Or"— and she's almost afraid to say it as no one so far has taken her up on the lassi— "a lassi?"

"Lassi?" Pablo says. "I love lassi."

Lottie, who's been curious about the lassi since it was first mentioned, chimes in with, "Yes, I'd like to try some of that too!"

Several more guests jump on the lassi wagon as well, which gives me hope that things are finally starting to lighten up. At least Dorothy's happy. I watch gratefully as she floats into the kitchen to pour a tray of lassis.

❖

Dorothy's Indian spread is a hit. Of course Richard keeps saying things like: "All these little bowls sure do make eating complicated," but he's filled his plate twice, and, he's sprinkled more peanuts on his curry than anyone else.

Food, I make a note to myself, is a safe topic. And if there's one thing everybody's sticking to, it's safe topics. They've talked about people's employment, movies, sports, and travel; they've even had the courage to talk about the next day's Love Happening, what's expected of them, and how Nina and Rick chose Slater Park. What they haven't talked about is me. Not one word.

I remind myself that I've come in the wrong order. First comes love, then comes marriage, then comes a baby in the baby carriage.

It doesn't help.

After clearing the plates and bringing out a tray with coffee and fixings, Dorothy presents a chocolate silk pie. "My mother's recipe," she says. This is followed by lots of ooohing and aaahing as the pie gets cut and passed around.

Once everyone's served, Lottie raises her coffee mug and says, "To Nina and Rick! May their love be everlasting."

I watch as they raise their mugs in the air and do their phony smiles. Just eat your damn pie, see if I care!

Then to my astonishment, Hester adds, "And to their little baby!"

Rick's neck flushes.

He glances at Nina.

Although other people's mugs hang in the air with uncertainty, Nina's is still proudly thrust forward waiting for someone else's to meet it. Rick glances once at Richard, then pushes back his chair and stands, his glass held high. "To Spanky!" he says, defiantly. And as if things couldn't get any better, Nina repeats, "To Spanky!" Then Lottie stands. "To Spanky!" Then Missy. "To Spanky!" Then the rest of the Sisters in Solidarity. "To Spanky!" "To Spanky!" "To Spanky!" Before I know it,

Dink is up and so is Pablo. "To Spanky!" "To Spanky!" Then Harvey, then Dorothy. Even Charlotte and Iris toast me. They're shooting off like fireworks.

So what are they waiting for? Why aren't they clinking their mugs?

Ah. Now I see. Richard is still sitting with his eyes locked on Rick's. The two of them are staring each other down like bull and matador.

Come on, Richard! All you have to do is raise your mug in the air and say, To Spanky! What's the big deal? You don't have to mean it. Iris doesn't. She's just "coming to terms" with me. Now raise your stinking mug, dude.

The weird thing is, he wants to, but his bones tell him that a baby preceding a wedding is nothing to cheer about; he simply can't reconcile his desire to join in with his stupid principles.

A small hand slips into his. "Come on, Mr. Hale," Hester says. "Don't you want to toast your grandbaby?"

Of course he can't say no to this, not to a grandchild. Eyes never leaving his son's, the Man of the Hour slowly rises from his chair and raises his mug. "To Spanky."

What a relief! For everyone. They clink mugs, all beamy and warm. Nina's eyes even brim with tears. And the best part is, once my name has been spoken, it *keeps* being spoken.

"When did you start calling her Spanky?" Missy asks.

"Spanky's just for now," Nina says. "Until we decide."

This is news to me. But so what? They're talking about me!

"I, for one, am hoping you'll use a family name," Richard says. "Maybe my mother's or your great aunt Candy's."

Candy?

"She'll be our first little Sssistaaaah!" Lottie says, accompanying this by wagging her pinkies, which set off a rash of pinky action around the room.

Hester pipes in, "Hey! I'm going to be Spanky's aunt! Maybe I'll get to babysit! We can play dress-up together."

Dress-up? How about tossing a ball around?

"We should see about enrolling her in preschool. The good ones have long waiting lists," Iris says.

Preschool?

"I've heard there's a new line of baby's clothes that's made from hemp," Lottie says.

"And of course you're going to breast-feed," Rhonda says.

"There's a great exercise workshop for mothers and babies…"

"I've heard of a ballet class that takes kids as young as four…"

No wonder babies cry so much, I think. They have nine months of backed-up retorts.

By the time the dessert plates are cleared, the conversation has swerved away from me—and boy, am I glad.

The Sisters in Solidarity pull Charlotte aside to show her her costume. Out of context, it does look outrageous: a lavender cape with a gauzy shapeless dress beneath. She imagines she's going to look like a giant grape in the middle of an otherwise normal wedding. As the Sisters try to explain to her that they'll all be wearing fantastical outfits, that it's not a traditional wedding but more of a theatrical event, she drives her teeth into her lower lip to keep from crying.

I can relate. It sucks when people try to get you to be what you're not.

❖

Everyone is gathering up their bags and talking about tomorrow's Love Happening.

Richard, warm from the beer and Indian spices, nudges Pablo. "I'm surprised none of these lovely ladies is at your doorstep. Or are you too smart to get yourself hitched?"

Pablo rests his elbow on Richard's shoulder and says conspiratorially, "You have no idea how smart I am. I've figured out a way to never get married."

Richard chuckles. "Good for you, son. Because believe me, women can be tricky."

Pablo leans in closer and whispers, "To tell you the truth, sir, men can be pretty tricky too."

Richard laughs a giant roar of a laugh and slaps him on the back. "I like you, son! We think the same."

Dink, thoroughly buzzed, stands by the door, checking out Lottie's shapely legs. She shakes her head and promises herself to cut down on the alcohol. Pablo joins her. "We survived," she says.

"We still have tomorrow," he says.

She smiles in a way that seems a bit devious. "Don't worry," she says. "I've got tomorrow all figured out."

I consider scanning her brain to see what she's up to, then decide I don't want to know. It's been a long night as it is.

I zip over to Nina and Rick.

Nina's just poked her head into the kitchen. Rick's standing by the dishwasher looking at the huge pile of dishes. "People are starting to leave," she says.

He turns his back on the dishes, thinking, *Mom can handle it*, then says, "I'll come out."

"How do you think it went?"

"My dad never even said a word to me, except that he thought I might be a pansy."

"At least he came. And he did join in the toast." She takes hold of his waistband and pulls him to her. "You know, in his own curmudgeonly way, he's kind of charming."

Rick kisses her. "He's an insurance salesman. It's part of his job."

"Well, he showed up." She kisses him. "Anyway, you know what they say in the theater biz: a lousy dress rehearsal makes for a great opening night."

He smiles. "Come on. Let's close this puppy out."

As people say their good-byes, Hester comes right up to Nina's belly and says, "Bye, Spanky. See you tomorrow."

This prompts others to join in. "Bye, Spanky!" "Bye!"

I love having a name.

Chapter Twenty-five

In less than one hour I'll be legal. I swear, having to be married before having a baby is one of the stupidest rules I've ever heard. I suppose it's there to protect me. But does getting married really make two people stay together, be responsible parents?

At the moment, I'm hanging with Nina behind one of several ribboned-off backstage spots behind a rhododendron at Slater Park. Through the clumps of schmoozing wedding guests, I take in the weathered, wooden Activities Stage, which the Sisters in Solidarity have tried to transform into a "magical shrine."

Nina's more impressed than me. The green and gold chiffon they've draped everywhere looks like sheets hanging out to dry. The amber vases of star lilies framing the pulpit are nice enough, but the handmade pulpit of curly willow and raffia gives the feeling it could topple over if a person so much as coughed. The Sisters have closed off the stone benches around the stage with ribbon so the forty-odd guests have to enter what's being referred to as the "The Love Circle." The aisle is strewn with dried lavender and rose petals.

Reverend Sky walks by. She's what they call a nondenominational reverend and has pretty much let them do whatever they want. She nods at Nina, but makes a point of giving her space. She's big on giving people space. Earlier in the week when she met with Nina and Rick, she said—several times—"This is your day, give yourself the space to appreciate it." Today she's giving herself space on account of she's jonesing for a smoke. She just quit and her nerves are sizzling like loose wires. Walking toward the stage she smiles at Hester, then at Iris, who's halfway through a smoke. Reverend Sky takes a deep breath of air hoping for a shot of nicotine.

Hester is driving Iris nuts with her squirming. She points to a large lump of fabric taking up the back right side of the platform. "What's under there?"

Iris sucks smoke from her cigarette. "It's probably something that belongs to the park. Gardening equipment or something. I don't think you're supposed to notice it." Iris drags Hester directly to the front row of the Love Circle. She doesn't want to have to chat with someone. She abhors chatting.

"How can you not notice it?"

Iris doesn't answer. She's tired of saying "We'll see" and "I don't know, honey" to Hester's million questions. She pulls a last drag from her smoke and flicks it into the bushes. Last night's dinner made her feel inadequate as a mom. She peers over her shoulder to see if "Dorothy-the-wonder-mother" is chatting like she should be doing, but she doesn't see her.

"Have you seen your dad?" she asks Hester.

I zip over to Harvey. He's outside the Love Circle, his face a cloud of confusion. He knows it shouldn't bug him that Nina doesn't want him to give her away, but it does.

"Uh, Mr. Kalina?"

Harvey focuses on Missy, who he vaguely remembers from the night before. "Yes?"

Missy hands him two scarves of green silk batik. "You and Mrs. Kalina wear these through the ceremony, then fling them at the stage once they do their kiss."

"Fling?" Harvey asks.

"To represent your letting her go."

He lifts the corners of his mouth. "We'll do the best we can." He watches her whisk off with two more scarves for the Hales, then stuffs the scarves in the pocket of his sport jacket. His thoughts are pretty much along the lines of: *How can I let go of what I've never held?* When he steps into the Love Circle he almost bumps into Richard Hale, who's holding a purple silk scarf at arm's length like it's a poisonous snake.

"Hey, Harv! What do you think of these crazy kids?"

Harvey laughs. "This is going to be some wedding!" And then he makes like he can't wait to give Iris her scarf. He hates being called Harv.

I spot Pablo by himself in the back row. He has his feet up on the stone bench in front of him and he's acting all aloof.

Dude! I want to say. *You think you have it bad? They're trying to cover me up. Literally. Have you checked out Nina's dress?*

Something brushes by Pablo's ankle, startling him.

"Franklin! Franklin! Slow down! Honestly, I don't stand a chance at keeping up with you." Viola's flowered-out in a summer kimono decorated with cherry blossoms and a broad-brimmed straw hat sprouting a bunch of silk daisies and one silk rose. "Why hello, Pablo. Do you remember me? I'm…"

"Nina and Rick's landlord."

"Viola Waltz." She places her big floral bag on the bench and plops down next to him. "Whew! You don't mind, do you?"

Pablo decides he doesn't.

She rummages through her purse and comes up with a pack of Chiclets. "Gum?"

He shakes his head, then says, "No thanks," like she's dim or something.

Viola is impervious to his attitude. "Don't mind me, I had garlic for lunch," she says, popping a Chiclet in her mouth. Then she levels him with her crinkly eyes. "This must be a rough day for you."

"Excuse me?"

"Well, you being a," she leans in and whispers, "homosexual and all."

Pablo, unable to believe what she just said, can't think of a response.

"Don't worry," Viola says. "Nina didn't tell me. I knew it the minute I saw you. I'm not sure I ever mentioned this before, but Franklin is a homosexual too. He's out of the closet, though. Has been for years."

Pablo shifts his attention to the porker dog rooting around guests' ankles.

"Before Franklin," she continues, "I'd never really given homosexuals all that much thought, but he's really raised my consciousness. Now I can spot a homosexual anywhere. And they're all over the place! But of course you know that." She leans into him. "And they are always the nicest people." She laughs. "Of course you know *that* too." She places a wrinkled finger with red nail polish on her chin. "Now that I think of it, this kimono was given to me by an old queen I met when I was out walking Franklin. His name is Martin. His companion's name is Rochester. A Pomeranian. Straight as a pin, wouldn't you know! Won't give Franklin the time of day. Isn't that just how it goes? Martin and I get along famously, though. He's just two years older than me and we have so much in common."

Pablo pretends that something fascinating across the park has got his attention.

"Oh, have I upset you, dear?" Viola places her hand on his knee. "Sometimes I am just too forward. I know it. But at my age, I've lost all my reasons for holding back."

The something fascinating that Pablo's staring at turns out to be the Sisters in Solidarity huddled behind a rhododendron.

"What's up with Dink?" Rhonda asks.

Lottie has just applied the final touches to Rhonda's makeup. "Weddings are hard for some people."

"But she's acting extra strange."

They all look at Dink, moping under the dogwood slowly turning a leaf in her fingers. She's wearing Howie's dress uniform with a tiny American flag sewn upside down on the sleeve—Rick's idea—her hair combed back like a boy's.

"She sure has changed since St. Theresa's," Missy says.

Lottie laughs. "I hope we all have!"

I zip over to the groom's tree where Nina's just snuck over to talk to Rick. "You okay?" she asks.

"Yeah. Just kinda trippin'." He doesn't tell her that he's worried about what his coworkers from Jack's are going to think about the "creative" nature of the ceremony. He didn't even want to invite them, but Nina mentioned the wedding to Chad over the phone and then Rick had no choice. Now he can't stop thinking about Wednesday when he gets back to work and has to listen to them taunt him about how gay the whole ceremony was. *Why did I let myself get talked into the white tails and top hat? I feel like the freakin' Mad Hatter.*

"You still want to do this?" Nina asks him. "You have about two more minutes to change your mind."

"I just don't know about all this hoopla…"

"The audience is going to love it, trust me."

"Audience?"

"Guests."

"Friends and family."

"Right. Whatever. Let's just you and me try to really be here, you know? Really see each other when we're up there."

He holds her at arm's length. "I see you. I just don't like being in front of people. I'm not a theater person."

"Just keep your mind on me. And on Spanky." She kisses him lightly on the lips. "I'd better get back to the bride's bush."

He smiles. "I'm pretty fond of the bride's bush myself."

She laughs. "None of that until after the wedding."

Right, I think, *like they've been holding back.*

Nina looks around. "Shouldn't Dink be here with you?"

Rick tips his head in the direction of Dink's dogwood. "She's been over there since she got here."

"She looks kind of spaced."

Rick shrugs. He wishes Howie were here instead of just his clothes.

"All right then, I'll see you up there!" Nina blows a kiss before sneaking back through the foliage.

Guess I should check on Dink. She does look pretty spaced standing there twirling that leaf.

Whoa.

This is strange.

She's not looking at the leaf; she believes she *is* the leaf. The veins of the leaf, she believes, are *her* veins, the experience of the leaf, *her* experience. She feels, deeply, the leaf's sorrow at being detached from the tree and its life force slowly leaking out. No longer is she a woman forlorn, a woman about to hand off her true love to a man she loves as a brother. She's a leaf fallen from the tree of life…and there are other leaves…and twigs…and blades of grass and ants…

She's high as a kite! And not on pot either. It's acid.

I wonder if Pablo knows. If that's part of what's eating at him.

I check.

He doesn't. Dink was afraid he might freak out.

Duh.

Dink twists the leaf's stem between her fingers, thinking she knows how it felt when it was ripped from its mother. *Just like me*, she thinks. *And now we're both slowly dying. Me and the leaf. Leaf and me. Sheleaf...*

Oh brother.

Lottie blows the opening conch shell and guests hurry to their places.

Dink thinks the sound was the tree mourning its long lost leaf. She's dimly aware of Rick walking over and trying to tell her something. Her eyes focus on the undulating buttons of his shirt.

I force myself to focus on the tinkling chimes wafting through the thick afternoon air, on Hester twisting around on the bench trying to see who's doing it, on Iris putting her hand on Hester's leg and telling her to settle down. Anything but Dink.

A recording of Howie on his electric guitar crackles through the speakers and three of the Sisters begin down the aisle. They're supposed to look like pagan goddesses, dressed in the same green and gold chiffon from the stage, their hair all wrapped in ivy—but they're more feral looking than pagan. They dart here, then there, all the while heading toward the stage. Occasionally, one of them shakes a ceramic rattle. One of the guys from Jack's Tires has to pinch his nose to keep from laughing. Another looks on, rapt, as if he's seeing Mother Earth herself.

Rick, mistaking Dink's strange behavior for stage fright, tries to coax her into walking down the aisle with him. "Come on, Dink. Twenty minutes and this will all be over."

Dink puts her hands on his shoulders. "No matter what, man, I love you. You're like a fucking brother to me. And you getting Nina, it's like, perfect, you know? You and Nina are like two leaves that have escaped the rake..."

Rick is too nervous to wonder at her bizarreness. "Let's go. We've just got to walk down that aisle. No big deal."

Dink nods somberly, but her mind is still shooting out crap: *He doesn't see the perfect web of coincidences that have brought us here. He doesn't know. He's perfect in his ignorance. He's as perfect as the breeze...as the clouds...*

"Dink, we've got to do this."

She grins. "Of course. It's time we align ourselves for the next experience."

Erg!

Halfway down the aisle, Dink starts to get paranoid about all the people watching. She focuses on her legs. *Hut two, hut two!* Gazing at Rick's white tails, she tries to regain her composure. She talks herself through the steps up to the stage. *Foot up, foot down. Foot up, foot down.*

Reverend Sky smiles without showing any teeth and Dink is sure that the reverend can read her mind and knows she's tripping. She takes her place to the right of Rick. She looks constipated.

A young woman in a flowing rose dress steps on stage and walks over to the lump of fabric. With a dramatic swoosh she pulls it off, revealing a harp.

Hester gasps. "I knew it wasn't garden equipment!"

"Settle down, Hessy," Iris says.

The rose-draped harpist sits, raises her arms, and awaits her cue.

The guitar music fades. More costumed Sisters flit down the aisle. One of them, Lottie, carries a bowl of burning incense. The rest have rattles. A few guests cough.

Harvey places his hand on Iris's knee, feeling a surge of relief that he *wasn't* called into duty after all. *I might have had to wear tights*, he thinks.

The harpist begins to play.

More clearing of throats.

Charlotte, wearing her purple cape and holding a staff with stars and moons cascading down its length, begins down the aisle. To her credit, she's trying to play the part of She Who Bears Witness. She holds her head high, her eyes trained forward, but it's difficult for her to remain stoic as she has to periodically yank the cape out from beneath her feet.

But nobody's looking at her; their eyes are on Nina. Compared to Charlotte, she seems to float down the aisle, the fabric of her gown so light it hovers. Fixed onto the back of her dress are two silver wings winking with sunshine. Tiny metallic stars surround her eyes.

Hester gasps. "Look at her, Mom. She's beautiful."

My stubborn girl, Iris thinks, *reincarnated as an angel.* She reaches a hand out to Harvey. He squeezes it. *She is beautiful*, his hand says.

"Today we are here to witness a blessed event," Reverend Sky begins and then goes on and on about a bunch of stuff I don't even bother with. I'm waiting for her to get to the part where she lifts her hands in the air and announces, "And now you're allowed to have a baby!"

She never says it, though. She doesn't say anything about babies. Not even: And if you should choose to have a little baby someday, you have to promise to take very good care of her because she's not going to be able to do much more than poop, eat, and cry when she first gets to you. All Reverend Sky does is talk about Nina and Rick loving and respecting each *other*. Not a word about loving and respecting me. The whole thing is a big waste of time. It gets mildly interesting when Nina walks around Rick three times, and he does the same around her. Richard whispers to Dorothy, "What is this, a goddamn cattle auction?"

Franklin, sitting between Pablo and Viola, places his head on Pablo's new trousers and grunts. Pablo shifts, trying to get Franklin to move. Franklin nuzzles in closer. *A gay dog*, Pablo thinks, *too fucking weird.*

"The ring," Reverend Sky says.

Everyone looks at Dink who, to my relief, reaches for the ring. Then she gets sidetracked by her hands. They no longer look like her hands. They're larger and sunburned, and dirt is caked under her ragged nails. A foreign thought passes through her mind: *My last mission. I must usher my friend into wedded life.* She reaches into her breast pocket, but feels no breasts, just a hardened chest like a boy's.

Holy mackerel. She thinks she's Howie back from the dead! She pauses with her hand in her breast pocket and looks out into the row of guests, her eyes stopping on Howie's mother, Candace Hartman.

Mrs. Hartman thinks Rick must have told Dink who she was and wishes he hadn't. It's painful enough to see this girl dressed in Howie's clothes, but to have her stare at her this way is exceedingly uncomfortable.

But Rick didn't tell her, so how dies Dink know who Mrs. Hartman is?

A tremor runs through Mrs. Hartman's body and releases a sensation she hasn't felt in weeks: warmth from the sun. A sob lurches from her throat. A friend sitting behind her places a hand on her shoulder.

"The ring," Reverend Sky repeats.

Dink whispers, "I told you that you could snag the actress, man."

Wait. How could she know that Howie said these *exact* words to Rick that night out by the Dumpster?

I try to get inside Dink's brain, but am blocked out.

Something weird is going on.

Rick knows it too and a chill runs up his spine. His eyes fill with tears. *Get a grip*, he thinks. *She's not Howie. She can't be.*

"The ring," Reverend Sky says one more time.

Dink flushes and steps back to keep from tipping backwards. *Damn, I'm fucked up. For a moment there I really thought I was...* She feels the box with the ring in her hand and thrusts it forward. "Here. Here's the ring. I got it. I got the ring."

Hand shaking, Rick takes it and turns toward Nina. *What the hell just happened?* he thinks. *I feel like I've just seen Howie.*

When he looks into Nina's eyes, he's glad she chose not to wear a veil. Her eyes center him. He begins reciting his vows, but all that's really happening is his mouth is wrapping around the memorized words. He doesn't hear a word he's saying. He's too tripped out. Nina, on the other hand, tries so hard to be sincere during her vows that it makes me wonder what she's trying to convince herself of. Not that it matters. All Rick hears are a bunch of consonants and vowels, and the guests can't hear much of anything at all due to a plane that passes overhead. Fortunately, Rick manages to utter "I do" when he's supposed to, as does she.

When it's time for the kiss, the Sisters in Solidarity step in with lighted sparklers and kneel in a circle around the newly married couple, framing their faces in lights.

"You gotta admit they have style," Viola whispers to Pablo.

Pumped full of adrenaline, Rick strays from what he and Nina rehearsed and takes her head in his beautiful hands and kisses her lightly on the forehead.

She tilts her head up to see what's gotten into him. *Is he going to kiss me for real?* she wonders.

A huge grin spreads across his face, which then spreads onto hers. They step into one another. She rises up onto her toes and puts her hands on his shoulders. He wraps his arms around her waist. And at last, their lips meet in one long, whopping, soppy kiss.

Viola throws her hat in the air. "Encore!" The rest of the guests burst into applause.

Busting with pride, Rick and Nina turn to walk back down the aisle where the guests have begun blowing bubbles. For a moment I think Iris, Harvey, Dorothy, and Richard are going to forget to fling their scarves of attachment, but Lottie waves her arms frantically and gestures to the strips of fabric, reminding them of their duty.

The scarves drop to the ground like kites on a windless day. Nobody but Lottie notices. Or cares. The Kalinas and the Hales have merged.

I notice Dink rubbing her temples. Is it possible The Known let Howie's soul hang around long enough to make one last appearance? I had no idea this was an option…yet it's so perfect. I got his blessing. And I have a family! I'm legal!

Chapter Twenty-six

Nina flops down on the too-firm king-size bed in the honeymoon suite at the Babbling Brook Inn. "I'm exhausted!"

Rick places their suitcases on the luggage stand and flops next to her. "Ditto."

"Would it be too anticlimactic if we took a nap?"

"Sounds great, wife."

"Okay, hubby."

They begin shucking their shoes and clothes. "When do you suppose I'll start collecting holiday aprons?" Nina asks.

"When I start obsessing over my lawn."

Naked, she slips between the crisp white sheets. "Let's not ever be that way."

He joins her. "We won't."

Moments later, they're conked out like an old married couple.

I long for a little shut-eye myself, only I don't have eyelids yet. I have managed to grow my own tiny set of fingerprints, but you'd never know it without a powerful microscope. Still, I think they're pretty cool. I especially like the spiral on my right thumb.

Fingerprints. Such a blatant stamp of separateness, of individuality, of me-ness.

What if Nina and Rick don't like me? What if they think I'm boring or hyperactive? Or not girlie enough? It worries me that they got to choose each other, but I just foisted myself into their lives.

❖

Nina wakes two hours later to Rick drawing with his finger on her swollen belly. She pretends to continue sleeping while he gives me a spelling lesson. M.O.M. he traces. “That’s who to call when you’re hungry.” Then, D.A.D. “That’s who to call when you need a good story.”

Is it time to start calling him Dad? Her, Mom? Do I dare? It seems so optimistic. There are still so many things that could go wrong… Then again, I’d hate to evaporate without ever having experienced the feeling of having a mom and a dad.

Here goes.

Dad’s attention shifts from Mom’s belly to her nipples, which are standing up like gumdrops. Dad cups Mom’s breast in his callused hand and whispers in her ear, “I’d love you even if you did collect aprons.” He nips her nipple.

Mom runs her fingers through his hair. “Slow,” she says. “Like it’s our first time.”

In between nipples, Dad utters, “We didn’t go slow our first time.”

“So let’s tonight.”

“I’ll try.” Dad sits up, lifting Mom onto his lap. He cuddles her buttocks.

Mom pushes him onto his back. “I can see I’m going to have to instruct you in the art of slow.”

“Teach me, Mrs. Kalina-Hale.”

Mom, now straddling Dad, says, “You might want to take notes.”

Ick. Calling them Mom and Dad changes everything.

I shift my focus to the picture above the bed. It’s a golden retriever with a raised paw. La la la la la…

Once Mom and Dad are finished, they lie in a pile of rumpled sheets with silly smiles on their faces. Mom leans over him to reach the room service menu on the nightstand. “Let’s use some of our wedding money to live it up. How about we have some beef?”

He drums a light rhythm on her tush. “You didn’t get enough just now?”

She laughs, then orders two porterhouse steaks with baked potatoes and mixed summer vegetables.

They dine dressed in plushy white hotel robes. They’d been too wound up to eat at their Love Happening, so now they’re starving.

"Your father gave me a very sweet hug," Mom says, her mouth full of potato.

Dad pierces a zucchini slice. "Hmph."

"I think he's trying."

"How about that toast he gave, saying how proud he was?"

"I thought it was nice."

"It was bullshit. He was saying it because he thought that's what fathers *should* say."

Dad thinks back on that day at the garage when Richard implied that I might not be his, that Nina was just marrying him to get herself out of trouble. Fortunately, he keeps his mouth shut.

"Well, he showed up. That's what matters," Nina says.

Dad piles potato onto a bite of steak and shoves it in his mouth.

Mom thinks, *I'm going to help him heal his relationship with his father.*

What a crock! She can't even sort things out with her own parents, yet she's certain she can help Dad with his.

Mom calls in for an order of baked Alaska. When it arrives they feed it to each other, licking it off each other's fingers and lips and…

More quality time with the dog portrait.

When they finish this time, Mom curls up with her head on Dad's shoulder and he listens to her breathe. He's thinking about Howie. "What do you think happens when we die?" he whispers. But Mom is already asleep.

FINGERS AND TOES

Chapter Twenty-seven

Mom and Dad have been married for two months and already they've sunk into a routine. Dad works at Jack's five days a week; and when he's not doing that he's doing odd jobs for Viola to help offset the rent; and when he's not doing either of those things he's hanging out with us. This doesn't leave much time for his music. Last week he saw a posting on the computer about some guys putting a jazz band together, but he was too busy to make the audition. He keeps thinking about it, though, wishing he'd been able to squeeze it in. He also thinks he's going to have to get a new job. Here's what he's come up with so far: firefighter, ambulance driver, park ranger, disc jockey, or run a small business. He needs a new job because I'm going to be expensive.

Mom's still doing occasional temp work—filing, answering phones, making copies—but she hasn't committed to any one job because she's going to be a famous actress. Once I'm born, she'll spend the first few years at home with me. This will make me healthier in the long run. Then, when I get a bit older, I'll accompany her to rehearsals. She imagines stage managers helping with my math homework, while actresses help with English. They'll all be such good influences on me and will teach me to think for myself and feel real feelings. And, on nights when rehearsals run late, I'll stay at home with Dad, who'll have a good job by then, one that pays plenty of money, but that will also allow him to have nights free.

But what if Dad gets into a band that rehearses at night? Who's going to take care of me then? Or what if the stage manager is bad at math, or the actress sucks at English?

Besides these worries, I've got the construction of my body to keep up with. Every day there are huge changes, new additions.

My pee-pee, for instance.

It's an innie.

Which is really no surprise, but I guess I was still kind of holding out for a miracle.

On a lighter note, I'm starting to be able to manipulate my facial muscles. So far I've managed two frowns and several squints. Both frowns were in reference to the aforementioned setback. But I'm determined not to fall into the common trap that most people in The Land of Forgetting fall into: thinking my body *is* me. We are so much more than our biological headquarters! We are physical manifestations of The Known, inhaling and exhaling consciousness, our bodies simply vehicles to help us gain experience—knowledge.

With this in mind, I figure I should get in as much last-minute astral travel as I can. If I'm lucky, I'll be able to remember some of my adventures after I'm born—even if I do have to go to a hypnotist to recall them.

❖

Tonight we're at a cast party for a musical called *Jesus Christ Superstar*. It's a flashy crowd and the music is blaring. Jacques, Pablo's dancer friend, is playing one of Jesus' disciples and he invited Pablo, who invited Dink who invited Mom who invited Dad. And then Lottie, who ran into Dink at a stationery store, asked if she could come too, because, like my mom, she wants to make more connections. She even told Dink she'd drive, which turned out to be good because the party is close to an hour from home and Dad's Duster has begun making a strange ticking noise that he thinks he should have checked out.

So now we're all here at this crowded party.

Mom is wearing an empress-cut tunic to disguise me, but it isn't working. People can definitely tell I'm here, which is getting in her way as she tries to make her connections. As she gloms on to a bunch of disciples and their boyfriends, none of them is taking her inquiries seriously. For one thing, they've just come off the stage and are pumped up. Also, Mom didn't see the show, which is making it hard for her to join the conversation. The main reason these guys are blowing her off, though, is me. Being pregnant doesn't make her particularly castable; and once she has me, they assume she won't be able to swing the late nights of the profession. This makes me feel a tad guilty, but it makes Mom mad. "So, did you have to be union to get an audition?" she asks.

I'm glad she's not giving up. I'll come with her to rehearsals. I'll even try not to cry too much. Or maybe we can get Dad to babysit.

Speaking of Dad, he's standing alone by the fireplace drinking a beer and feeling sorry for himself. He looks over at Mom surrounded by gay guys and wishes he hadn't come. *This is her scene, not mine*, he thinks.

"Some party," a tall man next to him says.

Dad thinks this guy might be trying to pick him up, so all he says is, "Uh…yeah."

"These things can go on all night," the stranger says.

"Sounds like you come—have gone to a lot of them."

"I'd have to say yes to that."

"I see," Dad says. "*I'm* not a regular." His words draw an invisible line between him and the man.

The man doesn't seem to notice. "When you're married to Mary Magdalene, you don't have much of a choice," he says.

"Excuse me?"

"My wife. She played Mary Magdalene."

"Oh!" Dad says, and boy, is he relieved. Too relieved, if you ask me. What would have been so hard about just saying "No, thank you, I like girls"? I try frowning, but can't quite get it to work. Shoot! I need more practice so I can express myself at will.

The man takes a swig of his drink. "Yeah. That's her in the feather boa. Last show, she played a hooker too, only blond. *Threepenny Opera*. I told her pretty soon I'm going to start claiming a cut. You know? As her pimp?"

Dad laughs so hard he starts coughing.

"Damn! I knew I was funny, but I didn't know I was *that* funny! My name is Steve Williams."

"Rick Hale. Glad to meet you." *Now* my dad likes the guy. *Now* he thinks they could be friends.

I see Dink hanging out at the bar by herself. She's wondering what the audience members would think if they could see Jesus Christ's disciples after hours—*Flamers, all of them!* She sighs. *But these are my people. Even though I still haven't kissed a girl!* She shakes her head and chuckles.

Lottie sidles up next to her. "What's so funny?"

Dink sobers up. "Nothing."

Lottie refills her glass of wine. "Mind if I hang out with you? Or would you rather continue laughing at your own jokes?"

Dink doesn't know what to make of Lottie's request; she thought Lottie came to make connections the way Mom did. She shrugs. "No. I mean, sure. You can hang out with me."

Lottie takes Dink's hand. "Come on. Let's go find a place to sit."

They pass two women slow dancing and Dink can't figure out why she feels so tongue-tied. But I know why. She's thinking what it would be like to slow dance with Lottie. Dink thinks Lottie looks pretty in her black minidress, red platform shoes, and pink granny glasses. She pulls a smoke from her pocket and lights up, never once letting go of Lottie's hand.

But what's this? The door pushes open and reveals three men who completely blow my latest theory about girls being the ones to wear uncomfortable clothes. Out front is a tall coffee-colored man with a platinum blond wig. He's cinched into yards of shimmering turquoise chiffon with itchy-looking turquoise feathers on the bottom edges of his bell-like sleeves and skirt. Huge rhinestone clusters are clamped onto his earlobes. And behind him are three men in matching gold lamé gowns and short-cropped auburn wigs. Their starched circular collars stand high behind their heads, digging into their collarbones. When they merge together they create one giant setting sun. These guys' outfits take the cake! They *look* like decorated cakes. And their shoes seem super uncomfortable, like Lottie's, and hard to walk in too.

Since when do boys get to wear dresses? How did I miss this?

Lottie, who's guided Dink to a window seat covered with pillows, whispers, "Would you check out the fabric that just walked through the door? That is some pricey stuff. The beadwork is amazing…"

Dink is listening to Lottie go on about the fabric, but this is what she's thinking: *Would it be okay to put my arm around Lottie?*

I hope she does. It might bring her out of this mood she's been in.

Lottie leans against her.

Dink's heart starts to accelerate. She brings her smoke to her mouth, trying to appear cool, but she's afraid to even look at Lottie. She gazes out onto the party without seeing it.

"I think gay people are hot," Lottie says.

Dink blurts, "I'm gay," before realizing that her lips are even moving. She clears her throat, hoping her blurt sounded more relaxed than it felt, like this isn't her first time to say she's gay since telling Pablo.

"I thought you might be," Lottie says. The electricity coursing between them snaps and pops like the bowl of Rice Krispies my dad had for breakfast.

Lottie takes Dink's hand with the lit Marlboro and brings it to her own mouth. When she takes a drag, she brushes Dink's fingers with her lips. Dink's panties get moist.

This is great! Lottie wants Dink to kiss her. And if Dink does it, and it's a good kiss, she might quit thinking about being in love with Mom and get on with being my aunt. It's okay by me if Lottie is my aunt too. I like Lottie; she has style. And having lesbian aunts would be groovy.

A guy swaggers by with his arm around his girlfriend.

Wait! It's not a guy. It's a girl who dresses and moves like a guy. Her hair is greased back in a ducktail and she's wearing a killer motorcycle jacket and leather pants. She and her girlfriend join some friends by the refreshment table. They're all talking and laughing—Hang on! One of the guys *used* to be a *girl*, and most of them know it, and they don't care. This is amazing! I had no idea this option even existed. The Land of Forgetting is so much more complex, so much richer, than I imagined…

My musings are cut short by the music shutting off and the host of the party standing on a chair and yelling, "Jesus would like to make a toast!"

The room quiets.

The host steps off the chair and offers his hand to the man in the turquoise dress, who flutters his false eyelashes like butterflies while stepping up onto the chair. "Well, it's not a toast really…"

Steve Williams whispers to Dad, "He looks really different in a tunic."

"That's Jesus?" Dad asks.

"God's only begotten."

Jesus continues. "I mean..." he whispers in a throaty tone that sounds like a girl's voice. "I just think it's time we add a new commandment."

"Tell it like it is, sister!" someone yells from the crowd.

Sister? Did someone just call him "Sister"? I love this!

"I just think it's time we add an *eleventh* commandment." More whoops and catcalls. "And the eleventh commandment should say..." He, rather, *she* brings her hand up to fix her hair. "It should say..." Her eyelids close for a moment, displaying a lot of silver-blue eye shadow, then, like a rolling window shade, snap back up, revealing eyes that blaze anger. "Thou shalt *not* stick your *ugly* noses into other people's sexual affairs. What they do in the bedroom is their *own* damn business!"

Everybody whoops and cheers. Me included. In fact, I think I'm experiencing my first crush. I love Jesus! She doesn't care *what* people think about her really being a boy. She's a knockout and she knows it.

I glance back at the circle of friends talking with the boy who used to be a girl. He looks so happy, so sure of himself—and everybody in the group seems to love him. But what's this? A couple of women have joined the group, and they're about to have a baby—together. They're talking about the father and his organic farmer boyfriend. How awesome is that?

I decide to try smiling, but it comes out like my squint. Darn! This would have been a perfect moment. I've found my tribe!

❖

On the way home, I have to try hard not to let my parents' mood ruin the night for me.

Dad is mulling over "that bull dyke" at the party. He's mad because when she went into the bathroom after him, she gave him shit for leaving the toilet seat up. *I hope Nina doesn't expect me to go to too many more theater parties*, he thinks. *The people are too off the wall.*

I want to scream, *But that's one of the things you liked about her when you met! Her bohemian scene! Why are you changing your mind now?*

And Mom is just plain pissed. She's heard tales of a "gay mafia" that dominates the theater scene, but this is her first exposure to it. The director of the play would not give her the time of day and neither would the producer. *So stuck up!* she thinks. *But I'll show them.* She's also obsessing over the fact that Lottie is letting Dink drive her van. Lottie never lets anyone drive her van and now here's Dink in the driver's seat driving. What's more, she and Lottie are holding hands. Mom can see it plain as day because their hands are clasped in the opening between the two seats. Mom can't take her eyes off the way Lottie's thumb keeps caressing Dink's palm. *They're just acting that way because of the party*, she thinks.

Dad puts his arm around her.

She glances over at Pablo. He's out cold, his head tipped onto his shoulder. Mom returns her attention to the sight of Dink and Lottie's hands intertwined. She scoots down in the seat, trying to pretend she doesn't care.

When we reach Pablo and Dink's, where Lottie is supposed to let everyone off, Dink doesn't get out from behind the wheel.

Mom stands in the back open doorway of the van. "Dink, aren't you coming?"

Lottie twists in the seat to face Mom. "She's spending the night at my place. I have to dye some fabric in the morning and she said she'd help out."

Mom slides the van door closed—*Whap!*—and takes Dad's hand.

"You okay?" he asks.

"I'm fine."

They watch the van drive off.

Mom turns toward Pablo. "What was that all about?"

He yawns. "What?"

"Those two suddenly acting gay."

He rubs his eyes. "Dink *is* gay."

"Since when?"

"Since forever. I don't know about Lottie." Pablo pulls his keys from him pocket. "Now, I've got to go to sleep. 'Night, guys."

Mom and Dad walk down the street to their car. "I don't believe it," Mom says. "She would have told me."

"At least she's not all *gay* gay," he says.

Mom's too tired, and too consumed with jealousy, to ask what he means by this.

And Dad…his attitude is bugging me big-time.

How could such a fantastic night have gone so horribly sour?

Chapter Twenty-eight

Eyelids! These are going to come in handy. I'll be able to choose what I want and don't want to see. And I'll be able to sleep. What a joy to block everything out and retreat into dreamland. It's exhausting to be stuck in this constant state of wakefulness.

I wonder why our other senses aren't provided this courtesy? Like, why no ear flaps? Or nose plugs? Maybe if I had a flap for my heart it wouldn't hurt so much.

Dink doesn't love us anymore. That's what Mom and I think.

Right now, Mom's folding laundry while Dad flips channels on his TV. Mom is mad at Dad because Dink hasn't called her in six weeks. Well, that's not how Mom would explain it. She'd say she's mad because he didn't tell her that he had lunch with Dink last week and she had to hear it from Pablo. But it's Dink she's mad at. Dad just happens to be in the way.

She smoothes a T-shirt out on the couch and folds the sleeves toward the middle. "Why didn't you tell me?"

"There was nothing to tell. I ran into her at the deli. We ate lunch together. Big deal."

"It *is* a big deal. You know she hasn't been returning my calls."

Dad has a headache. "She's probably been busy."

"Did you ask?"

"Why would I? That's between you and her."

"Rick!"

Mom gives up folding his T-shirt, wads it into a ball, tosses it into the basket, then goes to the bedroom and shuts the door. *Dink is my friend*, she thinks, *not his.* She picks up her cell phone and dials Dink's number. It rings five times, which means the machine is going to pick it up. Again.

At first Mom isn't going to leave another message, then she decides to.

I zip over to see if Dink is screening.

She is. Just like last time.

She's standing in the doorway of her bathroom with a wet paint roller in her hand.

"Dink, this is Nina. It's really starting to make me feel weird that you're not returning my calls. Do you think I don't want you to be gay? Is that it? Because I'm glad you're gay. Or not glad. I'd like you just as much if you weren't… I'm just trying to say it doesn't matter to me whether you're gay or not. You're my friend and you always will be. Or maybe this isn't about the gay thing at all. Maybe there's some other reason you're not calling me. Did I say something wrong? Or do something? Please call. I'm trying not to get my feelings hurt, but you're making it hard…" There's a pause on the line. "Oh, and I've got a midwife. I'm going to have a home delivery. My dad is totally freaked, but it's what Rick and I want." Another pause. "If it makes any difference to you, my midwife's gay. Anyway, call me. Okay?"

Dink waits for the sound of the click, then dips her roller into the pan of paint and climbs back up the ladder. *Fwwwwip! Fwwwwip! Fwwwwip!*

Pablo steps into the doorway, careful to stay out of the spray of her roller. "You should call her."

"Did you get the paint thinner?"

Pablo holds up a deli bag. "That and lunch."

"You god, you!" She climbs down the ladder and is about to step into the hall when he blocks her way.

"Don't! You'll track paint."

At first she's annoyed, then she sits on the bathroom floor, followed by Pablo. They unwrap their sandwiches. Pablo pulls up a corner of bread to make sure it's the ham and swiss. "Now, what was it you said you needed to whine at me about?"

Dink leans against the tub. "I'm having girl problems."

"And you want *my* advice?" He bites into his sandwich.

Dink plucks a strip of lettuce from her turkey and avocado and stuffs it in her mouth. "Let me rephrase: I'm having gay problems. Last night Lottie told me she wasn't a lesbian."

"And?"

"We'd just had incredible sex."

Pablo puts his sandwich back on the wrapper and picks up his soda. "You gonna eat your pickle?"

"Pablo!"

"So she's bi, what's the big deal?"

"But why would she tell me right after we made love? And I mean *right* after."

Pablo puts his finger on his chin and pretends to think. "Mmm… Because she wants to leave her options open? Or, ah, maybe the sex wasn't as incredible for her as it was for you. Or maybe it *was* and that scared her." He leans forward. "Now, seriously, do you want that pickle or don't you?"

If she's not going to talk about Mom I'd just as soon go home.

Mom's lying on the bed staring at the ceiling.

Dad pokes his head in. "It got awfully quiet in here. You okay?"

"I just wish she'd tell me what I did."

Dad sits on the edge of the bed and kisses her forehead. "If I run into her again, I'll ask."

Mom starts to smile, but her eyes fill with tears.

Dink doesn't want to be in our family anymore. The woman who was going to be my cool Auntie Dink has turned out to be a big promise-breaker. If I could cry, I'd join Mom.

❖

Okay. Maybe I spoke too soon. Dink's been coming around again, dropping by occasionally, or calling, but she always acts like someone's making her do it. And she's always got someone with her, usually a girlfriend. And she never asks about me. One time I even heard her call Mom and Dad "The Breeders" behind their backs, and me, "Little It."

I hate her.

This afternoon, she's here with her newest girlfriend. This one's name is Gaia and she has blond dreadlocks and a sarong tied over her tattered jeans and big hoop earrings. The two of them woke Mom up from a perfectly good nap; one she needed. Mom needs lots of naps lately because she has to pee about eight times a night.

Iris and Harvey are coming over for lunch before we all head to the Hales'. They're due in an hour. We have a big day planned. Mom,

Dorothy, and Iris are going shopping for me while Dad, Richard, and Harvey get to go to a football game. Dad just went for sandwiches.

Mom, who's gone into the kitchen to make coffee for Dink and her new girlfriend, lays her head down on the countertop and uses her arms as a pillow. She feels like she could fall asleep standing up.

"You giving birth in there, Nina?" Dink calls out.

What do you care? I think. *You're not my aunt anymore.*

But Mom laughs a phony-sounding laugh and peels herself off the counter to fill the coffeepot with water. "Does your friend want cream and sugar?" She knows it's rude to say "your friend" instead of remembering Gaia's name, but she's too tired to care.

If I had the ability to forget names, I would *for sure* forget Gaia's. I might even forget Dink's.

Mom watches the water drip through the filter, wishing that she and Dink could talk like they used to. She pulls two mugs from the cabinet, pours the coffee, then puts the filled mugs, a pitcher of milk, and a bowl of sugar onto her favorite tray and heads into the living room. "So…what did you say your name was?"

Gaia doesn't seem the least bit perturbed that she's already told Mom twice. She fiddles with a bead on one of her blond dreadlocks and says, "Gaia."

Dink puts her arm around Gaia. "She chose the name herself."

"Oh." Mom is not the least bit impressed. She thinks Gaia is a big fake.

Gaia picks up the pitcher of milk. "Is this dairy?"

Mom nods.

Gaia puts it back down and smiles. "I believe everyone has a soul name." She scowls at the sugar. "I don't suppose you have any honey?"

Mom ignores her. "Do you have a soul name, Dink?"

Dink shifts uncomfortably on the couch. "Not yet."

"I see." Mom eases herself into the chair.

The lock on the door rattles and Dad comes in carrying a couple of sacks from the deli. He's surprised to see Mom awake and visiting.

Dink stands. "Hey, Rick."

Dad glances at Mom, hoping for some signal that she and Dink have worked things out, but Mom's pursed lips are pulled to one side. "Let me put these down," he says to Dink, "so I can give you a hug."

"This is my friend Gaia."

Dad puts the deli sacks on the table and shakes Gaia's hand. "Nice to meet you." He continues to act like Dink's not loving us is no big deal.

"They're on their way to picket the army recruitment office," Mom says.

"Very cool," Dad says.

"I have to do something," Gaia says. "My brother's in Iraq."

"Rick lost his best friend," Dink says.

Gaia's hand flies to her chest. "I'm so sorry…"

Dad shrugs. He doesn't want to talk about Howie's death with a stranger.

"You should come with us," Gaia says, kicking off her sandals and wrapping her legs underneath her.

Dad glances at Mom. "I wish we could."

"Don't let me stop you." Mom gets up and walks over to the deli sacks.

"I just meant we have your family—my family too…"

She rummages through the bag. "You didn't get egg salad? I asked you to get egg salad."

"Honey, chill. They were out."

Gaia is so clueless she doesn't get that my parents are having a hard time. "They're already making plans to invade Iran," she says. "It's a fucking war machine."

Dink pats Gaia's thigh. "We should go."

"I'm sorry, did I say something? I just get so worked up."

Dad walks behind Mom and circles his arms around her. "We're both just tired. And a bit cranky."

Mom leans into Dad. She likes how he can take her full weight, even with me. She rests her arms on top of his. "We do wish we could go. Both of us. We're just a little tied up at the moment." Then, to my horror, she gestures toward me as if *I'm* the reason they're so short-tempered with one another.

Sure, blame me, I think. *What have you got to lose? I'm the only one without a voice to defend myself.*

Then it occurs to me I *can* defend myself.

I give Mom a good swift kick.

"She's kicking." Mom smiles.

"You should feel this," Dad says to Dink. "It's amazing."

Surprising all of us, Dink gets up and places her hand on Mom's belly.

I give it the old one-two.

"Whoa!" Dink says. "That Spanky's feisty."

Mom laughs. "You're telling me. She kept me up half the night."

And for the first time in a long time, Mom and Dink look into one another's eyes. "You doing okay?" Dink asks softly.

Mom's eyes tear up. "It's all happening pretty fast."

"Rick," Dink says, "this wife of yours needs a shoulder rub."

Rick laughs. "She's all yours." He goes to unload sandwiches.

Mom's eyes flick over to Gaia. "Dink, you don't have to."

Dink claps her hands and begins rubbing them together. "You would say no to one of Dink's world-famous shoulder rubs?"

Nina sits and lets Dink massage the tightness from her shoulders.

Gaia says, "I sure didn't mean you should go to the demonstration in your condition."

Mom tunes her out.

Dad and Dink exchange smiles.

Gaia slips off the couch, kneels at Mom's feet, and begins a foot massage. At first, Mom's muscles tense, but it feels so good, Mom can't help but give in. She closes her eyes.

"Are you going to breast-feed your baby?" Gaia asks, yanking matter-of-factly at her toes.

Mom is so far off in Never Never Land that she doesn't realize Gaia is talking to her.

"Nina?" Dink says.

"Huh?"

"Are you going to breast-feed Spanky?"

"Of course," she says followed by a long groan.

"I was just asking," Gaia says, "because I know a woman who makes a special nipple salve from honey and beeswax. I could get you some if you want."

Beeswax? You've got to be kidding me.

But Mom thinks it sounds nice and opens her eyes to send a smile to Gaia. "That would be great."

Gaia releases Mom's toes to stand. "Hang on. I've got her business card in my car."

Once she's out of the apartment, Mom asks Dink tentatively, "So you and Lottie aren't seeing each other anymore?"

When Dink's hands momentarily stop kneading, I think, *Here it goes, Dink's going to bolt again.* But she doesn't. She starts back up with the massage. "We still see each other occasionally. It's kind of weird, though. I don't think she's really…um…gay."

"Like you."

Dink tips her head back and does a little smile. "Yeah. Like me."

They're both silent for a few seconds. Then Mom says, "You deserve someone really great."

Dink laughs and gives my Mom's shoulders a final squeeze. "I'm going to get another cup of coffee."

"Would you pour me a tiny one?"

Dink cocks her eyebrow. "No way. We don't want Spanky doing the jitterbug down there."

Who needs caffeine? I'm already buzzing with adrenaline. I got Auntie Dink to love us again. All it took was one well-timed kick.

Chapter Twenty-nine

Time to face the music. Shopping for a baby. Where the first lines of gender territory are drawn—in powder blue and powder pink.

The day was Dorothy's idea and started with the notion that I was going to need a bunch of stuff that Nina and Rick probably couldn't afford. She called Iris and said wouldn't it be fun if the two soon-to-be grandmothers took Nina on a shopping trip. This didn't sound fun to Iris, who generally dislikes shopping, but she said okay. She didn't want it getting back to Nina that she'd shirked her grandmotherly duties. With this small success under her belt, Dorothy went on to include the men, suggesting they could use the day to get to know one another as well. Richard, who after the wedding seems to have forgotten all about disinheriting Rick, agreed immediately and suggested they go see a local college football game.

My thought was to stick with the guys and do a little shirking of my own, but football is turning out to be agonizing. That's because we have to stand around the snack bar and "shoot the shit" with the guys first, which is really boring because the only one who has any shit to shoot is Richard.

"Fred, Chuck, you remember my son. Well, guess what? He finally tied the knot! And imagine! The girl's father is still speaking to me!"

Fred and Chuck laugh; Dad looks down at his shoes; Harvey tries to appear interested; and Richard segues into what he calls customer relations. "How's that policy working for you?" He sees another pal. "Dan the man! Working hard, or hardly working?"

Dad's ready to pull out his hair. Harvey is too.

During a lull in shit-shooting, Richard turns to Harvey. "I tell you, I sell more policies out here at a game than I ever do at the office!" He looks over to Dad. "Isn't that right, son?"

Dad shrugs. "So you say."

Richard puts his soda on a white plastic table, places his hand on Dad's shoulder, and looks him squarely in the eye. "Son, now that you're married, you'll learn how important the men in your life are." He elbows Harvey. "Am I right, Harv? Or am I right?" He doesn't wait for Harvey to respond. "A man's got to have a place where he doesn't need to tiptoe around. Where he can be all man and not offend." He burps loudly. "You catch my drift?"

Dad glances self-consciously at Harvey, then crushes his empty soda can with one hand as if it's no big deal. "What do you say we lay off the lectures for one day, Dad?"

Richard roars with laughter. "Would you get a load of this kid? Thinks he knows every goddamned thing." He waves his finger at Dad. "But you'll see. *You'll* see."

But Richard is the one who's not seeing things. The changes in his and Dorothy's relationship have him so anxious that the crack-shot shit-shooter has had to make two trips to the doctor about his ulcer.

Unable to stand his theatrics any longer, I decide to do what I swore I wouldn't: Check in with the shopping.

❖

I arrive just as Mom, Iris, and Dorothy are entering Little Darlings, an upscale baby store.

It's worse than I imagined. It's decorated with babies riding rainbows, babies with flower petals sticking out of their heads, and babies sleeping on clouds. Boys' stuff is on one side and girls' stuff all the way on the other. Like they don't want them to contaminate each other, like it would be the worst crime in the world for someone to mistakenly pick up a girl's outfit for a boy.

Dorothy leads them to the back of the store. "Let's get the big stuff first, then we can do the fun part."

By "big stuff" she means instruments of restraint. They pick out a highchair, a bassinet, a car seat, and a scary-looking thing called a playpen. The designers of these malicious cages have decorated them in bright colors with goofy toys that dangle and ring, but they can't fool me, I know they're all about keeping me in line. I pacify myself with the thought that I'll grow out of them in a few years, leaving Mom and Dad with a bunch of junk.

We move on to the clothing section, where even Iris gets sucked in by the cuteness of the displays, cooing over a pair of tiny mittens, a palm-sized pair of silver slippers. I'm relieved to find that the newborn section includes some unisex items for expectant parents who don't already know the sex of their child, but since Mom does know she goes straight for a pink romper with a sparkly unicorn on it. "This is soooo cute." It doesn't occur to her to stroll across the aisle to check out the rompers with rocket ships and racecars. Nor does she see the cool Indian moccasins or engineer pajamas.

She picks up a hat that will turn my head into a tulip.

I give her a nice strong kick.

She smiles and says to Dorothy, "I think Spanky likes it."

Dorothy puts it in the basket.

I wonder if the football has started yet.

❖

Wow! It has, and it's better than I could have imagined! There are guys running, guys throwing things, guys crashing into each other, more running, more kicking. The best part, though, is all the yelling. Dad, Richard, and Harvey are hooting like nuts.

"Go! Go! Go!" my dad screams to one of the green team running toward a goal.

He, Richard, and Harvey are standing in the bleachers with their fists ready to fling above their heads. Then a blue team guy crashes into the green team guy and they both tumble to the ground. A bunch of other guys, green and blue, pile on top. It's awesome! They're all yelling at each other and a guy wearing black and white has to come over and break it up, and one of the guys on the green team starts screaming at the black-and-white guy, and the black-and-white guy blows his whistle and gestures something that gets everyone in the stands angry.

"Are you crazy?" Richard shouts.

Harvey and Dad groan.

A group of sturdy women in front of us, who've been getting drunker and yelling louder than anyone else here, yell obscenities.

A half an hour later the same green team guy runs down the field with blue team guys diving at him, but they never get him and he makes it all the way to the end. He throws the ball on the ground, hard, and it bounces way up into the air and Harvey and Dad and Richard and everyone else in the bleachers leap to their feet and yell and hug and jump up and down, shouting, "Yes! Yes!" And the green team guys on the field are all jumping around too—and jumping on each other. It's a blast!

This is what I want to do when I grow up. I want to suit up in a helmet and pads, go out on the field and crash into guys, just like that green team guy.

❖

Mom, Iris, and Dorothy are just now returning to Dorothy's to wait for the men to get back. Mom is so tired that Dorothy sends her upstairs to take a nap. Well, first she excuses herself to remove her personal belongings out of Dad's old room. She doesn't want Mom or Iris to know she's not sleeping with Richard anymore. But once this is done the grandmothers have drinks while Mom and I go upstairs.

Sitting on the bed that used to be Dad's, she looks at the sloped wall with dormer windows punched through and imagines Dad sleeping here. She pulls up a folded quilt from the bottom of the bed and covers her legs, then reaches down to the bag of stuff they bought today. She removes a simple lavender onesie that says SWEET, a pair of tiny pajamas decorated with hearts and butterflies, a bib with a tiara on it, and her favorite, the tulip hat. She spreads them out on the bed. "What do you think, Spanky? Do you like?"

All I can say is, I hope I'm not too big a disappointment.

Chapter Thirty

With each new day, the fear of crossing over magnifies. Thankfully, my eyes won't be able to focus right away. I'm sure the sight of me dressed in that ruffled pink romper and tulip hat would give me a heart attack.

Will I let them brainwash me into being all girlie only to have my real self reemerge years later during a midlife crisis? Or will I be the kind of girl who doesn't have any friends at school because I have a mega-chip on my shoulder?

Mom and Dad's obsession with finding the perfect name for me isn't helping either. Sophie, Chelsea, Hannah, Elizabeth, and—puke—Tiffany have all been considered. Could they be more clueless? *Spanky!* I want to scream. *What about Spanky?*

And then there's the lack of money. What if Dad never gets another job? It seems I've already put them in red numbers and I haven't even taken my first breath.

Another thing I hadn't considered: bacteria, viruses, cancers. You can have a perfectly healthy body and get smacked by one of these, and before you know it you're covered in pus-filled sores or puking yourself to death. I don't have enough time to sort through my gazillion genes, but one thing I've already discovered: I'll need Coke-bottle glasses before I'm ten. Thanks, Harvey. I'll be real popular with those.

But what if there's more? What if I have some evil mutant gene lurking in my genome, one that makes me grow too fast, too tall, not tall enough, or sprout hair from my eyeballs?

What if Mom and Dad regret having me?

What if I get bullied at school?

What if I have nightmares like Dad?

What if I can't make it through that hole?

If only I could enter into this life remembering that Mom and Dad didn't choose me. I chose them. It might make me less likely to spend a bunch of years blaming them for stuff—like they do with their parents. It's such a waste of time.

Maybe forgetting is as simple as it sounds: for *getting*. Maybe I'm supposed to empty out, become a hollow vessel of sorts, so I can be filled with…with…what?

❖

Our midwife Dinah has been coming over a lot lately. She's a voluptuous woman with more colorful head wraps than anyone I've ever seen. She has a blue one, a red one, a lavender one with gold threads, and a ton more. She also wears rings on seven of her fingers and one thumb, has a tattoo of a phoenix on her forearm, and has the annoying habit of saying "And?" whenever Mom says something she thinks is important. I find this unnerving. It's like she's trying to squeeze out some dark hidden truth.

Dad has missed our last few visits because he's working extra hours at Jack's. But Mom and I are here. And so is Dinah.

"How's the heartburn?" she asks.

"Better," Mom says. "Smaller meals have been helping."

"And?"

"Well…I'm still getting gas pains."

"Try increasing your water intake."

Mom nods. She didn't sleep well last night. "I wish she'd quit kicking my bladder."

"Did you try the Kegels?"

I'm appalled that they're even having this conversation. Two weeks ago, Dinah struck fear in both our hearts when she said to "contact her immediately" if I was "less active than usual." Needless to say, I've been kicking my heart out since then. So now I should stop kicking?

Mom mentions her recent contractions for about the third time and Dinah assures her, again, that they're Braxton Hicks. What a stupid name. Braxton Hicks. Rehearsals or Dry Runs would be more accurate.

I've been running them for about a week now. I want to be sure that when the big day comes I'll know what to do.

Dinah starts packing up her stuff to go.

"Do you happen to know Dink Raz?" Mom asks.

Dinah tucks a loose end into her silver and lavender head wrap. "I don't think so…"

Mom tries to think of a way to mention that Dink, her best friend, is gay too. "Just wondering."

Dinah takes Mom's shoulders with her meaty hands. "I have a good feeling about this birthing."

Mom wrinkles her nose. "That's good."

"And?"

"Nothing."

"Come on…"

"I'm just so happy to have someone…you…to see me through this."

Dinah lets her bag drop from her shoulder to the floor. "Nina. Everything is going to be just fine. You hear me?"

"Yeah."

"If there are any complications, we've got a plan, right?"

Mom nods. "Don't mind me. I'm just tired."

"Nina, it's important to be with this one hundred percent. If your intuition is telling you something, speak up now."

The look in Dinah's eyes scares me and I can't help but think she's speaking from an experience, about a time when someone *wasn't* 'fessing up to an intuition. I choose not to investigate. The last thing I need to see is a birthing gone wrong.

BIRTH DAY

CHAPTER THIRTY-ONE

1:15 a.m. They chose my name tonight.

Lucy.

Could be worse.

Maybe I can get my friends to call me Lou.

If I have friends.

If I'm not covered in pus-filled sores from some virus.

What am I waiting for? I'm sick of hanging around here, sick of worrying. I'm ready to forget. Can't *wait* to forget! Who cares if my due date isn't for another week? Every toenail is a masterpiece, each eyelash a marvel. Besides, nobody consulted me about any frickin' due date.

I switch on the oxytocin. My placenta obliges by pumping out the fatty acids, prostaglandins. There's no going back now.

❖

3:05. Mom sits up abruptly in bed with a contraction.

Morning, Mom! Want to have a baby today?

When my little calling card subsides, Mom, sure it's another of my rehearsals, rolls back over and goes to sleep.

❖

3:20. Mom wakes with another contraction. She's annoyed. She'd barely gone back to sleep after the last contraction and now here I am waking her up again. She waits it out, then snuggles closer to my snoring dad and falls into a dream where she's playing Titania, fairy queen, in *A Midsummer Night's Dream*, only she's carrying a bag of groceries.

❖

3:35. Ding Dong! Contraction time! Anybody home? Mom rolls over and opens her eyes. The wall has a crack of light, precise as a blade, slicing it in half. She looks over to the window. The curtain isn't completely closed. She decides to go to the bathroom. Sitting on the toilet, she considers the possibility that I might not be kidding this time.

"Everything okay in there?" Dad croaks.

"Fine. Go back to sleep." Mom gets off the toilet and walks over to the cracked curtain. The moon is almost full. She opens the drape, slips off her nightgown, and stands naked with her palms open to the universe.

After a few minutes she puts her nightdress back on and climbs into bed because she's cold. She snuggles up next to Dad.

3:50. Another contraction.

4:05 Another.

4:20. Another.

This isn't the first night I've kept her awake. I ran a similar practice drill last week. And even though she'd been able to sleep through some of those contractions, she thinks tonight is like that.

❖

6:00 a.m. Dad rolls out of bed. It's an inventory day at work. It was scheduled for next Sunday, but he requested they move it forward—just in case.

Mom listens to Dad making coffee. "Honey?" She wants to tell him about the contractions, but he doesn't hear. *Just as well*, she decides. *No need to worry him. Not like last week.* She listens to him put up the dishes and flip through the paper.

Another contraction. A beefy one. She sits up in bed.

Dad comes in to grab his wallet and keys. "You okay?"

She speaks with her eyes shut. "Rough night."

"Can I get you anything?"

"I'm trying to find the energy to go to the bathroom."

"What else is new?" He kisses her on the forehead. "So, you sure you don't need anything?"

"I'm fine."

"Well then, I'm outta here. See you when I see you." He picks up his Navy pea coat, pulls a knit cap over his head. "Pray inventory goes fast."

"Is your phone on?"

"It will be."

"Don't forget."

He sits on the edge of the bed. "Hey…you getting nervous?"

"Just tired. What time do you think you'll be back?"

"Hopefully not too late."

"You gonna be warm enough?"

"Warm in that garage is an oxymoron."

"Wear gloves."

Mom listens to the soft click of the door, swings her feet off the bed and into her slippers, then pads her way to the bathroom. She's sure it's just another false alarm and is glad she didn't trouble him. She pulls up her nightdress and sits on the toilet. When she wipes, her toilet paper comes up moist—too moist—and there's a streak of blood. Dinah warned her to look for this. She called it the Bloody Show and said it's a sign that the contractions are the real thing.

Mom wipes again. More blood. "Shit! Oh shit!" She bolts to the window.

Dad hears Mom rapping on the window and looks up from scraping a thin layer of ice from his car windshield. The sun in his eyes, he squints and puts his hand to his forehead, but he still can't make her out. He smiles and waves bye-bye, then gets in his car and pulls out of his parking space.

Panicked, Mom tries to figure out how to get his attention. She grabs a paperweight off the desk and lobs it through the apartment window. Smash!

Dad's car comes jolting to a halt, then starts backing up, fast, bumping up onto the curb. He flies out of the car, slamming the door shut behind him, and disappears into the building.

Seconds later he's thumping down the hall and bursting into the room.

Mom turns toward him. "Lucy's coming."

Dad's eyes bulge and his heart starts racing. "Now? Are you sure?"

"Well, not now…but soon."

"Well, we gotta…I gotta…Have you…"

Now that Dad's worrying, Mom doesn't have to. She picks an apple out of a bowl on the table. "It's still early, honey. I just thought you'd want to know." She bites into the apple.

He looks at her like she's bonkers. "Of course! Of course I want to know! I'll call Dinah." He pulls his phone from his pocket. "Or…do you need anything?"

"No, I'm fine. Call her." Another bite from the apple.

Dad can barely make the phone work. His hands are suddenly too big for the tiny buttons. "Shit!" He cancels and starts over. Finally it rings.

One ring.

Two rings.

Three rings.

Dinah picks up right before the fourth ring. "Dad?" she says.

"No, er, this is Rick. You know, of Rick and Nina."

"Yes, Rick, of course. This is kind of bad timing."

"Nina's having her baby."

"Now?"

"Well, not now, but…"

"Rick, my mother's had a stroke and I need to get on a plane to Florida. You're going to have to call the maternity ward."

"What?"

"I'm sorry, Rick. Can you put Nina on?"

Rick relays the information to Nina, then hands her the phone.

"Dinah?"

"How far along are you?"

"The bloody show…"

"See if Dr. Ryan is on today. If not, ask for Dr. Keen. She's wonderful."

"Dr. Ryan. Dr. Keen…" Mom says flatly.

I curse myself for not checking on Dinah before getting the ball rolling.

Mom flips the phone shut.

Dad takes it back. "I'll call the hospital."

"No. Not yet."

"What? Why?"

I'm wondering the same thing and am about to plunge into her mind when she says, "No hospital. I'm going to have Lucy here."

Dad looks as though he's just seen Mom's head spin around on her neck. "Honey…"

"I'm so clear about this, Rick. Lucy needs to be born here." She punctuates this by waddling matter-of-factly back to the bedroom.

Dad stands, motionless, his mind zooming around like a freeway cloverleaf gone mad. Thoughts are breaking speed limits, banking off curves, cutting each other off, braking, accelerating, flipping turn signals randomly on, then off, then on again. Dad charges after her. "Nina! This is crazy."

Personally, I don't see what the big deal is. What does it matter where I'm born? But Dad doesn't see it like I do.

"What if there are complications? What if she doesn't just squeeze out like toothpaste?"

The more Dad tries to talk Mom out of her plan, the more sure she becomes. "Having a baby is natural. Women have been doing it without hospitals for centuries. And I've learned so much from Dinah. I've been reading a lot too."

"Reading?" Dad repeats. "*Reading?* This is real life we're talking about, Nina. Not some book. This is our baby!" He stares at Nina and her half-eaten apple, visions of boiling water and bloody sheets swimming through his head. *What the hell is the boiling water for, anyway?* he thinks. *They never show that part in the movies.* "Honey…" *Hic!*

Now Dad's got the hiccups.

"I'm not bending on this, Rick. It's too important."

Dad remembers the phone in his hand and storms out of the bedroom. He speed-dials Dorothy.

"Hello?"

"Nina's having the *hic!* baby!"

"Now?"

"The midwife can't come and she won't *hic!* go to the hospital!"

"How close are her contractions?"

He yells into the bedroom. "Nina! How close are your *hic!* contractions?"

"Every ten or fifteen minutes! And I don't think I'm dilating yet. Or at least not much."

Dorothy tells Dad to relax and that she'll be right over.

Dad calls the Kalinas. Harvey picks up. "Hello?"

"Nina's having the baby and the *hic!* midwife can't make it and now Nina won't go to the *hic!* hospital."

"What was that, son?"

Dad repeats himself.

"Where are you?"

"Here. Home. She won't *hic!* leave."

"Put her on the phone."

"Your dad wants to talk to you."

"Tell him I'm busy."

Dad thrusts the phone at Mom. She shakes her head. He brings it back to his ear.

"She's not being very cooperative. *hic!*"

"How long has she been having contractions? When did this start?"

"Honey? How long *hic!* have you been having contractions?"

"A few hours maybe? I didn't look at the clock."

"A few hours."

"Tell him I've had the bloody show," Mom says.

"The bloody *what?*" Dad wasn't there the day Dinah talked about the bloody show and the sound of it freaks him out. "She said something about a show. A bloody one. *hic!*"

"How close are her contractions?"

"Honey? *hic!* How close are your contractions?"

"I just told you. About ten or fif—fif—hang on!"

Dad panics. "I think she's having one *now*!"

"Tell her she needs to get to the hospital."

"Honey? Your dad says we need to get you *hic!* to a hospital…Did you hear me? Neen?"

"Tell him I'm having my baby here."

"She says she's having it here."

"Call the maternity ward. I'm on my way."

The doorbell rings. Although it's impossible for Dorothy to have gotten here so quickly, that's who Dad thinks it is. He dashes for the door and flings it open.

It's Viola in a floral robe and slippers that make her feet look like two sunflowers. Franklin is parked by her ankle. "Did you hear breaking glass?"

Dad is so happy to see another human that his hiccups stop. "Nina's having the baby!"

Viola lights up like a hundred and fifty–watt lightbulb. "Jiminy Crickets! I knew it! I knew it was going to be an extraordinary day when I woke up, but old Mr. Dark Cloud here," she gestures to Franklin with her head, "*he* wouldn't believe me! He thought I was just being…"

"She's having it now!"

"This second?"

"In the bedroom!" Dad grabs Viola's hand and pulls her into the apartment. He has no idea what he's doing. It's like a poltergeist has taken over his body and is making him do things. When they reach the bedroom, he's annoyed to see Mom lying there as if everything is normal.

Mom smiles at Viola. "Lucy's on the way."

Dad can't believe how calmly Viola receives the news. She walks over to the bed and takes Mom's hand. "What a beautiful day to have a baby."

"I need to call the hospital," Dad says.

"No, you don't," Mom says.

"Your father said I should."

"*He's* not having the baby."

"But *he's* a doctor!"

"That's why he thinks I should be at a *hospital*."

Dad looks to Viola to see if she has any more understanding of the situation than he does, but she's gazing at Mom, as if she herself were a lowly shepherd and Mom, the Virgin Mary. "I think having the baby at home is a wonderful idea," she says. "I had one of my boys in a hospital and the other in a van. The one born in a hospital came out Republican."

Dad drops his head into his hands and groans.

Mom laughs. "I'm glad you're here, Viola. You really put things into perspective."

Two against one: Mom and Viola in favor of having me at home, Rick not.

I'm unsure which way my vote should go. Dad's anxiety is starting to rub off on me. What if something *does* go wrong?

Viola stands. "What we all need is a strong cup of tea."

Dad, believing the tea is a ploy to get them alone, follows Viola to the kitchen. Franklin brings up the rear. *Click! Click! Click!* go his toenails.

"So what are we going to do?" Dad asks when they're out of earshot.

"Have some tea. You're about to become a father."

The doorbell rings. Dad races to answer it.

This time it is Dorothy. Her hair is a rumpled mess. Dad drags her by the hand into the bedroom.

Mom is lying on her side, blankets tossed back.

Dorothy sits on the edge of the bed and looks lovingly at Mom. "So today's the day."

"Seems so." Mom pushes herself up to sitting. "My contractions are getting longer. They don't hurt too much yet. More like major cramps."

"Well, there's still time." She's certain that once the contractions get more intense, Nina will change her mind about the hospital.

Two for home birth. Two against. Me still undecided.

Viola enters the bedroom carrying a tray with a teapot and mugs. "Hi, Dorothy. I'm Viola. We met at the wedding."

"Yes, nice to see you again." Dorothy stirs a teaspoon of honey into a cup of herbal tea and hands it to Mom. "Rick tells me your father's coming?"

"Uh-huh. I'm hoping…" Mom's sentence stops abruptly. She puts the tea on the night table, arches back, and starts grunting.

Dad looks on in horror.

Dorothy looks at her watch.

Viola puts a hand on Rick's shoulder. "Her noises are perfectly natural. It helps her with the pain. When you…"

"Forty-five seconds!" Dorothy interjects like a sports broadcaster announcing a new record.

Viola cheers.

Nina swallows hard. "Wow. That was a good one!"

"Should we…?" Dad begins, but has no idea should we what? He fiddles with his goatee.

Mom laughs. "I'm fine, sweetie. It's not that bad. Really."

Not yet, Dorothy thinks. *Not yet*. She's concerned that once Mom's contractions get really painful they won't be able to get her down the two flights of stairs and out to the car. She's grateful that Harvey, a doctor, is coming.

That's right; Harvey's a doctor. He should be able to help get me out.

While Viola and Dorothy prattle on and drink tea, Dad stands by the window unsure what to do.

Nina puts her hands on her belly and tries to communicate with me telepathically.

Lucy, can you hear me?

Of course I can hear you! And quit calling me Lucy.

Talk to me, Lucy. Tell me where you want to be born.

You're asking me? I'm the baby here. Remember? But since you asked…I'd prefer not to have a bunch of strangers see me covered in guck with a long blue rope poking out of my tummy, thank you.

The doorbell rings. Dad jumps.

"That's Pablo," Mom says, taking her tea from the nightstand.

Dad looks at her questioningly. "Pablo?"

"He was going to come for coffee between cycles."

No one has any idea what she's talking about. Me included. Dad raises an eyebrow.

"It's his laundry day?" When Dad still doesn't get it, she adds, "The Laundromat down the street?" Her tone implies we're all idiots for not understanding.

Dad heads to the door. "Right. Like I would know that."

Pablo has the paperweight in his hand. "What's with the broken glass?"

"We're having the baby."

"Now?"

"Well, not exactly. We're contracting."

Mom yells from the bedroom. "Pablo? Is that you?"

"The one and only!" Pablo pulls off his red wool cap. "Perhaps I should come back at a more convenient time."

Dad slaps his head. "*Shit!* I forgot to call work!" and abandons Pablo at the door.

Pablo debates leaving. He has no desire to spend his day watching me get born. In fact, he's not planning on having any relationship with me at all until I'm well out of diapers and on to discussing literature but, out of loyalty to Mom, he decides to wish her good luck before heading back to his laundry.

Franklin's tail begins to wag like crazy when he sees Pablo.

Viola turns to see what's got Franklin's attention. "Pablo. I should have known. Franklin's got quite a crush on you." She lifts her crinkly palm. "Don't worry, I didn't tell him you were gay."

Pablo watches Dorothy pretend she's not shocked. "Hello, Mrs. Hale."

"Hello, Pablo. Nice to see you again."

Pablo cracks his knuckles. "So when does the midwife get here?"

"She's not coming," Mom says matter-of-factly.

Pablo takes in Dorothy's grim-set mouth and Viola's twinkling eyes. "Well, Neen. Just wanted to wish you luck." He turns to go.

"Oh no, you don't. You, of *all* people, need to be here. This baby was conceived in your bed."

Pablo stops in his tracks and spins around. "I told you not to use my bed."

"Don't worry. We washed the sheets."

Dorothy pastes a ridiculous smile on her face.

Viola shakes her head and slaps her thighs. "All this steamy talk is making me hungry. I'm going to get dressed and fix us something to eat."

Dad enters the room just as Viola and Franklin are leaving. "The guys at Jack's give you their best."

Pablo resigns himself to sticking around until his laundry is done. "You got any coffee fixin's?"

"Great idea," Dad says. "I could use a cup too."

The two of them troop off to the kitchen.

"So what's going on?" Pablo asks.

"The frickin' midwife can't make it and now Nina's gone all anti-hospital. She's refusing to go, saying she wants to have the baby here."

Pablo shakes his head. "I vote we just pick the wench up and carry her there."

The hospital team takes the lead.

❖

10:30 a.m. Dad greets four Kalinas at the door. "Wow. You *all* came."

"Don't ask," Harvey says, charging past him. He stops short when he sees Mom setting out plates and silverware.

"Oh good, you made it in time for breakfast," she says.

Charlotte smirks. "I told you she just wanted attention."

Mom gives Charlotte a look of withering contempt, then goes back to setting the table.

Iris drops her purse to the floor. "Charlotte, please."

"I tried to tell her she should rest," Dorothy says guiltily.

"Moving feels good," Mom says, heading into the kitchen for glasses. "We've never had so many people here at once. We're going to have to use some jars."

Hester knits her brows. "I thought you were having your baby."

"Soon," Nina says. "Anyone want coffee?"

Harvey and Iris pull Dorothy aside. "How close are the contractions?" Harvey asks quietly.

"About every ten minutes. They're getting stronger too."

Dad joins them. "Is this normal? Her feeling all tired one minute, then all manic the next?"

"It can be," Harvey says. "Have you alerted the hospital?"

"I've called the maternity ward and told them what's going on. Apparently they're swamped, but said to bring her in when the contractions get closer."

"What does she say?"

"There's no way in hell she's going."

Harvey pinches the bridge of his nose. "Jesus!"

It frightens Iris to see Harvey this uneasy. She places her hand on his arm. "Everyone's doing the best they can."

Harvey wants to scream: *You're not the one everyone's looking at to solve this! You're not the doctor here!* Instead he directs his words to Mom. "Nina, honey, I'm sure the birthing rooms at your hospital aren't as scary as you're making them out to be."

Mom looks up from pouring orange juice. "I'm not scared, Dad. I just don't want to go. The feng shui here is perfect for Lucy's arrival."

"Nina. This is no time to be stubborn."

"Hang on!" Mom grabs onto the counter and shuts her eyes. "Uuuuhnnn…"

No one moves except Hester, who tugs at Iris's sleeve. "Is she having her baby?"

Iris doesn't answer.

Finally Mom takes a big breath. "They're actually lightening up a little."

Dorothy and Iris meet eyes. They know what it's like to have a baby. In fact, Dorothy is having a particularly strong memory of giving birth to Dad. The nurse had to restrain her when she tried to rip an IV out of her arm.

"Order up!" Viola shouts from the hall.

Dorothy rushes to open the door.

Viola and Pablo enter with trays covered in steaming bowls. "Breakfast is served," Viola says. "We've got quite a day in front of us, folks. We're having a baby!"

"Thank God," Mom says. "I'm starving."

Like a pack of bewildered sheep, everyone, save Iris and Harvey, drifts toward the food.

"What should we do?" Iris asks Harvey in a sharp whisper.

"What *can* we do?"

"We need to talk some sense into her."

"And when did that *ever* work with Nina?"

Iris wipes a bit of dried shaving cream from behind Harvey's ear.

He glances at Mom, then sighs. "Time is on our side. Let's have some breakfast."

The table is covered in food: a big bowl of scrambled eggs with scallions, tomatoes, and cheese, another bowl with steaming home-baked corn muffins, and a giant platter of home fries with onions and sausage. But everyone's eyes are on Mom as she piles her plate so high it looks like it could topple. "Where's the pepper?" she asks.

"I'll get it." Dad strides to the kitchen.

Once her plate is full, Mom lowers herself to the couch and begins shoveling food into her mouth like she's a state fair pie-eating contestant.

Hester and Viola, their plates also full, join her in the living room. "This looks really good," Hester says, scooping up a mouthful. "I've never had eggs like this before."

Harvey adds a muffin to his plate. "Nina, you might want to—"

"Dad, I don't want to talk about it."

"I was just going to say you might want to limit your eating."

"Why?"

"Let's just say…when it comes time to push, you want to make sure you're not pushing out any more than your baby."

"Daaad!" Hester moans. "That is soooo gross!"

I couldn't agree with her more. That was definitely a case of TMI.

"I just realized," Viola says, "your baby's going to be a Pisces. Like Franklin."

Iris gets up from the couch, thinking, *It's not a birthday party, for Christ's sake!* She walks to the broken window to light up a smoke.

"This is a no-smoking apartment," Mom says.

For a moment it looks as if Iris is about to object, but she stuffs her smokes back into her purse and forces out a fake-sounding, "Sorry."

Franklin starts humping Pablo's leg. He gives Franklin a shove with his foot and pushes out his chair. "Would you all excuse me? I need to make a phone call." He takes his plate to the bedroom with Franklin in hot pursuit. *Click! Click! Click!* Pablo glares at Franklin and whispers, "Look, buddy, if you're going to make it anywhere in this world, you've got to read the signs. And I'm not interested. Okay?"

Franklin flops down dejectedly with his head on his paws.

Pablo pulls out his phone and dials.

"Copy room."

"Nina's having her baby."

Once Pablo explains what's going on, Dink, like everybody else, freaks.

Which doesn't exactly do wonders for my self-confidence. Why is everybody so worried? I mean, come on. We currently have *three* people who've had babies, *one* doctor who's assisted in delivering babies, and *nine* people who've all successfully crossed over. What more do they need?

"I'm on my way," Dink says.

Pablo enters the living room right as Mom is heading to refill her plate. She's hit with an extra-big contraction and stumbles over to the couch to grab the back of it. *"Ooooooo-ooooh!"*

Everyone springs up, their napkins dropping to the floor like tiny fallen angels. Dad takes her plate. "Honey," he says, "I really wish you'd—"

Mom raises her hand in a swift gesture to silence him. *"Errrrrrrr..."*

When her hand finally releases the back of the couch there are five dents in the foam. Mom takes a few slow breaths to regain her composure, turns to her family, and says breathily, "Hear ye! Hear ye! On this day of March..."

"Fourth!" Hester chimes.

"Two thousand seven, Nina Kalina-Hale proclaims to her husband, family, and friends that she *will* have her baby at home. All those objecting, speak now or forever hold your peace."

Dorothy, Iris, Rick, Harvey, and Charlotte all began to speak at once.

"One at a time, please."

"This is silly," Iris begins.

"Purely subjective," Nina counters. "Next?"

"What if something goes wrong?" Harvey asks.

"As Mom always says, you can't live your life on what-ifs. Besides, we're only five minutes away from the hospital."

"Ten," Dad says. "And if we count getting you down the stairs..."

"Whatever. It's close. And if there's any sign of a problem, I *will* go to the hospital. I promise." She looks at Harvey. "Dad, you've done this. I don't know what you're so worried about."

"Nina, I'm a pediatrician, not an obstetrician. I would feel much more comfortable if—"

"If what? A perfect stranger who's never even met me delivers my baby?"

Viola steps from behind the breakfast bar with a stack of dishes to take back to her own kitchen. "Whatever you decide is fine with me. But should you decide to stay here, you're welcome to use my apartment as a waiting room." Having said this, she and her dishes leave the apartment.

"Does she have to be here?" Iris asks.

"She's my friend," Nina says.

Iris notices a shard of glass on the windowsill and picks it up. "Sorry. I'm just keyed up."

"Nina," Harvey says, "I don't think you've really thought this out."

"There will be a lot of pain," Dorothy says.

Mom fingers the edge of her kimono. "I know. That's why I want to be here, surrounded by all of you." She turns toward Dad. "Especially you."

"But I'd be allowed into the birthing room, Neen. I checked."

"Still. It wouldn't be the same. Not like this. In our home." Dad's about to object when she takes his hand and says to everybody else, "Excuse us for a second." She pulls him into the bedroom.

"You've got to stand by me on this."

"But, Neen—"

"Think how amazing it would be to have Lucy here, with all of our friends and family. And my dad's a doctor! He'll know what to watch for."

Dad looks at the bed they angled into the corner of the bedroom for easy access, the small mirror above the door for good feng shui, the rose quartz pieces placed strategically on the windowsill. "I'm worried, that's all. I don't want anything to happen to you. Or Lucy."

"It's basically no different than with Dinah. I mean, if we have complications we'll rush to the hospital."

"But—"

She puts her finger on his lips. "Please?"

They look into each other's eyes and Dad's objections start melting.

"Okay. If you can convince your dad, I'll back you up."

She kisses him. "Thank you, thank you, thank you, thank you!"

They come out of the bedroom holding hands. "Rick's with me on this."

"*If* your dad says he'll do it."

Everyone looks at Harvey—except Charlotte. "I don't know why you're making such a big deal about this," she says. "Everyone else goes to hospitals to have their babies and they live through it."

But the tide is changing.

Iris thinks, *Surely, Harvey is more qualified than a midwife.*

Dorothy thinks, *The hospital is close.*

And Harvey doesn't so much think as feel, his heart swelling with pride. *My daughter wants me to deliver her baby, so why the hell not? I've got my emergency medical bag in the car.*

He looks to Iris. She returns an almost imperceptible nod. He turns to Dorothy. She does the same. He sighs. "All right. We will do this. But you must promise me—*promise* me—first sign that anything, and I mean anything, is even slightly irregular, and we pack you up to the hospital as quickly as I can say 'now.'"

"Oh, thank you, Dad! Thank you!" Mom starts to throw her arms around Harvey, but his words stop her.

"Hold on, we're not done yet." His eyes fix upon her. "Put out your hand, young lady." Mom does, and he takes her small hand in his big one. "You have to trust me. If I say we go, we go." Eyes locked, they unclasp hands, each spits on their own palm, then they re-clasp them for a slimy handshake.

Mom's eyes brim with tears. "I trust you, Dad, and so does Lucy."

Right at this moment I have a most disturbing realization.

CHAPTER THIRTY-TWO

I'll never again know my family as it is now.

Once I cross over, Mom and Dad will be nothing more to me than two warm blobs, one with magical orbs of satisfaction, one without. By the time I get old enough to understand how important a mom and a dad are, Dad will probably be working so many hours at Jack's I'll never see him. Or maybe he and Mom will stop loving each other and Dad will only be around on weekends. And I'll think I never knew Howie. I'll probably roll my eyes whenever Dad talks about him, and utter insolent remarks like, "Yeah yeah, Dad. We've all heard the story about your old soldier buddy."

What if Richard's heart finally bursts? Or Charlotte disowns her family and joins a cult? Or Dorothy becomes a famous essayist? I'll have no memory of how brave Dorothy's first scrawled words were. How miserable Charlotte was. Or of Richard's endearingly cantankerous ways. I'll have no context.

❖

It's 1:15 p.m., ten hours since the first contraction, and I would do anything to change the course of what is about to happen. I *want* to remember—everything.

I gaze down at my family sprawled around Mom and Dad's apartment. To look at them, you wouldn't know how tense they are. Iris reads the paper while Hester sits on the floor texting a friend; Pablo's got his laundry to fold; Harvey is on his laptop catching up on e-mail; Dorothy is recording thoughts on a paper bag; and Charlotte, dear Charlotte, is madly trying to finish a cap and blanket she's knitting for me. Meanwhile, Mom and Dad are camped out in the bedroom. He's massaging her feet and timing contractions. She's trying to stay relaxed.

I love them. All of them. And I want to remember them just like this, when they banded together as a family to usher me into life.

I'm aware of a presence in the hallway. I go to check who it is. It's Dink. She's brought Lottie Yang with her.

"If it's too weird, we won't stay," Dink says.

Lottie applies a fresh coat of gloss to her lips. "Tell me, of all those girls you've dated, did any one of them kiss as good as me?"

Flustered, Dink reaches past her and punches the doorbell.

I wonder how it will turn out between these two. Will I ever know?

Mom shuffles into the living room to greet Dink. "You came."

"You're supposed to be in the grips of labor."

Mom laughs. "Not yet." She looks down at her belly. "Lucy, look. Now your Auntie Dink *and* Uncle Pablo are here."

Charlotte looks up from her knitting. "Oh, are Hester and I not the only aunts now?"

Iris folds the world news section of the paper and is about to speak when Mom grabs Dink's shoulder and starts growling. Dad races from the bedroom and eases Mom onto the couch. Harvey puts his computer aside and stands like there's something he should do, even though he checked Mom's dilation minutes ago.

Nina finally relaxes. "Whoa! That was a whopper."

Harvey claps his hands together. "It's time we get you isolated. A little less excitement for you—and for me—would not be a bad thing."

"That lady said we could use her house," Hester says.

"Her name is Viola," Dorothy says, standing. "Why don't you and I walk over there and see if she's ready for us?"

"Okay." Hester jumps up and bolts past Dink and Lottie.

Suddenly, it occurs to me we're missing an important person: Richard Douglas Hale. His first grandchild is on the verge of being born and nobody's even thought to call him.

I decide on one last astral trip to say good-bye.

I discover him sitting behind his desk at White's Insurance. He's thinking how glad he is that they never got around to installing glass walls in the offices. He's having a rough day and would just as soon do it privately. He picks up a picture of himself, Dorothy, and Dad at an office picnic. Dad's in diapers and is holding Dorothy's hand to keep from tipping over.

The phone rings.

Richard stares at it absently.

It rings again.

He wills his mind to attention and picks up. "Yes, Josie?"

"Mr. Hale? I've got your wife on the line. She says it's urgent."

He sits up straight, thrilled that Dorothy would call him in a time of crisis. "Put her on, Josie."

"Richard?"

"Yes, sweetheart."

"Nina's going into labor."

He slides his chair out from behind the desk. "I'm on my way."

"Actually, I need you to pick up some folding chairs from the house."

"What?"

"Viola doesn't have many chairs."

"Fo—folding chairs?"

"In the garage, by the washer."

"I know where the goddamned chairs are, Dorothy. I just don't understand—"

"If you could just bring them. We're at the kids' apartment."

He neatly prints out the words FOLDING CHAIRS on his notepad. "I'll be right over—" But before he can finish his sentence, Dorothy has hung up.

Will I have no memory of them together?

❖

Back at Viola's, I try to memorize the painted flowers on all the walls, the floral fabric on the furniture, the coffee table in the shape of a daisy. By the time I'm old enough to appreciate her quirky world of flowers, she probably won't be around anymore. People can't live forever, no matter how much you love them.

She fills glasses of lemonade for Hester to pass out. "Isn't this exciting?"

Hester nods. "After Lucy gets born, I'm going to have all my friends call me Aunt Hester."

Viola smiles, then sits, massaging an arthritic hand.

Lottie, who's just activated the phone tree for the Sisters in Solidarity, takes a glass of lemonade from Hester. "Thanks, kid."

"Um, I like your hair," Hester says. "Mom let me dye mine pink on Halloween." With a final doting look at Lottie's blue stripe, she goes on to deliver the next glass of lemonade.

Lottie turns back to Dink. "Juniper and Rhonda are on their way."

Down the hall, Harvey, Iris, and Dorothy are in our living room talking quietly. "I'm going to need someone to assist me," Harvey says.

"How close is she?" Iris asks.

"Hard to tell. She's at five centimeters."

Iris crosses her arms. "I'd just as soon it not be me. I'll just make everyone nervous."

"I'll do it," Dorothy says. "I was a candy striper in college."

Iris breathes a sigh of relief. "Thank you, Dorothy. Really."

"Dad?" Mom calls from the bedroom.

Harvey peeks his head in. "Yes, sweetie?"

"I just had a really big contraction."

"I'll be right in. You timing these, Rick?"

Dad has a stopwatch in his hand. "Yes, sir."

Voices waft up from the street, one of them Richard's.

He's arrived with the chairs.

❖

Richard brings the last of the chairs into Viola's apartment. "So they're over at the kids'?" he asks.

Charlotte, who's unfolding and setting up the chairs, says, "She's really done it this time. She's forcing my dad into delivering the baby here."

"Nuh-uh!" Hester says. "They did the spit handshake, that's why. And Mrs. Hale gets to be the nurse!" She spins around backward on one foot. "I told Dad I wanted to be nurse, but he said I can't be a nurse *and* an aunt."

Lottie bursts into the room behind him. "Nina's water broke!" Viola cheers, while others, especially Iris, listen to Lottie's next words anxiously. "Her contractions are coming every five minutes and Dr. Kalina says she's going into active labor."

"How far has she dilated?" Dink asks, wiping a spot of soda from her shirt.

"She's still at five centimeters."

Charlotte pulls out her knitting. "The whole thing is insane! What is she thinking?" She rams her hand into he knitting bag and jams her finger. "Fudge!"

Richard's face twists into a knot of hurt and confusion. *Why was I the last to know about Nina's labor? Why am I always the last to know about everything?* Out of the corner of his eye, he spots several of the Sisters in Solidarity in a serious discussion with Pablo. A particularly attractive girl waves and smiles.

Richard, vaguely remembering her from the rehearsal dinner, smiles back, and feels bolstered by the attention. He returns his attention to Charlotte. "It's no big deal, Charlotte. Women in third world countries pop 'em out in rice paddies all the time."

Charlotte's eyes begin to burn. *Is everyone so stupid they can't see that Nina's manipulations have finally gone too far? It's one thing for Nina to risk her own life, but to risk the life of her baby?* Then Charlotte does something I wish I'd never forget.

She closes her eyes, drops her chin to her chest, and prays. Not to a God she's learned about in church, because Iris and Harvey never took her to church, but to a God she's created herself; a God whose love of order is even greater than hers; a God who notices how hard she works and how unappreciated she is; a God who cares. She is certain that her God will balance the scales, has, in fact, been tracking her suffering like a casino dealer tracking a growing pile of chips—and she's confident she's owed. So, on this afternoon, the day of my birthday, my sweet Aunt Charlotte cashes in all her tokens of anguish, handing them up to her God with one request: that I be born safely.

Hester throws her arms around her sister. "Don't worry, Charlotte, everything is going to be okay. Pretty soon we're going to be aunts."

"I know, Hessy," she says. "I know."

❖

Harvey and Dorothy wring out the towels they used to clean up after Mom's water broke. Once that's done and the towels are draped on various chair backs, Harvey fills a pot with water for coffee. Dorothy marvels at his ease in the kitchen, at his strong arms that still seem, somehow, soft. "Do you ever have the feeling that you might, all of a sudden, wake up out of your life?" she asks.

Harvey laughs. "Like now?"

"I suppose."

He rests his hip against the counter. "When the girls were young I used to wonder how I got stuck in a house full of females. Not that I don't love them all, but I don't mind telling you, I really wanted a son."

"Well, we certainly don't get to choose."

"And that's a good thing," Harvey says. "Because my girls have been good for me. In some ways they've softened me, and in others… well, I think they've helped me understand what being a man really means."

Dorothy nods. "I guess we get what we need."

Will I be what Mom and Dad need? Will I help them learn something?

I need to check in with them.

Dad is standing next to the bed and Mom is on her knees with her hands on the headboard. "Does that feel better?" he asks.

She's had a powerful contraction. They've been more painful since our water broke. "I don't know. I'll try it for a while."

"Maybe you should lie back down. Try to sleep."

"I can't."

"Do you want me to push on your back again?"

"No. Maybe I should try to sleep."

Dad doesn't say that he just suggested this and she said she couldn't. He just helps her onto her side and begins stroking her head. "Do you need more ice?"

She nods.

He takes an ice cube from a small green bowl and holds it to her lips.

"This isn't working. I need to walk around. Help me up."

He puts the ice cube into his own mouth, and reaches out to help her stand.

Another contraction hits.

She leans into Dad with such force he's afraid he'll tip over. He steels his legs—and his will. "You can do it, honey. You can…" He's said this so many times that the words no longer make sense to him.

Out the window, I spot Dink and Pablo on the front lawn having a smoke.

One of these days, Dink thinks, *Pablo's going to have to break down and buy his own pack of smokes.*

"How long do these things usually take?" he asks, flicking an ash onto the new grass.

"These things? God, Pablo. It's a baby, for Christ's sake."

"Sorry."

"It varies. She could pop it out right away, or it could take hours. That's what Lottie says anyway."

"It's already been hours."

"You got something better to do? I mean, *besides* supporting one of your best friends—a family member—through this miracle… this genesis of a being…this scientific marvel…this life-altering experience."

"I never said I wasn't going to stay."

Dink takes in her friend, the long black ponytail, the thin gold bracelet around his slim wrist. *If only he were a girl*, she thinks, then folds over the tip of her cigarette and stuffs it in her pocket. "Shall we?"

I think to myself, maybe none of us is one thing or the other, but a little bit of both—some more girl than boy, some more boy than girl—like the recipes Mom uses when she cooks. Maybe I shouldn't be worrying about gender at all. Maybe I've let myself be too influenced by the narrow-minded thinking of The Land of Forgetting.

But that's just it, they *can* be so narrow minded—and cruel. Am I ready for this?

❖

Plastic deli tubs and half-eaten sandwiches litter Viola's living room and kitchen. Conversation is sparse. You can almost hear the digestive enzymes gurgling.

Iris and Richard are sitting on folding chairs, each holding a cup of coffee.

"We're very close to the hospital," Richard reassures her. "And my keys are rarin' and ready." He takes them out and jingles them. "You can count on me."

Iris finds his wink a tad patronizing, but thinks to herself, *Choose your battles, Iris*. She takes a swig of cold coffee.

"Thanks for the grub, Mrs. Kalina."

"It was my pleasure, Juniper."

Viola pulls a book of English poetry off her bookshelf, opens it, and is delighted to discover she's chanced upon a very appropriate William Blake poem. She begins to read aloud.

"Little Lamb, who made thee?

Dost thou know who made thee?"

Hester, who's been quietly fashioning pieces of deli paper into hats, whispers to Charlotte. "Look at me and Franklin. We're twins!"

Charlotte drops a stitch. "Don't you have homework to do?"

"Gave thee such a tender voice,

Making all the vales rejoice?"

Iris gets up and goes to the window wondering if it's too soon to step outside for another smoke.

"Little Lamb, who made thee?

Dost thou know who made thee?"

Missy, Rhonda, Juniper, and Cathy sit in a circle braiding one another's hair. "Is it normal for it to take this long?" Juniper whispers, not wanting to disrupt the poetry.

"My mother said I took fifteen hours," Cathy whispers back.

"Well, I can't stay all night. We've got a big gig tomorrow. Thirty lasagnas for a Rotary Club fund-raising dinner."

"Little Lamb, I'll tell thee,

Little Lamb, I'll tell thee."

Pablo, sucking a butterscotch, lies on his back on the floor and listens to Viola read. He notices that the flowers on her ceiling are hand painted and marvels at the thought of Viola standing on a ladder to do this.

"He is meek, and he is mild;

He became a little child."

Dink's in the bathroom looking at herself in the mirror. She brings her face within an inch of her reflection, hoping to get close enough to see into her soul.

"Little Lamb, God bless thee!

Little Lamb, God bless thee!"

❖

10:30 p.m., nineteen hours since the first contraction. Mom is lying on her side, shivering and nauseous. Dad presses a cool washrag to her brow. I'm practicing words in hopes that I'll take some with me. Applesauce, Alpha-fetoprotein, Accelerator, Brainwash, Barbecue, Bottle, Cabbage, Cracked wheat, Corpuscle…

Mom pushes the rag away. "I can't do this."

She's said this several times in the last ten minutes and Dad wonders if this time she means it. "Should we—"

"What? What do you think I want?" She looks at him accusingly, as if he were a double agent secretly working for the hospital. "How can you know what I—" She grabs his sleeve. "Eeeeerrrrrrrrrrrrrrrrrr…" Her eyes plead with him to care for her.

Exhausted, Dad tries not to blink as her eyes bore into his. "You can do it. You can do it, sweetie," he says.

Harvey steps into the doorway, wanting to check how much she's effaced, her dilation, our vitals. Last check she was only six, maybe seven, centimeters, but it looks to him like she's transitioning. *Is it possible?* he wonders.

"Just come *out*," Nina moans, her body shaking.

Easy for her to say.

Once the contraction is finished, Harvey sits on the end of the bed to see how things are progressing. "You're doing so well. I'm so proud of you." Rick slides in and cradles her from behind so she can see her dad. She's the most relaxed when she knows what's going on.

Harvey's eyes narrow.

"What?" Dad asks.

"We're at ten."

Adrenaline shoots through Dad's veins. He yells to Dorothy in the other room. "Mom, she's at ten!"

Dorothy strides in and pulls a chair up to the bed. She takes Nina's hand, then glances at Harvey as if to ask permission to speak.

He nods. They've talked about her, a veteran, coaching Mom through this next part.

"You're doing a great job," she says, her voice soothing.

Mom's bottom lip quivers.

"And I know it seems impossible that there's more to come…"

Mom tries to smile, but her eyes are as big as bottle tops.

"…but Lucy needs your help now. You need to start pushing."

Another contraction.

Mom grasps Dorothy's hand with a bone-crushing grip and begins breathing in short pants. A drop of perspiration rolls down her forehead.

Dad looks past her to Harvey. "Is she pushing?"

He shakes his head.

Dad, Harvey, and Dorothy wait out the contraction in silence.

When Mom's finished, she gasps, "I didn't push."

Dorothy pulls a sweaty lock of hair from Mom's cheek. "That's all right. Take your time. But pushing will help Lucy drop down."

And what if I don't want to drop down? What if I'm too scared?

But Mom can't keep this up forever. Her body isn't strong enough. It's time for me to move out.

With her next contraction, we join forces and push, hard, giving it everything we've got. Grrrrrrrrr!

…

…

…That was it? I expected to pop out like toast.

I ready myself, bracing my muscles for the next push.

Again—Puuuuush!

Again—Nada.

Apparently, one has to prove one's allegiance to life with more heave-ho than I imagined.

❖

We've been pushing for twenty minutes and I'm still in here.

Mom and I can't find the right position: on her back, on her side, on all fours—we try them all.

"Breathe…Breathe. You can do it!" Dad coaches.

Sometimes, in between pushes, Mom drops off into a sleep-like state where she imagines meeting me on the edge of life—like Persephone and Demeter. Once, we're dolphins speeding through the briny sea. Another time, she's an oyster and I'm her pearl. When she wakes from these dreams, she thinks she's slept for hours. "How long was I out?"

"A minute. Maybe two," Dad says.

Before she can sort this out, the next contraction hits and the pushing, now with a will of its own, takes over. Like a runaway big rig powering three heavy trailers down a steep incline, there's no stopping it.

Suddenly, I panic.

Dad notices Mom's eyes soften as if she's looking at a distant horizon. "Uh…Harvey, what's going on?" Dad asks.

"I'm not sure."

"She's stopped pushing."

"I know!" Harvey snaps and reaches for his stethoscope.

"She's tired," Dorothy says, trying to mask her alarm. "Aren't you, sweetie?"

"I don't hear the baby's heart," Harvey says.

What?

Dad's stomach seizes up. "What?"

Harvey moves his stethoscope, perspiration dripping down his collar.

For a moment I'm so freaked, I actually believe him. *Good-bye, world! Good-bye, life!* Then I realize he's holding the stethoscope to my feet.

Mom's pretty sure everything is okay, and says, "Dad…"

But Harvey's had enough and rockets to his feet. "We need to get her to the hospital. *Now!*"

Lottie pokes her head in the door. "Any news?"

"Get a car. We're going to the hospital."

"On it!" Lottie says and flies back to Viola's.

"Nina," Dad says firmly, "we need to get you up."

Mom can't imagine standing any more than she can singing an aria, but the expression on Harvey's face is clear—she has no choice. She heaves herself to sitting and prepares to stand.

Dad swoops her up in his arms.

"Careful, Rick!" Dorothy says.

"Call the hospital," Harvey says.

Dorothy grabs her phone. "Got it."

I hear everyone trooping down the hall from Viola's.

"I knew this was a bad idea," Iris says.

"Everything will be all right," Richard says.

"What's going on?" Dink asks.

"I don't know," Pablo replies. "They're taking her to the hospital."

"Shit!"

As Dad carries us out of the bedroom and toward the door, I hear Mom whisper, "Come on, Lucy. We can do this."

Really?

We're about to pass through the front door to the hallway.

"Lucy?" she says. "Don't be scared. I love you."

You promise?

To my astonishment, she says, "I promise."

Dorothy's words about parents getting what they need, flashes through my mind. *Okay, Mom. I'll try. But I hope you're ready for one shit-kicker of a girl.*

She wraps her arm around Dad's head to anchor herself, and we begin to push. She squeezes Dad's head—tighter, tighter, and for a moment I think he's going to drop us.

"Uh...Harvey?" Dad says.

But Harvey and Dorothy have raced ahead wanting to make sure the car is ready.

Mom twists and turns in Dad's arms. Afraid he's going to drop us, he sinks to his knees and lays us on the entry rug.

Harvey and Dorothy, momentarily distracted by Richard and Iris rushing down the hallway, don't notice.

"What's going on?" Iris wants to know.

Then in one move, Mom howls, flexes her legs, and kicks the door shut.

Dad, Mom, and me, are now on one side of the door and my grandparents and everybody else is on the other.

"Rick! What's going on?" Harvey yells.

"She's pushing!"

"Open the door!"

"I can't! She's bracing her feet against it!"

Mom is determined to have me and takes a giant breath. She pushes super hard. "Yeeoaaahhhrrrgghargh!"

"Rick! Let us in!" Iris yells, her voice, raw panic.

"I can't!"

I hear the others making their way down the hallway. "What's happening?" "Why aren't you bringing Nina to the car?"

My body is thrumming with the belief that I'm just what Mom and Dad need. I'm just what Mom and Dad need. I'm just…

"A screwdriver," I hear Dink say. "Where can we get a screwdriver?"

"EEEEEEEEOOOOORRRRRGGGGGAAAAAAAHHHHH!"

Whoa. I see a splinter of something harsh. Dazzling. Light! It must be light! I'm crossing over. Oh! Something is tingling. I think it's… My head! It's the crown of my head!

"Oh my God! Oh my God! Something is coming out!" Dad yells.

Such a chilly sensation. Air?

—Whoa. Wait. I'm sliding backwards! Why am I sliding backwards? Forward. Forward. More light! More air!

"Come *on*, Lucy," Mom says through gritted teeth. "HHHHAAARRRRGGGAAAAH!"

"I see a head!" Dad screams.

"Rick!" Harvey yells. "Keep her pushing!"

"No problem there, sir!"

I'm just what Mom and Dad need. I'm just what Mom and Dad need.

We push again. Harder this time. "UUUUUNNNNNHHHH"—Mom sips some air—"UUUUUNNNNNHHHH"—she sips some more—"UUUUUNNNNHHHHHHH…"

My head! My head is squishing through! We're doing it, Mom. We're doing it!

Ouch. My eyes hurt.

Lids down. Much better.

My whole head is tingling, including my face.

Lids up. Oh! Still too bright.

Lids down.

"How much can you see?" Harvey yells.

Dad wants to answer but he can't. He can already tell I have Mom's nose.

"Rick!" Dorothy screams.

"How much of the head can you see?" Harvey yells again.

"The whole thing!"

"Oh, my God," Iris gasps.

Everyone's super quiet. Is everything okay, I wonder. Do I look normal? Has he noticed my exceptional features?

"Everything all right?" Harvey asks, echoing my thoughts. *"Rick!"*

"I have no idea! I've never done this before."

"Feel around the neck and make sure the umbilical cord isn't wrapped around it." There's a pause. "Nina, can you hear me?"

Mom nods.

"She can hear you, sir."

"Tell her to pant."

"Pant?"

"Like a dog."

Mom starts panting. It's not easy. She's tired.

Come on, Mom, we can do this.

"Hold hands," I hear Viola say to everyone in the hallway. "Let's pull in some good energy." She starts humming.

Dad's afraid to touch me. I'm too small. But he lifts Mom's foot, which is still braced against the door, and slides under her leg so he can get to me. He props himself up on his elbow and stares at my head sticking out.

I'm at the edge of an abyss. On both sides of a window. The beginning and at the end.

An extraordinary gentleness cradles my head. It's warm and cool all at once it's… Touch! My dad's touch!

Lids up. Bright / Shadow / Bright.

Lids down.

Blood pulses through his fingertips.

Da-dum. Da-dum.

Or is this my blood?

Da-dum. Da-dum.

I don't know. But I'm no longer afraid. I *want* to be born. Life is impossible. Magnificent. Breakable. And I will do anything to obtain it.

"Rick!" Harvey yells.

"No umbilical cord!" Dad yells back.

"Good! Now—gently!—take the head in your hands."

Dad is breathing hard. I can feel it on my head.

"Honey?" he says, and I don't know if he's talking to me or Mom "We're almost there."

Mom smiles weakly.

"Just one more push."

This is it. Time for me to do what all infants ultimately must if they want to survive: trust my parents.

For Getting. For Getting.

Good-bye, everyone. Next time I see you, we'll be strangers.

"Don't be scared," Dad says.

I think of beautiful Jesus in her turquoise dress. Wish me luck!

Mom grits her teeth. "Don't say I never did anything for you."

I won't. I pull my shoulders in to get as compact as possible and together we push, one more colossal push. "EEEEEERRRRRRRIIIIIIAAAAAAHHHHHHH!"

The rest of me squeezes out into my dad's hands like toothpaste.

Chapter Thirty-three

Weird. I still remember everything.

I can see myself through Dad's eyes. I'm shriveled and blue.

I try to use my eyes to look back at him, but they're not ready. All I can see is a shadow of a shadow, the inside of a halo.

But somehow I've crossed over and not Forgotten. I've done it! I've done it! The first baby to ever—

Hey, wait. Shouldn't I be breathing?

I open up my tiny mouth to gulp at the cool frothy blend of nitrogen and oxygen.

Oh! Oh! What's going on? I'm spinning like a top, a colossal tornado, a corkscrew of flame. Round and round I go…the centrifugal force pulling me apart. I'm spiraling to the heart of a double helix, strands of nucleotides spinning around me. Now I'm shrinking even smaller. I'm the nucleus of the atom, electrons whizzing by me at dizzying speed. It's too much! Too fast!

But wait. It's begun slowing down…slower…slower…

Stopping…

Still.

I'm deposited on a shore. Salty and warm. And it loves me. It's mine. Mine.

Me. My. Mine.

"She's turning pink."

Pink?

Do I know that voice? Do I?

A warm blob embraces me.

Oh no! It's in the air! The Forgetting is in the— Waaaaaaa!

About the Author

Clifford Henderson lives and plays in Santa Cruz, California. She runs The Fun Institute, a school of improv and solo performance, with her partner of eighteen years. In their classes and workshops, people learn to access and express the myriad of characters itching to get out. When she's not teaching or performing, she's writing, gardening, and twisting herself into weird yoga poses.

She's pleased to have recently completed recording an audiobook of *The Middle of Somewhere* with Dog Ear Audio.

Her third novel, *Maye's Request*, is coming out in 2011.

Contact Clifford at www.cliffordhenderson.net.

Books Available From Bold Strokes Books

Fever by VK Powell. Hired gun Zakaria Chambers is hired to provide a simple escort service to philanthropist Sara Ambrosini, but nothing is as simple as it seems, especially love. (978-1-60282-135-4)

High Risk by JLee Meyer. Can actress Kate Hoffman really risk all she's worked for to take a chance on love? Or is it already too late? (978-1-60282-136-1)

Missing Lynx by Kim Baldwin and Xenia Alexiou. On the trail of a notorious serial killer, Elite Operative Lynx's growing attraction to a mysterious mercenary could be her path to love—or to death. (978-1-60282-137-8)

Spanking New by Clifford Henderson. A poignant, hilarious, unforgettable look at life, love, gender, and the essence of what makes us who we are. (978-1-60282-138-5)

Magic of the Heart by C.J. Harte. CEO Susan Hettinger and wild, impulsive rock star M.J. Carson couldn't be more different if they tried—but opposites attract in ways neither woman can resist. (978-1-60282-131-6)

Ambereye by Gill McKnight. Jolie Garoul is falling in love with her assistant. The big problem is, Jolie is a werewolf. (978-1-60282-132-3)

Collision Course by C.P. Rowlands. Tragedy leaves Brie O'Malley and Jordan Carter fearful and alone. Can they find the courage to take a second chance on love? (978-1-60282-133-0)

Mephisto Aria by Justine Saracen. Opera singer Katherina Marov's destiny may be to repeat the mistakes of her father when she becomes involved in a dangerous love affair. (978-1-60282-134-7)

Battle Scars by Meghan O'Brien. Returning Iraq war veteran Ray McKenna struggles with the battle scars that can only be healed by love. (978-1-60282-129-3)

Chaps by Jove Belle. Eden Metcalf wants nothing more than to flee from her troubled past and travel the open road—until she runs into rancher Brandi Cornwell. (978-1-60282-127-9)

Lightbearer by John Caruso. Lucifer dares to question the premise of creation itself and reveals that sin may be all that stands between us and living hell. (978-1-60282-130-9)

The Seeker by Ronica Black. FBI profiler Kennedy Scott battles ghosts from her past, deadly obsession, and the evil that haunts her. (978-1-60282-128-6)

Power Play by Julie Cannon. Businesswomen Tate Monroe and Victoria Sosa are at odds in the boardroom, but not in the bedroom. (978-1-60282-125-5)

The Remarkable Journey of Miss Tranby Quirke by Elizabeth Ridley. When love enters Tranby's life in the form of a beautiful nineteen-year-old student, Lysette McDonald, she embarks on the most remarkable journey of all. (978-1-60282-126-2)

Returning Tides by Radclyffe. Insurance investigator Ashley Walker faces more than a dangerous opponent when she returns to the town, and the woman, she left behind. (978-1-60282-123-1)

Veritas by Anne Laughlin. When the hallowed halls of academia become the stage for murder, newly appointed Dean Beth Ellis's search for the truth leads her to unexpected discoveries about her own heart. (978-1-60282-124-8)

The Pleasure Planner by Larkin Rose. Pleasure purveyor Bree Hendricks treats love like a commodity until Logan Delaney makes Bree the client in her own game. (978-1-60282-121-7)

everafter by Nell Stark and Trinity Tam. Valentine Darrow is bitten by a vampire on her way to propose to her lover Alexa Newland, and their lives and love are placed in mortal jeopardy. (978-1-60282-119-4)